A DEAL WITH THE DEVIL

To Whom It May Concern: Should Mitchell New-land not survive the trail drive to the Territory of Montana, his ownership of the Twin N Ranch, of Cawlins, Texas, will pass to Corliss Bilks, also of Cawlins, Texas.

The simple statement was followed with three some-what straight lines. Bilks signed on the first line, Mitch-ell was to sign the second, and the third, for Hubert, was followed with the word "Witness" and once more the date.

"Is that all that's required to make this a binding agreement?"

"You bet it is, son."

Mitchell signed before Bilks and Hubert, and his hand shook a little. He bore down with the nib and poked a hole through the first sheet.

"Easy, boy, else you'll get ink on the baize." Bilks chuckled.

Mitch signed, reminding himself that it was busi-ness. Except that he could hear a far-off bell tolling, a big brass bell, cracked, to be sure, but it was there. It was a clanging sound only he could hear, back in the darkest reaches of his brain, warning him of something he did not want to hear.

RALPH COMPTON

THE TOO-LATE TRAIL

A RALPH COMPTON WESTERN

MATTHEW P. MAYO

BERKLEY
New York

BERKLEY
An imprint of Penguin Random House LLC
penguinrandomhouse.com

ISBN: 9780593333839

First Edition: April 2021

Printed in the United States of America
1   3   5   7   9   10   8   6   4   2

Book design by George Towne

*For my trusty trail mates,
Jennifer and Miss Tess.—MPM*

THE IMMORTAL COWBOY

This is respectfully dedicated to the "American Cowboy." His was the saga sparked by the turmoil that followed the Civil War, and the passing of more than a century has by no means diminished the flame.

———◈———

True, the old days and the old ways are but treasured memories, and the old trails have grown dim with the ravages of time, but the spirit of the cowboy lives on.

———◈———

In my travels—to Texas, Oklahoma, Kansas, Nebraska, Colorado, Wyoming, New Mexico, and Arizona—I always find something that reminds me of the Old West. While I am walking these plains and mountains for the first time, there is this feeling that a part of me is eternal, that I have known these old trails before. I believe it is the undying spirit of the frontier calling me, through the mind's eye, to step back into time. What is the appeal of the Old West of the American frontier?

———◈———

It has been epitomized by some as the dark and bloody period in American history. Its heroes—Crockett, Bowie, Hickok, Earp—have been reviled and criticized. Yet the Old West lives on, larger than life.

———◈———

It has become a symbol of freedom, when there was always another mountain to climb and another river to cross; when a dispute between two men was settled not with expensive lawyers, but with fists, knives, or guns. Barbaric? Maybe. But some things never change. When the cowboy rode into the pages of American history, he left behind a legacy that lives within the hearts of us all.

—Ralph Compton

CHAPTER ONE

T HE BULGE-EYED TEXAS longhorn snorted, her muscled red shoulders bunching and quivering in
counterpoint to her skittering eyes and heaving, lathered rib cage. Flecks of white foam dripped from her
trembling mouth. But it was the beast's foot-and-a-half-
long mismatched horns that Mitchell Newland kept an
eye on. She jerked her head and offered him a jaunty wag.

"If I wanted to cause you grief, missy, I'd have dosed
you with a lead pill long ago. Maybe I should have at
that, but your mama was ol' Broody Ethel, and Pa
would never have forgiven me if I laid low one of her
bloodline."

Somehow that got through to her, and the belliger-
ent beast eased her post-legged stance and swung her
head back toward the clot of scrub brush behind her.

Past her shoulder, Mitch caught a glimpse of what he
had expected to see—a tiny red-and-white mottled face
with drooped ears peering around the spiny branches.
"Good mama."

The young rancher eased his black gelding, Champ, three, then four cautious steps backward, but then the horse balked. "Let's give her space. She's doing what we'd want her to, after all, was a coyote to come along intent on molesting her calf."

If Champ understood or cared about what Mitch was saying, he didn't let on, and he didn't budge another step. Mitch dug harder with his heels. The horse offered a low snort, then gave in and they eased back, sidestepping until they were at a distance safe enough should the ornery young mother change her mind.

"My word," said Mitch, rubbing his sweat-stained fawn hat back and forth on his head. "Was a few minutes there I thought maybe we were going to have to duke it out. And you"—he patted the horse's neck—"you big lummox, all but let me down back there. What's gotten into the critters on the Twin N spread this morning?"

Mitch half-smiled and gave a look around, as if someone on the scrub-and-sand plain might catch him nattering away. Conversing with himself was a habit he'd had most of his twenty-three years, and one his pap, Jakey Newland, had encouraged.

"You go right ahead talking to you and yours. You meet better people that way, son," he'd say with a wink.

"Don't know about that, Pap," said Mitch, resuming his one-sided conversation. "But I can tell you the only other person who doesn't think it's odd is Evie. She is, as you said long ago, a keeper, and I'm pretty certain she feels that way about me, too. Only trouble is, I can't in good conscience ask her to marry up with me if this ranch limps along. We need rain, money, and more of both. In that order. But I'll settle for two out of three."

Mitch looked up at the morning's wide blue sky and sighed. His gaze fixed on the worn, flat trail before him, dust kicked up by a gust, carrying off whatever useful dirt the Twin N had left. Nope, Pap hadn't left much. Despite that, Mitch felt something deep inside for the place. A warmth different from the sun's unceasing heat driving down, day on day, week on month on year.

He shook off the tiring thoughts and drained his canteen. He was in sight of the cabin anyway. With luck, the pool at the creek would have collected more of its slow flow. It'd still be the silty color peculiar to muddied water, enough so that he told himself it was no different from creamed coffee. He'd much prefer to sip from a clear-flowing stream on his own property.

"We will again," he said as they trudged homeward. "All it takes is a little rain. Just a little rain." Mitch looked skyward once more, in case a stray thunderhead had lost its way and wandered over in his direction. Maybe it would linger above the Twin N and figure it was as good a place as any to let loose its precious cargo. But nope, nothing but blue above and brown below.

He sighed and urged Champ into a trot. "Race you home, boy," he said, smiling at the same old tired joke his father had always told to whatever horse he'd been riding. And somehow, the horse always won . . . by a nose.

CHAPTER TWO

"Papa, you know that's not true." Evelyn Bilks narrowed her eyes at her father, the single most annoying man she'd ever met. Of course, that didn't mean much, living on a dusty old ranch three miles from the limp little town of Cawlins, Texas. She'd been raised by her father, or so he thought.

It was Carmelita, cook, housemaid, and unofficial ruler of the house, who could take most of the credit for keeping the young firebrand from straying too far off the straight, if not always narrow path. And of course there were the dozen ranch hands always about the place whom she regarded as little more than annoying brothers.

Still, Evie had met enough men to guess her suspicion was true—her father was infuriating. And claiming Jakey Newland had been a liar and a cheat was two falsehoods too far.

"I knew Jakey about as well as I know Mitch, and neither of them has ever lied to me, nor cheated anybody I've ever heard of. Those claims of yours will be the first."

Corliss Bilks jammed the wad of ham and egg into his mouth and dropped the fork with a clatter to the china plate. Both Evie and Carmelita looked up, unimpressed with his tired display of annoyance.

"I about have had enough of you correcting me in my own house, young miss. And in front of the help, to boot!"

Evie suppressed a smile, as did Carmelita. To call the older woman "help" was like calling their nine-year-old bluetick hound, Golly, a feisty pup. The dog spent all his time asleep and farting on the ranch house's long, low porch. His only worth was as a conversation deterrent.

Evie hated it when her father talked with his mouth full of food, something he'd always done. She long ago gave up trying to change his ways where manners were concerned.

"Your mother never could, so leave off it," he'd say around a mouthful of steak and beans.

She shoved away from the table and threw her balled napkin on her plate.

"You ain't eat yet!" Corliss looked as though it was a high crime to skip a meal, an offense he'd not committed in many a year.

"I have lost my appetite." She turned to walk out.

"Where you going?"

"Riding."

"Yeah, to that cursed Newland spread. I have half a mind to forbid you from ever seeing him again."

Evie paused in the dining room's doorway. "You do and you'll never see me again, Papa." She strode down the long, cool hallway, her riding boots snapping hard on the polished planking.

Bilks shook his head. "Worse than her mother, she

is. Girl's going to cause me grievous harm one of these days." He ladled another serving of beans onto his plate.

As Carmelita cleared away Evie's setting, she muttered, "Evie is right and you know it."

"What was that?" said Corliss through his beans.

The cook sighed. "I said Evie is right."

"You, too, huh?" He gulped coffee, then wiped his mouth. "Gettin' so a man can't speak his mind in his own home else a passel of women descends screeching out of the skies like . . ."

"Eagles?" she said, not hiding her smirk as she walked out.

"No!" He shoved away from the table. To her back, he said, "Like vultures! That's what I was going to say!"

To the empty room he sighed. "One of these days I will have to do something about young Newland and Evie. I do not like where it's all leading. Not a little bit at all."

CHAPTER THREE

T. C. TRUNDLESON PAUSED in sweeping the board-walk in front of his mercantile and leaned on the broom handle. He dragged a sleeve across his forehead and sighed long and low. It was fixing to be another griddle-hot Texas day, like all the rest, and sometimes he wasn't so certain it was where he wanted to be.

He'd had his pick of places to settle himself after the war, but then he'd up and met Mabel, and that, as they say, had been that. Not that he minded all that much. But his thoughts did sometimes cat-foot away from him, leading down trails that often involved greener grass and women whose faces weren't so pinched. . . .

"T. C. Trundleson!"

He winced.

"What is it you find so fascinating that you have to spend more of your time every single morning of the year sweeping off the storefront porch?"

T.C. groaned. Mabel had a way of sneaking up on a fellow that set his teeth together hard. "Oh, being thorough, my little bluebonnet." The words didn't sound as sincere as they ought, but he didn't care. Then there she was, peering over his shoulder, then past him down the dusty street.

"Who's that?"

T.C. squinted. "Looks to me like Mitchell Newland."

"Jakey's boy?"

He sighed again. He wanted to ask her what other Mitchell Newland did she know of. Instead, he said, "Yes, dear, that's the one."

A sound as if she'd spat—a coarse habit in which Mabel would never indulge—bubbled up out of her throat, and she turned and made for the door. "Turning out like his father."

"Oh, I don't know about that. Mitch, he's a good boy. Never asks for more than he can pay for, and he has good manners. Come to think on it, so did Jakey. He let his credit build a little too much, is all."

T.C. turned to see how she'd taken his retort, but she'd gone back inside. T.C. shook his head and lingered with the broom a while longer.

"Women are something else, ain't they, T.C.?"

The shopkeeper turned to see old Bucky Folsom holding down his usual end of the split-log bench off to the side of the display window. A genuine skirmish-fighting hero was Bucky, though you'd never know it from looking at him.

He was half the height of most men, and when he stood, you could see why. He was bent right over like a question mark, as if he carried a load of stones swinging from his shoulders, tugging him forward and looking as if he might topple any moment. The other thing you noticed about Bucky was his beard.

It was a formidable, fluffed, gray presence made even more impressive by his stooped stature. In the midst of the mass of hair that wreathed his wrinkled face and flowed past his knees, Bucky's long, pointed nose dripped, anytime of year, anytime of day. He was forever dabbing it with an old blue kerchief.

"How's that, Bucky? Didn't see you there. Good morning."

"Morning, T.C. Women, I said."

T.C. nodded. They'd had the conversation before, and would again, no doubt. Then Mitchell Newland rode up and spared him the experience.

"Morning, Mr. Trundleson. Morning, Mr. Folsom." Mitch swung down out of the saddle and looped the reins over the rail. He stepped up onto the shade porch and lifted off his hat, and smoothed back his thick black hair.

Both older men nodded and replied in kind, but it was the young man's hair they were struck by, the same as always whenever Newland's infrequent town visits occurred. T.C. and Bucky were each as bereft of hair on top as a kneecap. That darn kid was tall, too, what the ladies all called "easy to look at."

Most irksome of all, though, was that the kid had no idea womenfolk found him appealing. Plus, he was so blamed nice, genuinely so, not like some of the smarmy youngsters who were forever grubbing around for something, then weaseling off to talk of you behind your back.

"Haven't seen you in a spell, Mitch. Keeping okay by yourself at the ranch?"

"Oh, yes, sir, Mr. Trundleson. You know, one foot at a time, one beef at a time." Same answer as always. The youth smiled, but they knew he was making light of a situation no one in town envied.

His father, Jakey, a good kid himself way back, had come home from the sea a changed fellow, found a hole in his life where his pretty wife, Irma, had been. She'd died of the influenza while he was away on his last trip.

He also returned to find his young son had been taken in by a kind but odd German couple who lit out for points west as soon as they turned Mitchell over to his father.

But Jakey had no heart for ranching, no heart for much after Irma died, other than drinking whiskey and not paying his debts, which he built up all over town. He did love his boy with an obvious devotion that fell short of staying sober. Eventually, though, the drink wore him down to a nub.

Jakey died of a whiskey-fueled accident when Mitch was fifteen, leaving a confused kid alone, up to his shins in debt on a hardscrabble ranch, to tend a handful of rangy, hide-on-bone cattle.

To everyone's surprise, young Mitchell shunned all offers of help. Most perplexing of all, though, he also rejected repeated—and not all that generous—offers from Corliss Bilks to purchase the meager four-hundred-acre Twin N spread.

The kid would have none of it. On his infrequent visits to town, he'd let slip now and again that he was determined to make the ranch a going concern, to do Jakey proud. Everyone tried to talk sense into the youngster, but he was as bullheaded about keeping that ranch as his pa had been about drinking away every day of his life.

Not only did he manage to hold on to the ranch, but the boy paid off his father's debts. Every last one. It took him six years, but he got there. Then he set to work buying cattle and building up a herd. Most folks who knew about such things knew the kid's critters were not much to look at, scrubby and balky and wild. But of late he had been running them with a half-breed Hereford bull, with an eye toward raising fatter, less ornery stock. The plan looked to be working, slow as an old man in a blizzard, but it was working.

Mitch Newland was also as determined to wed young Evelyn Bilks, and she him; a genuine match, everyone agreed. Everyone but her father, Corliss, the wealthiest rancher in the region. He wouldn't even talk of the matter whenever he clacked into town in his barouche, which was most every day, for a card game at Underhill's Tavern.

He owned half-share in the establishment, so Hubert Underhill couldn't say much about the food and drink Corliss consumed daily. But as it came at a significant cost, and thus was a vexation to Hubert, in his quiet way, he made certain the rest of Cawlins knew.

Sure, if you wanted to rile Corliss Bilks, you mentioned how so-and-so saw young, handsome Mitchell Newland courting Miss Evie down by the grassy bluff overlooking the all-but-dry bed of Ortiz Creek.

The chubby rancher's cheeks would fire up like a struck match and his pooched mouth would work that cigar of his like a banked fish works air. Then he'd shout about how nothing in his life was anybody's business, and that included idle chatter about his Evie!

The folks of Cawlins, wearing secret grins, would scurry and scatter back to their respective tasks, snickering and whispering.

CHAPTER FOUR

M ITCH STEPPED INTO the store, careful to ease the slam of the door behind him. If he didn't, that brass bell would clang and jangle, and he'd hear Mrs. Trundleson's theatrical sigh echo in his head the entire time in the store and throughout his ride back home.

He would be glad to be once more away from the old sourpuss, and he suspected most folks in Cawlins felt the same way. He could admit to Evie thinking such things, of course, but Pap had raised him to keep such opinions to himself.

Within minutes of entering the store on that day in July, a drummer of tonics and tinctures by the name of Reginald Chillicutty—a dapper, handshaking sort— had entered behind him to chat, as drummers do, before easing into his reason for being there.

The salesman talked to Mitch and to Mr. Trundleson as the latter's wife filled Mitch's order. Mitch soon found himself intrigued by the whelming news from the drummer.

"I see I have piqued your interest, young man." Chillicutty rocked on his heels and grinned, his red cheeks riding high on a smile.

"It's true, then, what they're saying about the gold-fields up north?" said Mitch.

"Oh, on my honor," said the drummer, pulling a solemn look and patting his chest. "Those gold camps up Montana Territory way are booming, I tell you. They're also desperate for fresh beef. Why"—he tugged on his braces and his look grew serious—"beeves this fall are expected to fetch forty dollars a head. The goldfields are so productive that many of the miners are planning on wintering over. That's why the beeves are proving so valuable. Those men need to eat!"

Mitch nodded, lost in thought, not quite looking at the messenger of these intriguing tidings.

Chillicutty went on: "They'll be paying top-dollar prices to anyone willing to drive a herd northward before the snows arrive. Of course the news comes too late for some of the herds that have already made the journey to the usual railheads, but for the rest? Oh, what a golden opportunity, as they say." Again, the man rocked back on his heels as if he himself had dreamed up this grand scheme.

Forty dollars a head? That was ten times the amount he could make locally. Of course it was all silliness, nothing more. Mitch came back to himself and saw the grinning drummer. Something about his earnestness struck Mitch as humorous and he let out a quick snort.

The man sighed and reached into his vest pocket. He tugged out a single-sheet newspaper and unfolded it and held it out. "See here?" He tapped it with a pink forefinger. "Dated but one month ago. Read that, my boy, and doubt no more." He held out the paper and Mitch took it.

Mitch read it, standing in the store as if rooted, ignoring Mrs. Trundleson's volley of sighs. He finished and read it through once more before folding it into its customary creases and handing it back to Chillicutty with a shaking hand.

Mitch had tried for months to interest one of the few nearby ranchers driving their stock to the railhead in Abilene to take along his meager herd of a hundred fifty head. He'd hoped he might be able, with luck, to double the four dollars per head he could make locally.

It would all but wipe him out of cattle for a pittance, sure, but he planned on sinking the profits into stock with stronger bloodlines. Better a fresh start with a small but strong herd than to continue with the stringy, ornery cattle he'd been running.

But none of it mattered, as he'd not found anyone willing to take on his stock, and the last of the herds had dusted out of town months before.

Montana, he thought. *Oh, Montana . . .*

All those ranchers had turned him down and left Cawlins without his cattle. All the drives were gone, save for Corliss Bilks' herd.

Mitch nodded goodbye and left the store with his few purchases. The door, despite his efforts, slipped from Mitch's fingertips and slammed closed, the annoying brass bell clanging as if struck by a peen hammer. But Mitch didn't hear it.

He was too busy indulging in a grand daydream, selling his stock for such a profit. He stood on the porch, shifting his paper-and-twine-wrapped parcels to the crook of his arm. So smitten was he by this notion that he mumbled aloud to himself: "How can I get my cattle to Montana Territory?"

"Drive them, boy! Drive them on up there." It was old Bucky Folsom. The old man's reedy voice, always sounding as if it needed the lubrication of oil to work smoother, pulled Mitch's gaze from the unfixed space he'd been staring off into, across the not so busy main street of Cawlins, Texas.

"What's that you say, Mr. Folsom?" said Mitch, still mired in the possibility of all that money waiting for him in the mine camps in Montana Territory. Heck, imagine if he could but get up there. Why, he could stay on for a while and try his hand at digging for gold, too! All those people wouldn't have trekked up there for nothing, after all. He might even earn enough cash to purchase his own fancy pedigree bull. Imagine that. . . .

The old man sighed and shook his head, but if anybody could have seen behind that voluminous shelf of hair flowing off his face, they would have found a smile. He repeated himself. "Boy, you got to drive your cattle to Montana Territory. Only way to get them there. But you'll need a whole lot more than your tiny herd to make it a worthwhile trip."

By then Mitch had come back to himself and walked over to stand before Bucky Folsom. "How many more do you think, to make it worthwhile, as you say?"

The old man shrugged. "Oh, if you had six, eight hundred all told, that would do it up, considering you'll lose some to dangerous critters, not all of them the four-legged kind, neither." He touched the side of his nose and nodded.

It was a habit Mitch had witnessed several times, and he didn't know how to respond. So he nodded back.

"Know where you can find another five, six hundred or so head of cattle, son?" Bucky said it with yet another hidden smile, but this time his eyes betrayed him.

"What are you getting at, Mr. Folsom?"

"Think about it, son. Think about it. You know folks, don't you?"

Mitch nodded. Of course he knew people. Who didn't?

"Okay, then. Except knowing folks ain't of much use if you don't use them once in a while, huh?"

That didn't sound quite sporting to Mitch, as his father used to say about dodgy deals.

There was a moment, then, that Mitchell Newland would recall in coming months and years, a moment in which nothing seemed possible, and then it was. And with a terrible clarity he wasn't so certain he liked. But it was too late, far too late, and he knew it deep in his bones. For once an idea entered a man's mind, it was there forever. That much he knew about himself. It was a curse.

Sure, it was an unreachable notion, that he'd make it to Montana Territory. In fact, he was already planning for next season. In spring, he might take the risk of sending his animals to another rancher, as early as possible, and hope the market would still pay more than four dollars a head. But he wasn't certain he could hold out that long. Not another whole season.

He'd already resigned himself to selling some of his stock locally, to limp through the coming winter. He'd do his best to keep brood stock and a few bulls in order to build up a herd once more.

But then that feeble thought had been chased off by the notion that Mr. Folsom was hinting at, and Mitch understood at once.

Bilks. Of course, he had to mean Corliss Bilks. Despite his many misgivings, Mitch's mouth dropped open and his eyes widened. Bilks. Now that was a thought. After all, he had heard from Evie in passing but a couple of days before that her father was still considering a late-season drive to the railhead in Abilene.

"Yeah, I figured you'd cotton to the idea," said Bucky. "Takes some folks a spell to catch on. And here I always figured you for a sharper pencil than that, Mitchell Newland. Could be my advanced age has hindered my ability to tell when a man's capacities are wanting."

But Mitch wasn't much hearing him, beyond knowing the old goat was funning him. He was thinking about how Evie's scrimy father had six hundred or so prime longhorns ready for market. Mitch also knew that Bilks had had a falling-out with another rancher by the name of Choto.

The man had agreed earlier in the year to drive their herds together to the railhead at Abilene, but Evie said Bilks had demanded too much in the deal and didn't offer half of the effort and investment the venture would require. And so Evie's stingy father was planning to send his men to drive his herd to Abilene on their own.

What if Mitch could convince him to drive them to Montana, along with his own? It was a much longer journey, sure, but they'd both make a pile more money than they would in Texas, especially since the bottom had dropped out of the local beef market years before. And from what Mitch could tell, it didn't look like it would ever be a thriving market again. They didn't have the customers, and the ones they did have were too poor to buy enough meat to keep the ranchers in business.

Mitch had to convince Bilks to drive his herd to Montana Territory instead of to Kansas. *It was that simple,* he thought with a snort.

Mitch turned to leave the mercantile's porch, dropped a tin of Ceylon tea, and bent to retrieve it. The old man leaned over until his beard's tip grazed the knuckles of Mitch's outstretched hand.

"You be cautious, Mitchell Newland." The old man's voice was low and even, steel sliding over a whetstone.

"Driving the cattle?" said Mitch.

"No, sakes alive, no." Bucky Folsom leaned back and fluffed his beard, stroking it briskly as he was wont to do when excited. "Be on your guard when you talk with that Corliss Bilks."

Even Folsom's voice, as bold a man as he was, dimmed when he pronounced the name of the powerful rancher who seemed to own an interest in much of the main street, such as it was, of Cawlins.

Mitch smiled. "Aw, thanks, Mr. Folsom. But Mr. Bilks, he's not so bad. A little angry at times, maybe."

"You bet he is. Don't you let none of it rub off'n you. You take my advice and keep your eyes open good and wide before you climb into a featherbed with that man."

Mitch didn't know what to say to that, so he nodded, touched his hat brim, and pinched his tin of tea tight under his arm. "Thank you, Mr. Folsom. I appreciate it. I really do."

He had to get going. It was still early enough that he might be able to track down Mr. Bilks in town. If not, he might have luck on the road. He'd be riding the same route the rancher took to get to town from his place on most mornings.

One way or another, Mitch planned to brace his wealthy neighbor and . . . say what?

From the porch, he heard Bucky Folsom shout, "You'd best get to it, son. Summer's a-wasting. Might already be too late."

He pondered all of this as he rode Champ down the street, moving one measured step at a time, eager to discuss what was fast becoming in Mitch's mind the most important notion he'd ever come up with. He couldn't wait to share his idea with Evie.

But she would have to wait, for Mitch spied her father's barouche drawn up tight between Underhill's Tavern and the stable yard to its right.

Mitch urged Champ to the hitch rail in front of the bar and swung down. "In for a penny," he said as he mounted the single step that led up off the dusty, sun-bright street. He paused and pulled in a deep breath, once more slipped off his hat, and ran a hand through, smoothing his black hair. He was sweating, to be sure, due to far more than the day's heat.

As his eyes accustomed themselves to the dark interior of the tavern, Mitch could see there weren't but two other folks in the bar besides Corliss Bilks. Hubert, the barkeep, and Florence Rakoff, a pretty number, even if she was about as old as what he guessed his ma would be were she still alive.

Mitch knew she'd been sweet on his pa and had taken it real hard when he died. She'd moped for weeks and gotten herself dismissed twice from her hostess duties at the bar. She was always hired back because Mr. Bilks liked to pat her backside whenever he had a full table and a cigar in his mouth. Which was much of the time.

Mitch set his shoulders and strode forward. Hubert nodded and Mitch did the same. He also arched his eyebrows and nodded toward Bilks' table. The barkeep nodded again. But there was something else in that look, too. Pity? Hidden laughter?

That's when Corliss Bilks looked up.

The fleshy face gazed right at him, eyes narrowed and far from friendly. And then the rest of the man's face broke into a smile. All but the eyes. They stayed narrowed.

Mitchell Newland knew right then there was more than the whiff of truth to all those stories about Bilks and his ruthlessness.

Such as the time Bilks had dealt with the family of squatters who'd encamped on a knot of land on a far-off corner of Bilks' ranch. He'd had them hauled to town, three children crying and the mother and father in wrist manacles. Bilks had insisted that a trial of law be held to determine what everybody already knew. The squatters had indeed trespassed on Bilks' land and lived there in a crude makeshift shelter. And yes, the man had hunted deer and other critters so his family could eat. But they'd not caused any lasting harm.

Though he'd had the family released, the circuit judge had been obliged to fine them the full twenty-five dollars Corliss Bilks had determined he'd been owed as compensation for something called "hardship fees." The episode hadn't earned Bilks any friends, but if that bothered him, he never let on. In fact, the legal win had puffed his sails, and he lorded over Cawlins as never before.

No one ever challenged the man, save for Evie. She was relentless in this, and had come close, as she told Mitch, to becoming disinherited. She said this would pain her not because of money, but because she believed the good father she used to know as a little girl was still there, buried beneath the bravado and money and power.

No one else saw it—not even Carmelita, and she had known Bilks longer than had Evie, as she had been hired by Evie's mother, Enid, when she was alive.

As Mitchell Newland stood before Bilks now, his wobbling resolve collapsed. Only Bilks' hard gaze and the fact that he was Evie's father drew Mitch to the table, a moth drawn to lamplight.

"Mitchell, my boy, what brings you here, of all places, on this fine morning? I didn't take you to be a drinker. I would've thought your father had lapped up enough booze for the both of you. I guess not. Set yourself down and I'll order a bottle. You can carry on the family line of work."

The bulky man leaned forward and, with a toadlike wink, said, "'Cause we both know it ain't ranching, eh?" The odd, hiccupping giggle Bilks was known for bubbled up around the cigar in his pooched pink lips.

The crack about his father could not stand. "I . . . I'm not here to drink, Mr. Bilks."

"Oh, well." The cigar drooped. It was as if the man had received disappointing news.

Everything about Bilks is false, thought Mitch. *And I should leave now.* Yet the opposite happened, and too late to bite them back, he spoke in a rush of words, wincing as he heard them tumble from his mouth.

"I'm going to drive my herd to Montana Territory and I wonder if you would consider, that is, I know you have about six hundred head. . . . I've heard you're thinking of driving them to Abilene. I've learned of this opportunity. . . . Montana Territory has all these mining towns, and cattle are going for ten times a head what we get hereabouts. I thought, with your herd and mine, I could get them there. . . . You'd make a lot of money, sir. I would, too, enough to . . ."

It was here, red-faced, tight-throated, and parched of mouth, that Mitchell reined in his rampant tongue. It would not do to divulge his intentions toward Evie yet.

He knew the man was aware of their fondness for each other, for Evie had several times mentioned to Mitch she'd told her father she was going to take up with Mitchell and move away. He still sighed inwardly at that, for he intended never to pull up stakes and leave his ranch behind. His father's legacy meant far too much to him.

Not as much as Evie did, of course, but, well, the ranch was different somehow, a thing not explained with clumsy, ill-worded sentiment. It was deeper, more meaningful. Surely there could be room in a man's heart and mind and life for two loves, a wife and a ranch.

If Bilks suspected where Mitchell had been about to venture, he did not let on. He sat erect at the baize table, two stacks of papers before him, an inkpot and a pen jutting from it, a cup of black coffee at his elbow.

His hands, like newborn piglets, rested atop the

green tabletop, a slight leftward cock to his head, the creeping baldness of his scalp reflecting the low honey glow of the hanging oil lamp. His lips puckered around the ever-present cigar jutting from his round little mouth as if it were giving birth to the thing, blue smoke rising in faint trickles from its end.

Mitchell wanted more than anything at that moment to wipe away the drips of sweat stippling his face. He opened his mouth to apologize and get the heck out of there, but Bilks held up a hand that froze him in place and seized his tongue.

"Hubie, pitcher of water and a glass for our friend here, if you please."

Bilks held his hand up as if he were in the street halting a procession of wagons. He only lowered it once the barkeep nudged Mitch's knuckles with the tall, tepid glass of water. Mitch took it, sipped, then gulped the rest. Hubert set a glass pitcher on the table.

Mitch glanced at it. That meant he'd have to reach for it, as he was still standing, and there was no way he'd ever be able to move from this spot again. No way.

The entire time, he was aware that Bilks had been watching him, studying him, maybe, but also doing some sort of thinking. He suspected this because the man's eyelids twitched now and again as if he were thumbing through great sheafs of important papers in his mind.

Then he said, "All right, son. I'll do it."

YOU ARE CORRECT. I have six hundred beeves, more or less—the finest in Texas, I don't mind saying—and they are prime and ready for market. My crew had planned on driving them to the railhead in Abilene. There I will more than double the paltry fee I could net hereabouts, as we are in the grips of a vicious scheme to thieve livelihoods from hardworking ranchers.

"Enough said about that for now. But your news of the market for beef in Montana Territory, which I assume you came by legitimately, reinforces much the same information I have learned on my own about the opportunities in the far, frozen north. Until now I had been undecided about exploring all that Montana Territory's mine camps have to offer. Until now."

Mitch nodded, not entirely certain what he was hearing. He was about to respond, out of courtesy, when Bilks held up that hand once more and resumed speaking.

"As to the terms, I will supply the men, the cook and chuck, the remuda and wrangler, feed. In short, I'll fund the entirety of the drive." He stopped talking and looked at Mitch. The young man felt a powerful and immediate need to respond.

"Yes, sir. Uh . . . I have my cattle, two horses. I can take care of my own food. I can bring food, that is. . . ."

"Didn't you hear me, Newland? You'll be part of the team. In fact, as this Montana deal is your notion, I have half a mind to make you boss of the outfit, in title only, of course. It'll give you a leg up with the men. Of course you'll have the expertise of seasoned trail hands, as well as the current foreman. I believe you know him. Joe Phipps. The men call him Drover Joe, and for good reason. Phipps has been on more cattle drives than anyone I've ever met. He's lucky to have landed at the Bar B, I can tell you." Bilks leaned forward and sipped his coffee.

Seemed to Mitch it was Corliss Bilks who was the lucky one in that deal. Mitch did know Drover Joe Phipps, had for several years, in fact, since he arrived in the region and slipped into the employ of Bilks. But he wasn't about to quibble with Bilks. It was all he could do to keep his heart from crawling up and out of his throat, so hard was it beating.

"It's . . . well . . ."

"Speak up, boy. What you got to say? Two words spring to mind, but I'll let you ponder on it a moment."

"Yes, sir, well, it all sounds very good."

"Very good? Hell, son, it's downright miraculous."

"No, I mean, well, I don't have much to offer in the deal."

Bilks shoved forward once more, and a quick smile lit his fleshy face. "It's true. Let's not kid ourselves, son. Those beeves of yours ain't half the quality of my critters, are they? And your ignorance of the trail is no doubt going to be a hindrance. Despite all that, I am willing to give this a go—back the play, as they say."

Before Mitch could respond, Bilks leaned forward. "That's why I've come up with a solution for you. There's a condition, the only one I have. Should you, Mitchell Newland, not make it back to Cawlins, I will assume ownership of the Twin N Ranch, such as it is."

He said it as if he were saying, "I heard tell there's the possibility of rain sometime in the future. Somewhere."

At first Mitch didn't understand what he'd heard. He even looked over at Hubert briefly, but the man was busy wiping down an already dry and gleaming bar top. At that moment, Florence walked back into the barroom. She looked to Mitch and her smile faded. It must have been because of the look on his own face, or maybe the silence in the room. She said, "What's happened? Has someone died?"

This struck Corliss Bilks as funnier than anything said since Mitch had come in, and he yodeled that hiccupping sound until he teared up and coughed. He pounded a hand on the table, the water in the glass pitcher rippling and jumping in the center.

"Well, boy, speak. You looked about ready to glad-hand me not but a minute ago. Then I come to the terms and you look like you're about to give birth to a sack of nails."

Mitch shook his head. "Well, sir, no, there's no way that can happen. You see, I have plans. That is my ranch, my father's legacy, and it was left to me. I know what you think of him, what most folks do, but—"

He succumbed to that raised hand once more.

"Yes, I know. And everybody on God's green earth knows of your hard work to hold on to the ranch. I even know of your plans to marry my Evie. Oh, don't look so shocked. I'm not that thick in the bean, Mitchell Newland." Bilks rapped a pink knuckle against his equally pink temple.

"Fact is, I admire how you set to a task and see it through. I really do. That's why I think you're the man for the job, the man to get them cattle to Montana Territory, and that's also why I think you'd be a bigger fool than your pa ever was if you turn me down."

"But . . ."

"Ain't no buts about it, boy. With my terms, why, you can't lose!" He rapped both hands on the table, then plucked out the cigar he'd been talking around and set it in the thick glass ashtray at his elbow.

"Look at it this way—if you make it to Montana Territory, you and me will both make decent money on our cattle, yes?" Bilks nodded his head in a big, exaggerated up-and-down movement, smiling at the same time.

Mitch found himself nodding, too.

"Good. Then follow me now. That means you will also have proven to me and to yourself that you are

worthy of marrying my daughter, my precious Evelyn."
He paused and let that seep in a moment.

Mitch felt his ears and cheeks redden like a hammer-
struck thumb. All this was rolling faster and bigger
than he imagined it might. He wanted to say he'd have
to think about it, which really meant he wanted to talk
with Evie. She was smart, one for thinking things
through. He didn't always agree with her, but she
wasn't afraid to share her mind.

He didn't have time to speak, however, because
Corliss Bilks jumped right back in. "If, on the other
hand, you die along the trail . . . Lord forbid!" He held
up that hand again and puffed once more on the cigar.

Mitch's eyebrows rose like birds taking flight.

"I know, I know. Ain't no man alive who wants to
think of such things, but believe me, it happens to all
of us. But not thinking about it is as foolish as calling
a horse a chicken. So, say you die along the trail, right?
Well, with my terms, I will get your land and I'll put it
to good use, ranching it in high style as the Good Lord
intended. It will never be treated better—that I promise you. And I will also see to it that Evie is paired up
with a suitable suitor. I'm sure you want only the best
for her. Why, it's as if you were leaving the ranch
for her."

Bilks leaned back, thumbing the sides of his brocade
vest and puffing a blue cloud up at the ceiling. "It's business, son. It's all business. Odds are in your favor you'll
come back to us safe and sound—and you'd better. I'll
have a load of money riding on this. You agree to this
and we can sign a little something right here and now.
I'll write it up, we both sign it, and ol' Hubert, why, he'll
bear witness. Ain't that right, Hubie?"

The barman glanced at Mitch. He wasn't smiling.
But he did nod his head.

It looked to Mitch like a warning from someone

who had gone into a business dealing with Corliss Bilks and who maybe regretted it. His glance did not offer the encouragement Mitch had been hoping for.

"Business, son. Look at it that way, and it all becomes clear as the water in that there jug. Speaking of, pour yourself another glass full and sit down at the table. We'll hammer out the details."

Mitch, barely breathing and stiff legged, followed the man's advice, pouring water and swallowing in slow gulps, as Bilks busied himself writing.

"Now, I am going to make this short and sweet. We can always add to it, make amendments later. But for now it'll be something to get us moving so we each have a copy." He grunted and his breathing grew louder, almost as if he were in a deep sleep.

Mitch fought the urge to stand, to back away, to shake his head and bolt for the door. But was the deal really so bad? Of course he'd come back. His ranch was here and Evie was here; everything he loved in life and all he'd ever known were here. He'd only be off on an adventure, a lark. Something Pa had said all young men should do with their lives.

It had been one of the last things Pap had wheezed to Mitch as he lay dying. He'd made Mitch promise he'd get out, off the ranch and away from Cawlins, and see the world. "Get wind in your face, son. Feel the breath of far-off places. Get out of here."

He'd flopped back, and Mitch thought he was gone, but his Pa had surprised him by opening his eyes a squinch once more. "Should have sold this damn ranch and taken you away from here when I could. Been a fool, been a damn fool, Mitch. Don't you be a fool." And that had been it.

Mitch had knelt, holding his father's head in his lap, and said over and over, as if in prayer, "I will, Pap. I will, I promise. I'll do it. Anything. Only don't you leave me now. Don't do it, Pap. We'll go on that trip together. I promise you that, if you'll only stay with me, Pa. Stay a while longer with me."

But that had been a long time ago. Eight years now, and he'd been a kid. Yet those words had lingered in his mind. That request echoed, his father's last wishes, and his own promise to him, to the only parent he'd ever really known, the only person he'd ever really loved, until Evie. Now he was a man, but he could still follow those wishes.

And here he was in this dark saloon on a hot summer morning, seated before Corliss Bilks, of all people, the man who had hated his father most in the world and whom his father had hated with equal venom and vigor. Yet it was at that very moment that his dying father's wishes made the most sense to him.

He would go off and he would have the adventure Pap wished for him. But he was his own man, too. He'd come back from that lark, that youthful journey, with a whole wad of cash in his pockets, and he would ranch like he invented the very word himself.

Maybe he'd stay on in Montana Territory for a spell, and dig himself some of that gold. Maybe they rooted for such stuff in the cold months, too. Well, he'd worry about that later.

"I'll sign." Mitch heard his voice, barely a hoarse whisper, yet it sounded shaky, older.

From somewhere behind the bar, he heard Florence Rakoff gasp, and it annoyed him. After all, was he not a man, a man who knew his own mind? He cleared his throat and spoke again. "I'll sign that paper, by God. I'll sign."

Corliss Bilks looked up at him, smiling and nodding his head. "I know. I know you will." And he offered up a quick chuckle. As he wrote, his pink tongue tip sliding back and forth between his wet lips, he grunted again. Then, with a quick flourish, he tapped the pen a last time and looked up briefly.

As he reached for a second sheet, he said, "Hubie, bring a bottle and two glasses over here. The good stuff. None of that swill you pour down the throats of the locals. Ha!"

Underhill brought the bottle and two glasses and set them down, pausing long enough that Mitch looked up at him.

"It would pay to read both copies with care, Mitch."

Bilks smacked a hand hard on the green felt surface of the games table. The ashtray, the inkwell, and the little shot glasses all jumped and rattled. "And it would pay you to mind your own damn business, wouldn't it . . . bartender?"

The shout was a high-pitched bark, the words torn off and dripping with a flare of hard anger matched only by Bilks' lid-eyed look at his bartender business partner.

Corliss Bilks proved true to his word and the sheet of paper Mitch was handed bore the date and:

To Whom It May Concern: Should Mitchell Newland not survive the trail drive to the Territory of Montana, his ownership of the Twin N Ranch, of Cawlins, Texas, will pass to Corliss Bilks, also of Cawlins, Texas.

The simple statement was followed with three somewhat straight lines. Bilks signed on the first line, Mitchell was to sign the second, and the third, for Hubert, was followed with the word "Witness" and once more the date.

"Is that all that's required to make this a binding agreement?" Mitch asked.

"You bet it is, son."

Underhill stood grim faced.

"If you won't bear witness to this transaction, Hubie, I'll go find someone who will. And while I'm at it, I might drum up somebody who will also not mind being my partner in a certain public house."

Underhill draped the grimy bar towel over his shoulder. "Never said I wouldn't sign, Corliss. Only offered young Mitchell some advice, is all."

"Yeah, well—sign there and there—he wants any business advice I expect he knows who to come to. Ain't that right, Mitchell?"

Mitchell signed before Bilks and Hubert, and his hand shook a little. He bore down with the nib and poked a hole through the first sheet.

"Easy, boy, else you'll get ink on the baize." Bilks chuckled.

Mitch signed, reminding himself that it was business. Except that he could hear a far-off bell tolling, a big brass bell, cracked; to be sure, but it was there. It was a clanging sound only he could hear, back in the darkest reaches of his brain, warning him of something he did not want to hear.

CHAPTER FIVE

Hours later, back at his place, Mitch was still wearing his town togs—his blue shirt that Evie bought him to wear when he would accompany her to the infrequent dance, even though he hated dancing. Why did women love to dance so? It was about as natural as petting a snake.

Then Evie rode up. He met her on the porch; he was still embarrassed at the humble and tiny house—one room with a curtained corner in the back for sleeping—that he lived in.

"Mitchell Newland," she said, smiling and slipping off her goatskin gloves one finger at a time. He could watch her do most anything and never grow tired of it. "What are you doing in your best bib and tucker? You aren't stepping out on me, are you?"

Though he knew she meant it as a joke, he liked that there was the slightest edge of jealousy to that question.

"Why, no, Miss Evelyn Bilks, unless you count spending time with your very own father as such." He couldn't wait, knew he wouldn't be able to. Mitch handed her his copy of the signed agreement and watched her face. As soon as he did, he regretted telling her this way.

She was a quick reader, but she spent a whole lot of time on the brief document, too short to require that much attention, even from someone as slow at taking in the written word as he could be, though mostly what he took in was his father's volume of Shakespeare's sonnets.

He didn't understand many of them, but it didn't stop him from dipping into them now and again. Never seemed to matter. They were forever beyond his thinking, it seemed.

"Mitchell," she said, still not looking up at him. And then she did. And he saw in her eyes a stew of shock and anger and worry, stirred up and spinning. "What have you done?"

"Well, now, Evie, I see I've surprised you with my big news."

"Mitchell, what have you done?" Her voice rose and she wagged the paper. "What trail drive? What does this mean? And should you not survive? What"—she shook the paper again, crushing it in her white-knuckled fist—"is this?"

"Now, Evie, it's great news, really. You know I've been saying I want us to be married. But I can't do it like this." He raised his big hands to indicate the small, humble shack, then let them drop by his sides.

"But this morning, Evie, I talked with a drummer, a Mr. Chillicutty, when I was in town at Trundleson's. Anyway, he told me that a head of beef in Montana Territory is bringing ten times what I can fetch for it hereabouts."

He saw a hard, squint-eyed, pinch-mouthed look on Evie's face. She didn't seem impressed with his news about Montana Territory. He plowed on ahead and told her all he could recall from the newspaper article, even throwing in details about the place that a few cow-hands had told him of Montana Territory in the past.

He paused, waiting for her to say something. Anything. But she remained silent, eyeing him with that hard stare.

"Look, Evie, I have a hundred fifty head of mangy, rangy longhorns I can call my own. Any more time passes and they'll kill one another off out of sheer dumbness and spite. You know how much they're worth here? Four dollars a head, if I'm lucky and the wind is with me."

Evie recognized the phrase, something Mitch's father used to say, a holdover from his days at sea.

"So we're going to drive the cattle, my herd and your father's, to Montana Territory. Commencing Saturday. That gives us five days to gather the rest of his and all of mine. It isn't much time, but it's what we have. We're already late starting and we have a bit farther to go than Abilene."

"A bit farther to go? Mitchell, have you even seen where Montana is on a map? Hmm?"

Mitchell shrugged. In truth, he had no solid idea where Montana lay. He'd talked to a few cowhands over the years who'd summered up there, north in the Shining Mountains as the old-timers called it. He knew for certain it was a ways beyond Indian Territory, Kansas, and even Colorado. But how much beyond that, he'd no real notion. He shrugged again.

Evie shook her head and growled low, swung around as if to leave, his agreement with her father still balled in her hand. Then she spun back, walked to him, and looked up at his north-of-six-foot height. "Mitchell, why did you do this? You know I don't care if you have money. You know I don't care if we live here or in a soddy somewhere far from here. If it were with anybody but my father, I'd say we could make it work. But

I do not trust Corliss Bilks any more than I trust Champ to turn into a broodmare."

"You'll see, Evie. This'll turn out to be the best thing that could happen to us."

She was silent a long moment. "Well." She finally sighed as if defeated. "You might be right. It offers you, us, a way out of here. It's what I always hoped for. You can finally be your own man."

"What are you saying, Evie?"

"Don't you see? He's offering you a way out, freedom from the weight of this"—she waved her arms and, as he did minutes before, let them drop—"this place."

"But it's my land. My father left it to me. It's the only thing of value I've ever had, the only thing I can count on to build a future for us."

"What about me?"

He saw then what she meant: that she was, and always had been, the ace in his deck of cards. But what she was saying wasn't even worth considering. Couldn't be. How could he give up on the ranch?

"Mitchell, you stood right there and told me, not two minutes ago, that your new drummer friend's newspaper article said Montana Territory is full of green grass as far as the eye can see, broad valleys, mountains with snow on them year-round, rivers you can't hardly see across. You told me all that, and you still want to see it, then come back here and bake to death and chew rock and choke on dust and die in this forsaken place? Why?"

Mitch knew he didn't have an answer that would satisfy her. In fact, he couldn't disagree with her, except that the Twin N was his, the whole thing, for good or ill, and he had vowed to himself after Pa died that he was going to keep it. Work for it, then keep it, always. Pa hadn't liked ranching, but that didn't mean Mitch hated it. The opposite, in fact.

He wanted to show himself, to show the rest of the world, that he was a man who kept his word. But to Evie, all Mitch could do was stand there like the great big fool of a man he was—no, not even a man. More like a fool of a boy. An overgrown boy playacting at being a man. And now he was into something way over his head, a sand pit with the walls caving in on him.

Evie had that look as though she were reading his mind, something he had long ago grown used to. It reminded him of a mystical woman at a tent in a traveling circus Pa had taken him to see over in Plainfield back when he was nine years old. His father had said it would be a lark. He was in high spirits, having had a couple of glasses of beer in yet another tent Mitch hadn't been allowed into.

They'd parted red-and-black cloths and stepped inside a stuffy, small tent. There was a woman not much older than Pap, but dressed in black, with a lacy shawl on her head and hunched shoulders that made her look older. She'd said something to Pa that his father didn't much like, because he only grunted and dug in his coat pocket for coins.

Once paid, the woman motioned them to two chairs across the wobbly little crepe-draped table before her. But it was the glass ball, no bigger than a round goose egg, that she revealed with a flourish from beneath a lace hankie that most impressed Mitch. He remembered the woman had smiled when he said, "Oh."

She had run her fingertips over the ball, then paused and, closing her eyes, said, "You have brought shadow on this boy, on yourself, on the land." Then she opened her eyes and looked at Pa.

He stood. "Come, Mitchell, time to go. This was not the lark I intended for us."

"No, the boy must hear what the orb tells us."

"I think not. Come, Mitch."

But Mitch could not rise from the chair; somehow he couldn't muster the strength to do it. The woman spoke quickly. "You, Mitchell, will be a man of greatness. And thus the thorn begets a rose."

That last he heard as his father lifted him from the chair and carried him out of the dark, close tent and into the bright sunlight.

He looked at Evie now and wondered if all women had some weird power of vision that left men forever guessing. Likely so.

"Here's what we should do." She narrowed her eyes, watching him closely. "At least, here's what I am going to do. I am going to go along with you on this drive. I will pack up this house, such as it is, and if you won't do it, I will find us a spot in those shining mountains and settle us down there. Together we will build up a ranch, a family, all the things we've talked of, all the things we can be proud of. Not"—she stomped a dusty riding boot on the worn floorboards—"a patch of flat dust even the snakes and lizards can't wait to get shed of."

It took a moment for Mitch to find his voice once more, lodged as it was like a clot of dirt in his windpipe. "Now, Evie, I ain't even—"

"Haven't even."

He nodded. "Let me get this out, will you? I haven't even asked you to marry me yet. You're saying things a man ought to say to a woman, after they've . . . come to terms, an agreement of sorts. You see?"

She stared at him some more and he fidgeted.

"And besides, it isn't done. It just isn't done."

"What's not done, Mitch?"

She said that quietly and he didn't know why. "A woman going along on a cattle drive. I am not so sure it has ever happened."

"I doubt that," she said, pulling on her gloves. "And

if you're right, then it's time we change that foolishness." She walked to the door and turned.

Mitchell tried once more. "Evie, my pa, he gave me this land."

"Yes," she said, stepping outside. "And I curse him each day for it." She stared at him once more, then let out a big breath. "Goodbye, Mitchell Newland."

He followed her out, but she said nothing else as she mounted her bay and galloped off in a boil of dust, without once looking back.

Long minutes passed before Mitch walked back inside and closed the door.

CHAPTER SIX

Y OU LOOKING FOR work, you'd best take yourself to
the ranch house proper, yonder over that rise."
The man barely looked up as he spoke. He was a squat,
solid fellow with a grayed dagger beard, not acquainted
with a razor in some time. His was a face not overly
handsome, more pitted and cratered than a pox victim's, with a nose that looked freshly stung by a scor-
pion. The man's eyes were watery and bloodshot, but
kind. His bald head was topped with an old brown and
mouse-chewed derby hat, the best days of its life long
in the past.

"Hello, Cook."

The man squinted over at him. "I know you?"

Mitch realized he was skylined against the daylight
in the open doorway and stepped in and to the left.
"Better?"

"Mitch Newland, that you?"

"Yes, sir."

The burly man grunted. "Well, good." He slid a big

iron griddle across the stovetop. "Maybe you can set me straight on something. Because I heard it, but I don't much believe it."

"What's that?" Mitch knew what Cookie was about to ask. He'd known the man for years, at least ten, since he had set up his kitchen as the ranch and trail cook for Bilks' Bar B Ranch.

How a man from New Orleans ever ended up as a cook on a dusty, bone-dry ranch in Texas, he'd never know. Cook was surly, straightforward, quick to flash his Creole rage, as he called it, but always good for a cookie or three, one of several reasons why everybody couldn't help but like the man, despite his oddness. Mitch had long since forgotten, if he ever even knew, the man's real name.

"Foolishness is what I call it."

"You mean the drive?"

"Yeah, I mean the drive." Cook rattled a big wooden spoon in a massive pot perpetually brimming with whistle berries.

Mitch shrugged. "Not much to tell, I guess. I'm going to join up with your drive and—"

"Yeah, yeah, we all know that. What I want to know is, why? We'd all but gotten old Corliss hisself convinced the market up Abilene way was bound to be better next year and he was willing to let the herd age on the hoof right here on its own stomping ground for the winter season. He'd also heard tell of a buyer willing to come all this way and pay him more than whatever he was liable to get locally. Then you go and fill his head with notions of more cash to be found up Montana way than a man can carry in his pockets."

Mitch smiled. "That's what he said?"

"Near enough." Cook rapped the spoon's shaft on the pot's rim. "Now I got to outfit my chuck wagon all over again. Foolishness is what it is." He turned. "Sit down already. Got a doughnut or some such around here. I expect you're hungry. Young men are always hungry."

Mitch sat down, and as if by magic, a glass of cool milk and a small plate heaped with cookies, two muffins, and a stack of cold flapjacks appeared before him. "Best eat those before the flies settle. Can't do a thing with them once a bluebottle crawls all over them."

Mitch tucked in. Life alone was not so bad, but cooking had always been something he did to get through with it. First for Pa, then for himself. He mostly ate beans, bacon, dried fruit, and corn bread. His biscuits came out denser than cobbles. No matter the methods he tried, they would not rise to the occasion.

Around mouthfuls, he said, "I'm sorry about it, Cook. I never—"

Cook interrupted him. It had been a couple of months since Mitch had visited the Bilks ranch, and he'd forgotten about the man's habit of interrupting anybody anytime he felt like it.

"Aww, don't worry none. The chuck wagon was about loaded and rigged up anyway. Can't believe a thing I say, except for the true parts." He winked and plunked down with a groan and a sigh on a bench opposite Mitch. "Besides, gets me out of here. I ain't been up ol' Montany way in quite a spell."

Mitch paused in midchew. "You've been to Montana Territory?"

"Been there, huh. Course I been there! Got the limp to prove it. Coldest place I ever set foot in. Vowed never to go back."

"Well, that's where we're headed—"

"Long way 'twixt here and there, boy. Long way. Don't say you're somewhere before you get there. But it will be nice to get shed of this place for a spell. The nightlife in Cawlins ain't nothing more than a drunk cowboy shooting a rattler. Or his own foot or both. Can't believe I stayed here this long. Got me relations in New Orleans I aim to visit again one of these days. See to it you don't molder in one place before you git the nerve to explore, boy. Mark my words."

The sudden slice of advice reminded him of Evie, then his Pa, and Mitch's throat lumped. "Yeah," he said, his voice raw. "I'll see to it."

Cook stood and shoved back from the table. "Okay, then. You're in my way, in my hair, and in my kitchen. I got work to do even if you ain't. Boys are waiting on you, I expect. Bilks told them what we'll be doing, or Drover Joe did. Said if you should come by my kitchen, you was to hightail it to the horse pasture. One with the big corral. You know it?"

"I do." Mitch rose and wiped his mouth on the folded napkin Cook had set out with the snack plate. The man might look rough, Mitch noted, not for the first time, but Cook was known for quiet at his table, cleanliness among his diners, manners all around—and he was more than happy to "learn you some" should you fail to meet his expectations in that regard.

His own self was excused, apparently, from that list, as Cook looked like he never changed from the clothes he wore all week, cooked in, and spattered daily with bacon drippings, dough flecks, bean juice, and gravy drips. His beard wore the same decoration. Mitch nodded to him as he left.

Mitch heard the men before he saw them, as the land dipped low several hundred yards behind the big barn. Only when a man walked to the edge and looked down at the broad vista below him did he see the massive rail corral. A smaller version sat east of it, a worn snubbing post jutting at a slight angle from the center.

But it was at the bigger corral that a dozen men had gathered. Many of them stood on the rails, a couple perched along the top rail. Horses were tied here and there; others were picketed, but most milled slowly in a group inside the corral. A short, wiry fellow wearing, of all things, a black shirt and a black hat stood apart from the rest, arms draped over the rail.

"Must be roasting," said Mitch.

As though he'd been heard, a half dozen of the men swung heads in his direction. Pretty soon all of them did. He nodded at them and strode down the slope, making for a tall, solidly built fellow in jeans and a worn blue chambray shirt. His face sported oversize dragoon moustaches and a perpetual squint beneath a tall-crown, sweat-stained, fawn topper.

Drover Joe Phipps was foreman of the Bar B Ranch and a man Mitch had looked up to for years, though he expected Joe wasn't but a decade older than him. Something undefined, but straight and true about Drover Joe demanded and earned solid and abiding respect from his men.

Mitch stuck out his hand and gave the man a firm, quick shake, as Pa had always taught him to do. *It's a measure of a man,* he'd said, *if he doesn't try to squeeze your fingers until they pop off your hand. Neither should he give you a grip that's weaker than a child's. And for land's sake, look him in the eye when you shake.*

Drover Joe's father must have taught him the same, for he gave a solid shake in return as his gunmetal eyes regarded Mitch. "Mitch. Good to see you."

"Same here, Joe. Been a while."

"Yep." He turned back to the corral. "Pull up a rail. You know most of the crew. A few of the boys will be new to you."

Mitch nodded toward them all, smiled. He saw a few

familiar faces—Chicken Pete, Tully, Sycamore Jim, and Chet among them. He noted others whose names he couldn't recall right then, though he knew they'd been around at least a couple of seasons. As usual on a ranch that size, there were fresh faces. None of them looked overly pleased to see him. *Must be something Cook put in the breakfast beans,* he thought.

He looked to the corral. A swarthy man in a sombrero worked a lariat with impressive expertise.

"The vaquero's Rollo," said Drover Joe. "Solid wrangler. We're putting the remuda together for your big drive."

He shoved back away from the rail and turned. Mitch got the sense he wanted to talk. He fell in beside Joe.

"Well," said Mitch, "it's Mr. Bilks' drive. Me and my herd are more or less tagging along."

Joe rasped a hand over his freshly shaved chin "Not how we were told. Mr. Bilks said you came to him with a proposition, something he felt—How was that now? Oh, yeah, 'compelled to go along with.'" Drover Joe's eyebrows rose as he said this. "He also said you were the boss of the venture."

"What?" Mitch felt his face and ears redden. "No, no, that's not right."

Joe nodded. "Mm-hmm. Said you insisted on it as part of your—What did he call that? 'Tricky negotiations.' That's what he said."

"Oh." Mitch looked up to see they'd not walked but fifteen feet from the corral. Likely the boys had heard every word. From their faces, none of what he'd said was news. He got the impression not one of them wanted to go on a trail drive. And if they had to, they sure didn't want him to ramrod the thing.

"Can I talk with you a minute, Joe?"

"Isn't that what we're doing?"

Mitch thought maybe there was a hint of a smile on the cowboy's face, tough to be certain because of his big moustache.

Mitch's face heated up all over again. "I'll talk with Mr. Bilks. There's been some mistake, that's all."

"Now, Mitch, you know as well as I do that when Bilks sets his mind to a thing, there isn't enough dynamite in all of Texas to shift him. So," said Drover Joe, "let's get these horses sorted. Lots of work to do if we're going to hit the trail by Saturday."

CHAPTER SEVEN

T HE HERD BAWLED and butted and stomped on out
of sight of Cawlins, or rather the northern edge of
Bilks' ranchland, late on the first day. The slowness of
the day's events wasn't a surprise to Mitch, though he
hated it and knew he had to get used to it, and soon.
That's how these things were, slow, grinding, and
steady. Didn't mean it wasn't frustrating as all get-out.
He sighed and rubbed a knuckle in his eyes. It only
worked the dust deeper in.

Drover Joe rode over to Mitch. "What's it going to
be, boss?"

Mitch liked the sound of that word, but winced
when Joe said it. It wouldn't do, especially not when
the man who'd said it had been driving cattle while
Mitch was still in short pants.

"I was thinking about that," said Mitch, trying to sit
taller in the saddle. Every time he saw Drover Joe
Phipps, Mitchell found himself wishing he carried
himself more like the seasoned cowboy.

"Oh, boy, sounds like trouble."

Mitch's eyebrows rose. "Huh?"

"Thinkin'. Never amounts to much good for folks without money." Then he winked. "I was you, I'd—"

A sharp shout cut him off. Both men spun toward the sound to see a cowboy in a black shirt and a black hat pulled low, a red bandanna tugged up over the lower half of his face, flailing aboard a humped, crow-hopping dun that snaked as it bucked. Mitch recognized the man—and his black clothes—from that day at the corral.

"Damn kid," mumbled Drover Joe. "Told him to save the dun for later. He ever listens to me, it'll be the first time." Then he turned to Mitch. "What you want to do about him?"

"Me? Oh, right. Well, I guess I should take care of it." Mitch hesitated. "Anything else I need to know?"

Joe shrugged. "He's a hothead name of Stokes. Wants to be called the Kid, though."

Mitch kicked Champ into a lope, skirting a couple of dozen head of cattle poking along the frayed western edge of the herd.

Behind him he heard Joe shout, "Okay, boss. You settle his hash!" Mitch swore he heard a chuckle. But Drover Joe never laughed, did he?

Mitch was thankful, not for the first time that day, that Champ was a seasoned cattle pony, comfortable around cows. Longhorns were unpredictable critters, even when they were at their most docile. No need to carry on this way in the midst of a herd that hadn't gotten used to life on the trail nor mingled with another herd, no matter if Mitch's beeves were outnumbered nearly six to one.

"Hey, now!" shouted Mitch, neck-reining Champ and coming up along the clinging cowboy's hopping fool of a dun. "You want to get us all trampled this early on?"

The man in black was on the young side, perhaps Mitch's own age. He flailed with each hop the horse took. But he held on, his jaw snapping downward, then rocking back again. His hat worked loose and fell to his shoulders, held by the strap. It revealed a thatch of short, bristly red hair. Much of the man was hidden in a dust cloud, a quirt flailing off his right wrist, then slapping down on the horse's rump, over and over.

Mitch leaned out, snatched at the near rein, missed it, then on a second try managed to snag hold of the leather strap. The big brute horse about tore his arm off, but he held tight through another hop.

As soon as the Kid felt his mount beginning to settle, he jerked the reins hard to the right, sawing to get the dun back under control. The horse had other ideas. Mitch, still gripping the rein, slid in his saddle, felt air beneath his backside, and jammed his boot tighter into the right stirrup.

"Calm yourself, Kid!" he growled, and gave one last tug that pulled the dun closer to the now stomping Champ. That was a sign the big horse had had enough of this foolishness. Somebody was about to get bit.

Mitch let go of the Kid's reins, tugged on Champ's, and growled, "Easy now, easy, boy." Then to the Kid he said, "Swap that horse out. He ain't fit to ride right now."

The spark in the Kid's slate eyes told Mitch all he needed to know. Whoever this young cowhand was, he was about to cause him grief. Mitch sighed as the Kid worked the dun closer, then tugged the dusty red bandanna off his face and jammed his hat back on his head. His cheeks glowed red from the ruckus and his meager ginger moustaches wore sweat droplets.

"I don't much care who you think you're supposed to be, Mr. Fancy, but I work for Corliss Bilks and so for Drover Joe Phipps. I take orders from them and them alone!" The Kid shouted loud enough that Mitch was certain at least a couple other cowboys had heard him. Even the cattle seemed to quiet down.

Mitch sidled Champ closer and leaned over until he was a couple of feet from the black-hatted fool. He couldn't help but notice that, even a-horseback, the Kid was wiry but short. And his dun wasn't a giant, either. *Why is it always short men who seem to cause a ruckus?* thought Mitch.

No matter, Mitch liked the feeling of lording over this squint-eye fool. He sat a good head taller than the Kid and knew he'd be at least a foot taller than the Kid on the ground, too.

"Look, I know you know who I am. And Corliss Bilks isn't here, but I am. If that doesn't matter to you, think on this: I'm the one who holds the purse strings on this drive. If that's too much for you, why, you are free to ride on back right now. I'm sure Mr. Bilks will understand, you and him being so close and all."

For a finger snap of a moment, Mitch saw raw fear slip over the Kid's ruddy features, saw the sweat droplets caught in the kid's wispy ginger hairs tremble on his starter moustaches. Then the hard muscles of the Kid's red cheeks bunched once more.

As if jerked hard by an unseen chain, the Kid's left fist whipped upward and slammed high into Mitch's right cheekbone. Mitch's head snapped back and his vision dimmed, peppered with shots of pulsing stars. His right ear buzzed with a high, zinging sound. He could not have predicted such a reaction from the fool.

Then the Kid struck again, like a cornered rattler double-dosing its victim. The second shot hit lower, caroming off Mitch's thick shoulder, because the first rocked Mitch to his left, away from the Kid, and Mitch hadn't had time to jerk himself upright again.

Despite the buzzing in his ear, he'd heard the fist hit

him—a hard, smacking sound. It put in his mind times when he was a kid and the creek still had water in it, enough to bathe on a hot day. He'd slap the surface with an open hand, then shove a wave at his father, who'd threaten him with "an old-fashion dunking," something he never seemed to follow through with.

That second blow knocked Mitch's balance enough that he felt himself slide fast down the left side of the saddle, past the point where he could right himself, though he tried. But he was too dizzied by that unexpected first fist to the head. He grabbed for what he thought was the saddle horn, only to find it had already whipped past.

Somehow his right boot had freed itself from the stirrup, and he dropped faster, tumbled away from Champ, and hit the solid ground, feeling the whoosh as his wind left him.

Mitch landed hard on his backside, free of the horse. Rage and mortification boiled in him. As he squinted through the dust to avoid Champ's dancing hooves, Mitch thought that never could there be a more shameful situation to be in as a cowboy.

The Kid had thundered off before Mitch shoved upright, found his hat, and smacked it against his chaps. He would choke the life out of that young jackass and be glad to do it.

Champ hadn't stomped far and stood looking bored, waiting for Mitch to mount up once more. "Thanks for nothing," he said, wincing as his face pulsed with the effort of talking.

He rode back to where he'd been before the dustup. Within a few minutes Drover Joe dropped back once more and fell in beside him.

After a lengthy silence, Joe said, "Well, that was interesting. I've never seen a boss man so . . . indulgent."

Despite how he felt about Joe, the past ten minutes

had stretched Mitch thin. His jaw and shoulder ached in counterpoint with each other, and a bucketful of dry dirt had leaked into his jeans when he'd tumbled from the horse. No, he had to be honest about it; he hadn't fallen. That blasted Kid had shoved him from his horse.

Mitch looked at Joe, felt himself still shaking with renewed rage, and shook his head. It was the only thing he could do without shouting the man down.

"I'm inclined to let him go his own way." Mitch touched the tender right side of his face. "Seems that's what he wants."

Joe said nothing, but nibbled on his moustaches a moment. "Kid's good with cattle. He's an idiot, don't listen worth a wet match, but . . ."

"But?" said Mitch.

"We're already a small crew. Can't spare the loss."

Mitch sighed. "How many chances would you give him?"

"One. And that was it."

"Well, his thread's pulled pretty thin, then." Mitch spit a clot of blood and blinked dust from his eyes.

"About that matter we were discussing before you went to deal with junior there."

Mitch closed his eyes and nodded. "Right. We need to call it a day. We didn't make up much distance, did we?"

Joe shrugged. "We will. Always happens this way in the first days of a drive. Slow going, horses testing the men, men testing one another, cattle testing the men, the weather testing us all. We get it figured out, we can make up time."

"You don't seem too worried about that."

"I'm not. Yet." He tugged his hat low again and rode ahead a few feet. "Plenty of time for worry later. Right now you might want to consider whistling for us to ease off for the day."

Mitch sat up straight once more. Whistle? "Oh."

Mitch cleared his throat. He was dry as a plank. He'd also never been very good at whistling.

Joe nodded. "If you're all right with it, I'll give it a go tonight. Looks like your whistler's swelled up."

Mitch touched his tender jaw and winced. "Yeah, sure, if you don't mind, Joe. I'd appreciate that."

The older man touched his hat brim, then rode ahead, disappearing behind a cloud of dust. In a moment Mitch heard a sharp, long whistle that cut through the mismatched bawling of the cattle and the steady yips and growled urgings of the cowboys. A second sharp whistle followed, then a third, all the same duration, each one from a different direction.

Word, Mitch saw, passed from man to man and eventually the herd slowed, then stopped. He rode up to where he guessed Joe would be, and as the dust cleared, he was surprised to see, northeastward, that the cook tent was already set up. He felt shame redden his cheeks once more, then climb up and color his ears a hot red.

He needn't have been so worked up about the decision to stop. Tonight's stop had likely been decided long before by Joe and Cook. Joe, as true foreman of the drive, was showing him a kindness by teaching through doing. There was so much to learn he wasn't certain how he'd go about it, nor retain it once he did grapple it to the ground.

With that thought, he spied something that set his teeth together tight. It was the Kid on the dun, or rather the Kid who'd been on the dun. Now he was astride a black that looked a whole lot smoother than the dun had been. He rode not twenty feet away from Mitch and whipped a sidelong sneer his way as he trotted by.

Smirk all you want, damn you, thought Mitch, *but you went and swapped that mount, didn't you? Like I told you to.* Mitch let himself enjoy a thin smile.

He sighed again and felt the blood pulse in his cheek, right where that wiry little rogue had popped him. He'd give anything to get back the minutes before it happened. First day out, supposed to be the boss, or at least a boss of some sort, and he'd been knocked on his backside by a cock-of-the-walk runt kid.

He couldn't let the Kid walk on him like that. He knew it was expected of him to challenge the Kid and dole out a beating on him in return. And Mitch didn't doubt he could do it. But that wasn't his way.

Then his gut roiled and growled as he looked ahead at the chuck setup and smelled what would be the first of countless meals on the trail. If he wasn't mistaken, there were beans and biscuits, fresh baked and wafting to him along with the heady stink of powdered dung and dust. If that was the way he'd have to take his meals, so be it. He was so hungry he could gnaw the bark off a mesquite and come back for a second helping.

"First things first, Mitch," he said, glancing around to see if anybody heard him. The only soul was a cowboy a good twenty yards behind; the vaquero, whom he had noticed earlier, hadn't mixed much with the other men.

Rollo, thought Mitch. *His name is Rollo.* The man caught Mitch looking his way and bent his head, hustled his horse, a smooth-muscled roan, around toward the rear of the herd.

Champ whickered and slowed to a plod.

"You, too?" said Mitch. "I get grief from one more beast today, four- or two-legged, and you all will see what Mitchell Newland can get up to when he has a mind. And a dinner plate to lick clean."

He tapped the horse's barrel with his bootheels and made for the chuck.

CHAPTER EIGHT

S EVERAL DAYS LATER found Mitch accompanying
Drover Joe on a quick detour from the herd to
round up a stray steer. It didn't take long before the two
men heard something familiar, something they both
knew well and both hated.

The sound, like a half dozen dried gourds being
shaken, their seeds hard and rattling inside, could be
heard from forty, fifty feet away. But it wasn't seeds in
gourds, and it wasn't quiet. It was loud and menacing
and sounded as though it were all about the pair of men.

"Damn these strays," growled Drover Joe. "Led us
right into a snake field. Should have known better."

"I hate rattlers," said Mitch. He'd heard, seen, and
killed plenty of the vile things in his short life so far.
"From the sound, we interrupted their supper."

"We'd best retreat," said Joe. "Guide that horse
slow. See that big one, no, off to your left?"

Mitch nodded, drops of cold sweat beading on his

top lip. His hands shook, one atop the pommel, the other smoothing the reins slowly, over and over.

"Mitch!" barked Joe. "Pay attention to what I'm saying. I'll be right behind you. Now lead the way, and keep a sharp eye."

"What about the steer?"

"He's on his own. If he doesn't make it out, to hell with him," said Joe. "Might be he'll die so we can live. Enough talking—pick your path."

Mitch nudged Champ forward. The great horse's breathing came out loud and trembly. "Easy, boy, easy."

"Take care—watch that fat one to your right."

Before Mitch could see it, the crack of a revolver shot nearly unseated him, not because Champ reared up, but from his own sudden surprise. He finally saw the snake Joe was talking about—with a smoking hole bored in its flat wedge head, as if the thing had been hammered into the ground where it lay. Its wrist-thick body coiled and roiled under and over itself, the dozen-button rattle spasming, slowing before stiffening and rattling once more.

Champ surprised Mitch by not crow-hopping and dancing around in the foul, rocky place.

Then the cow they'd been making for gave a great, deep bellow, his head down and ears perked forward. He stood stiff legged, staring at something in front of him on the ground. Then that something launched itself at him and muckled onto his great rubbery snout. Before it could dislodge itself, the steer jerked his head side to side and the snake, like a great pulsing rope, whipped back and forth, snapping against his ribs.

The steer kept up a great bleating sound that tapered into a long, high-pitch squeal, as if he were being squeezed to death from one end to the other. He trembled and clots of white foam flecked his muzzle and slipped from his mouth. Still, the beef worked his head side to side, though slower with each pass.

"Oh, no, Spunk," said Mitch. "Not Spunk."

"Never pays to get yourself attached to a beef. Only let you down when you eat 'em."

Joe's words were of less comfort than if he'd kept his mouth shut.

"Keep moving. Make certain we're good and shed of this spot.

"But the steer . . ."

"Nothing you can do for him now!"

It was the second time in as many minutes that Mitch had heard Drover Joe raise his voice, and he wasn't sure he wanted to hear it again. It wore an edge of hard steel.

The two men guided their mounts, picking their way free of the weird, rocky snake ground, then halted. The beef was down on his front knees, his mewling pitiful, his mouth swelled nearly shut. Still, Mitch saw that foul snake curling and slapping away, stuck in the cow's nose somehow, unable to get free. To his right he saw Joe raise his rifle.

"Nothing we can do," said the cowboy.

Mitch knew. He'd been around snakes his entire life. In his estimation, they weren't good for much of anything, except for dying when you got the chance to kill them. He wasn't prone to taking a creature's most valuable thing, its life, but snakes rendered the notion of compassion a far-fetched thought at best.

Drover Joe shucked his rifle from its scabbard and squeezed off a shot. A thumb-size clot of deep red welled on the beef's temple, between the eye and the ear, and spilled a rivulet down the side of his long, smooth jaw. He leaned to his right but didn't topple. Joe levered another round and sent it close by the first. That did the job.

The critter slopped to his side, his hindquarters stayed upright a moment longer than the rest of him; then that, too, collapsed in a rise of dust. His topmost legs, those of his left side, trembled, straight outward, stiff as lengths of seasoned mesquite.

"Sorry, Mitch. I know how you feel about your cows."

"Yeah," said Mitch, turning Champ so he wouldn't have to look at Joe. "This life is not a good one for cattle. Hard, with a raw mess at the end."

He knew it was a bitter thought, but he didn't care. He'd caused that poor beast to die this way as surely as if he'd tossed the snake at his face. If he hadn't been so desperate to make money and better himself, and the ranch, that beef would still be alive. But for how long?

Mitch glanced back at the steer. It lay partially facing them, and though Mitch knew it had stopped breathing, he thought maybe he saw that great belly give one last shuddering sigh. The most unsettling part, though, was its swelling face; that muzzle had puffed up to four times its normal size.

"I helped birth him. He was a steer my father would have had a liking for, big and rangy and kindly, more or less. Hard to tell, it's been so long since Pap died. Tricky to remember as time goes on."

The tall man nodded, nibbled his moustaches. "I hear you. We all need reminders. No shame in that. I carry a locket in my traps that belonged to my mother. My father gave it to her when they wed. There's a little picture of him in it, and a tiny curl of hair from her head, long before it grayed." He shrugged. "Might be a day when I don't need such a thing anymore, but Mother's been gone these three years, so I reckon it'll take time. I'm in no rush to speed the plow."

"I reckon my reminder is the ranch itself," said Mitch. "Only thing he left me that's worth anything. Even that came with debt."

They rode in agreeable silence a while. Then Joe asked, "How'd he die?"

"Oh, my pap," said Mitch. He let out a breath he hadn't known he'd been holding in. "The short version is the bottle."

Joe nodded, said nothing.

"Long version is he fell off his horse. He'd been riding when he ought not to have, and riding hard, to boot. His horse, a pretty old black named Coal, snapped a foreleg in a rathole. Sent Pap flying, landed on his head, did something to his neck. He laid that way for hours until I found him. The horse was in agony. I had to do for him, then get Pap home. He couldn't move of his own will. He did talk some, at the end. Lingered for a couple of days."

"How old were you?" Joe's tone was straightforward, not prying.

"I was fifteen."

"That's a hard knock to take anytime. But so young, why, that's doubly sore."

Mitch shrugged. "It was a long time ago. So long ago it almost feels like it had happened to a different person than me."

They rode on in silence.

CHAPTER NINE

A S THE DAYS stacked up, the crew grew accustomed to one another and to the routine of life on the trail. Of the nine men, all but Mitch were seasoned hands who'd spent time on at least one drive before this one. Mitch groaned inside whenever he thought of how arrogant and foolish he must have sounded to Mr. Bilks when he'd first presented the idea to him.

He much preferred to let Drover Joe Phipps run the drive. Joe insisted on calling Mitch "boss," at least in front of the other men, something Mitch balked at. After a few days on the trail, the lanky cowboy motioned for Mitch to follow him. They stood off to the side, not able to avoid the heat of the day's growing sun.

"I'd hoped you would understand what I'm on about when I call you 'boss.' It's not because I'm going soft in the head. It's because oftentimes on a drive, you'll get the moneyman along on the trip—the real boss in life, if you understand what I mean. And he's called 'boss,' even though the ramrod does the thinking. It's for the benefit of the rest of the men, really. They'll never follow you as ramrod."

"Is it that obvious I don't know what I'm doing?"

Joe smiled and nodded. "Yeah, it is. But don't let that get to you. This way, they'll still give you the respect a moneyman deserves. Someday on the trail, that'll come in useful."

And that had been the way of it for nigh on a week, with Mitch keeping his mouth closed, responding to "boss," and learning everything he could about this side of the cattle business.

One early evening found a small handful of men at chuck, as it was their turn before spelling others so they might do the same. Mitch spooned in a second plateful of beans, amazed at how hungry he was on the drive. "Forever peckish" is how he described it, and he could only imagine how the horses felt, let alone the beeves, who existed, as always, on stubbly grasses, already nubbed from previous drives.

"Sycamore, huh?" said the Kid from across the fire. Then he made a short, sharp sound, as if he were spitting. "Sounds made-up to me."

Sycamore Jim's brows pulled together. "Well, if you're asking if my mother give it to me, then, no, sir, she didn't. Well, the Jim part, sure. But the Sycamore, I come by that natural. Was my uncle Samuelson who started calling me that on account of how I'd climb this big ol'—"

"I look like I care?" The Kid turned away, but in the fire's glow on the left side of his face, Mitch saw a thin smile.

Cruel, he thought. *He said that to be cruel.* Mitch glanced at Sycamore and the young man looked hurt, to be sure, but confused more than anything, as did the other two men. Cook, it seemed, was out of hearing range.

Mitch wished Drover was about, but stopped himself. If he waited for him, or anyone else, to fight his battles, he'd be a long time lost in this world. Before he could rethink his scant momentary plan, Mitch set his plate down, dragged a cuff across his mouth, and walked over to the Kid. "I'd like to talk with you."

He intentionally stood close, closer than was comfortable, to the shorter man. Mitch was a good head taller, and he looked down at him. "Over there." He nodded toward an empty spot on the far side of the fire, away from the wagon and the men.

"Why?"

Mitch noted the young man had lost the barest slip of that cocky grin, then gained it back as he glanced toward the other men, then back to Mitch.

"I'm eating. Bother me later."

Every single thing that annoyed Mitch about the Kid boiled up in that instant. Mitch's left hand swung upward and sent the Kid's tin plate wheeling skyward, biscuit spinning and beans spraying.

"Hey!"

That was all the Kid had time to say because Mitch's big hands snatched at the Kid's chest, balled the shirtfront and leather vest, and lifted him a couple of inches off the ground. He rammed forward, steering him around the fire to a clear patch.

The Kid lost all footing and collapsed backward on the ground, one elbow out, stopping his fall with a sudden jerk. He tried to rise, his boots scuffing and digging hard into the packed earth, but Mitch straddled him and bent low, the long fingers of one hand outstretched and jamming the Kid's chest back down.

With his left fist, he delivered a quick shot to the leering little fool's rangy chin. The young man's head whipped to the side, stunned for a moment.

The big man's right mitt gathered the shirtfront and

vest once more, and he jerked the Kid upward. The action brought the Kid around and he thrashed and bucked, slapping and cursing blue words. They were the sort Mitch had certainly heard but had never uttered himself, even when alone, mired in thorns and dung and surly beeves, out on the range.

But the sound of them, along with the windmilling whirr of the Kid's hard fist and the thrashing, muscled arms and legs pummeling him, only made Mitch more certain that he'd chosen the right course of action. He let the Kid have another one, and a third and fourth, the last from his hard right fist, for equal measure.

The Kid sagged under his clawed hand, still grasping the shirtfront, and Mitch drew his fist back for another battering right, when he felt a hard hand on his arm, a hand that gripped his arm firmly. He turned, fist poised in the air. It was Cook.

"Okay, Mitchell. He's had enough." The man winked at him. "For now."

Cook returned to the chuck wagon.

Mitch, still holding the dazed, lolling cowboy aloft by his shirtfront, saw the other men staring at him. He dropped the Kid, who crabbed on his back and shook his head. "What was that for?"

Mitch pulled in a big breath of air and was about to shout a list of annoyances and affronts that he'd given them all, but shook his head instead and said, "Everything." He walked back to his plate, flexing his fingers. He half-expected the Kid to jump him, but apparently the young hothead knew better.

The others, Sycamore and Tully and Chicken Pete, eyed him over their nearly empty plates. Mitch wasn't thinking of much as he spooned in the last of his now cold beans and sopped up the juice with his remaining biscuit.

No one spoke to him as he finished eating. His coffee had turned cold, too, but he didn't care. If the Kid didn't understand what a jackass he was, neither Mitch nor anyone else would get through to him. Ever.

He saw, with a sideways glance, the Kid rise, adjust his clothes, pat himself down, then do the same with his hat. He moved slowly, as if he were an old man, back toward his plate, facedown in the dirt. He stopped, stared at it a moment, then walked away toward his horse, saddled and waiting. He rode off.

For a moment Mitch thought the Kid might make southward, toward where they'd come from that day, and then homeward. But no, he rode toward the herd and his night rider duties.

After a few moments of silence, Mitch cleared his throat. "I'm sorry it came to that, fellas."

That seemed to crack the ice between them. Tully stretched his legs out. "Heck, my paw said never apologize for putting a no-count in his place. That Kid, he's been asking for that since he come to the Bar B."

Sycamore nodded. "That's a fact. Been riding me hard all the time. I don't know what it is about me, but folks seem to like to get my goat. I ain't never been brave enough to do what you did, though, Mitch. Much appreciated."

Mitch felt his face heat up. "I'd be lying if I said it was for you and not me, Sycamore. You all saw what he did to me that first day. I can't let that stand."

"That Kid," said Tully, "he's all bluster. His problem is he don't like to be told what to do."

"I guess he'll have to get over that," said Cook, walking up behind them with the coffeepot. "Anybody need a top-up?"

Every man held out his cup.

"Don't get the notion I'm always this nice. I happen

to be in a good mood because that pesky Kid got what he's been begging for."

"Now maybe we'll get some peace," said Sycamore.

"Huh," said the big Cajun. "Don't count on it. We ain't but just begun."

CHAPTER TEN

It was smoke that twitched Drover Joe Phipps' nostrils. He'd slid down out of the saddle a good twenty minutes before in order to give Trooper a rest from carrying his sorry hide all over creation.

He'd also been giving his back a rest from pounding up and down, side to side, in the saddle. How many more years would he be able to spend all his time a-horseback and still be able to walk upright once he'd finished for the day?

Joe walked along, keeping an eye on the dry earth ahead, taking in the dung piles and hoofprints of the last trail drive. He reckoned it had passed through nigh on a month before.

He let his mind mosey over to the tempting but seldom visited notion of someday. Would he ever marry? Raise up a few youngsters, perhaps a son? In truth he didn't care, boy or girl, as long as it was healthy and happy and not a vexation to him and the mama, whoever that might be.

Would this woman he would meet look as he hoped she did? Would her mind be her own and challenge him at every turn? Part of him hoped so. He admired the spirit of young Evelyn Bilks and envied equally young Mitchell Newland and his standing with one such as her.

"Someday," he said to Trooper. "Someday we'll find us a fine mate and look back on these days as one might a funny daydream, eh, boy?"

Troop whinnied and worked his head up and down like a pump handle.

"What is it, boy?"

Joe had been around horses most of his life and knew never to ignore their instinctive reactions. He followed the horse's sight line up, ahead to the northeast, and saw little more than he'd seen all morning since he'd ridden off before light, away from camp. He'd filled his neck with coffee and filled his pockets with fluffy sourdough biscuits and lit out for a few hours of scouting.

The sky had been a fine purple shawl spread high, the last stars winking down even as dawn cracked the horizon and revealed the broad reach of the plains toward Kansas.

It didn't feel as odd to Joe to be passing right by Kansas, leaving it to the east of them, as it likely did to some of the other hands who'd only ever driven stock to the railheads in Abilene and Thomaston.

He, for one, was pleased they'd be traveling all the way to Montana Territory. A long trip, to be sure, and not one for the weak of will, but he was not one for being cooped up on a ranch for months without end. Besides, this was a trip a man ought to make with a herd, if only to see for himself the vastness of this land before it was hacked apart by farmers and ranchers and trains and buggies and dandies all looking for their own piece.

He could hardly blame them, but sometimes he fretted for the future of this land, for what it was fast be-

coming and what it would end up as. Would there be
so many people here one day that the land would be all
but gone, chewed up by greed? The thought made him
shudder and he shook it off. *Enjoy the day, man,* he
reminded himself.

He was looking forward to seeing real mountains
once more. It had been too long since he'd set eyes on
the great Rockies, seen them loom large for days. They
never seemed to grow closer, yet they did the entire
time the drovers moved the stock forward.

Out of instinct as much as professional practice, Joe
Phipps stood beside Trooper, each with head canted
high, working their nostrils and sniffing a scanty breeze.

A thread of something carried on that breeze. What
was that? Joe closed his eyes and sniffed gently but
deeply. He snapped open his eyes and rummaged in his
saddlebag, then pulled out a brass telescope and yanked
it open, full length, and twisted the worn eyepiece as he
balanced the shaft on a scarred knuckle.

The honeyed metal warmed in the sunlight. "My
word," he said as his gaze settled on the edge of land
far to the northeast. The line of distant hills, with waving grasses between, blurred, focused, blurred as he
roved the spyglass left to right and back again.

Something tremored, disappeared, wriggled once
more into view before settling back into the lavender
vista he'd seen at first. But it was a vista of moving
clouds, too low, though, to be clouds.

"My word," he said again, and climbed back into the
saddle. In a moment, the only evidence he had been
there was a cloud trail of smoky dust.

J OE SLID FROM the saddle and tugged off his sweat-
stained topper. He shoved his palm up his forehead,
smearing back damp, sand-colored hair.

"What you doing back so soon? Run out of biscuits already?" Cook chuckled, then lost his smile as he saw Joe's face.

Mitch finished his coffee and set down his cup.

"Grass fire. Don't know what or who set it, nor why, but it's a fast mover. Gnawing up everything in its way, mostly dry grass and clumps of sage. And it's headed for us."

"How far?"

Joe nodded from where he'd ridden, northeastward. "Couple of hours that way." He made certain Trooper was getting his pull at the water trough before raising a dipper for himself from the barrel roped to the wagon.

"We in danger?"

Joe shrugged. "Might not be, but I'd hate to play that game."

"What do we do?" said Mitch.

"Only thing we can do." Joe hunkered and dragged a long finger in the dirt at his feet. "Here's where we are. Here's the fire line. We're headed thataway." He drew an arrow pointing northwest. "We keep on that path and we might outpace it. Depends on the wind and how fast we dare to push."

"We best get a move on, then. I'll tell the men." Mitch mounted up and was halfway to the back of the herd before he thought to second-guess himself. *Maybe Joe has more of a plan?* he wondered. He glanced over his shoulder but nobody had followed, so he kept riding, feeling that maybe he was getting a feel for driving herd.

Within another couple of minutes, he'd related the news to Sycamore and Tully. Mitch held drag with Sycamore while Tully rode around the east edge of the herd, telling the others.

Everyone knew the dangers of kicking the beeves

into a faster pace, but a prairie fire was too big a gamble. As long as they could keep the herd moving in the general direction they intended, there was a good chance they could keep control of it. If not, it could sprawl into a stampede.

"Nothing a harebrained steer likes better than a flat-out run to nowhere in particular. Why, I've seen 'em run themselves to death. Go and go and go until their hearts explode!" Sycamore rapped his chest with a bony fist and nodded.

In the short time he'd come to spend with Sycamore, Mitch knew that though the young man from Tennessee could spin a yarn when he was of a mind, in a situation as dire as this, he was apt to stick to the hard truth. Mitch accepted his words as useful wisdom, and wondered how on earth they could keep eight hundred head of bulge-eye beef cattle from tearing themselves apart in a blind, panicked run.

As if he'd read his mind, Sycamore said, "But that was a special situation. That was lightning or some such. No, no, now that I think on it, maybe it was a fire and a whole lot of smoke started by a lightning strike." He snapped his fingers. "Yep, that was it."

Then he realized that it was fire and smoke they were running from, and he shrugged. "Aw, boss, don't mind me. I talk a whole lot, but . . ."

His words were lost to Mitch as they separated, one splitting left, the other right, tending the fraying edges of the herd as it surged forward. The mass of beeves picked up its walking-and-grazing pace, and for the first few minutes, it seemed as if they might get away with the increased pace without mishap.

Then he saw a natural shift in the cattle that Mitch had seen twice before in the first uneventful two weeks on this drive—it was as if the herd was a single living beast undulating over the vast grassy plain before them.

The entire mass of cattle moved as one, and he'd learned that when they found a common rhythm, the danger level was at its highest. *And this isn't looking good,* thought Mitch. For instead of running at the urged pace set by the cowboys, the cattle bolted faster and faster, their constant bellowing even dwindled, replaced with a raspy, mismatched huffing, their eyes wide and white.

It was up to the boys near the front of the herd to keep them in check, and turn them in on themselves should the run bloom into a stampede. But that wasn't likely today, as it was fast becoming apparent they couldn't afford to lose any ground. Maybe a straight-ahead controlled run was the best.

The animals bawled, their dust and stink clouding all and rising into the blue sky. The men, bandannas drawn high beneath their owling eyes, coughed and snotted and rubbed at their dust-caked watering eyes. There wasn't a man among them who could see beyond his horse's ears, save for the darker, teeming mass of cattle before them.

Sycamore shouted something, but it was little more than a passing sound that peeled up and away. Mitch didn't even want to guess at the message. All he had to think about was how to get the cattle up the trail and out of potential danger's hard promise.

As he and the rest of the boys struggled not to lose complete control of the herd, a new smell tickled Mitch's nostrils. It was not the usual dung and dust, but the pungent tang of smoke. It took moments to reach all the men. It seemed to have a similar effect on the cattle, for they ran harder, packed together shoulder to rump, heads raised, horns clacking horns.

Mitch visored his eyes beneath his hat brim and thought perhaps that he could see it coming from the northeast, the very direction Joe had said. The line of fire shimmered as far-off flicks of orange-red that danced along the edge of the landscape. Then, in a blink, the fire was less distant than it had been, the flames taller, closer.

With them, the smoke made its presence even more obvious. Second by second, the great, roiling black-and-gray wall seemed to double in height, a ground-hugging layer of storm cloud, and it moved closer with each moment.

The distance from fire to herd looked to be less than a mile and closing fast. Stampede be damned, they had to get the cattle and themselves beyond the far end of it. There was a moment when Mitch lost sight of the fire, and he hoped that perhaps it had somehow met with an unseen river and had delivered itself unto its own demise, quenched by the cooling water.

Then the fire reappeared, closer still, the flames taller. He saw why he'd lost sight of it—a dip in the terrain that had hidden it from view for a few merciful moments had given him false hope. Now, though, he did not see how they could outrun the thing.

A steer, more red than white, rangy and determined to break free of the herd, slipped past him, pounding hard eastward toward the racing line of blaze before sensing its error and jerking itself in midstride back toward the storming herd. If the fire was useful for anything, it was in keeping this flank of the herd contained.

Between them and the low, roaring wall of licking flame, Mitch saw through the smoke something large churning forward, sharing their direction. A break in the thick smoke and dust showed him it was Cook in jouncing, howling command of his chuck wagon.

Mitch even fancied he heard the clanging and clanking of pots and pans and who knew what else slamming inside and hanging from the outside of the big man's normally tidy wagon.

If he could keep his mules, Romulus and Remus, at that pace, they might make it. The wagon was hitting some mighty big ruts and boulders, though, risking snapping a wheel or worse.

He doubted Cook was able to see the terrain ahead any better than the rest of them, but he drove that loaded wagon, tugged by a brace of lathered mules, as if he had a clear road. The sight emboldened Mitch.

The men coughed steadily, smoke raking in and out of their lungs with cruel, snaky fingers. They kept their heads low, drawing shallow breaths through sweat-soaked shirts, then rose up and growled and swore at the cattle before dipping down again, retching. All they could do was keep themselves up with the cattle and not get stomped under the thundering hooves.

It seemed to Mitch they ran for hours, as if the very hounds of hell were on their heels. And the entire time, the line of fire crept closer and closer, though they paralleled it as they raced northwestward. The fire knew no straight path, nor did the cattle, but with effort, the men were able to keep the herd stomping on the good, as yet unburned side of the plain.

Then, from ahead, to his right, Mitch heard a sound barely clawing its way above the others. Something of a shout and a yip. He didn't have time to wonder what that might mean, or who had uttered it, because in the time he'd looked westward and back again, the fire had leapt closer.

A vast patch of still green grass sat behind the pulsing flames as if it had defied the fire, at least for a short time. By leaping that sizable sward, for a reason unknown to Mitch, the fire had strategized and come up with a winning hand. *Now it's your turn,* the blaze seemed to say, without letup. *Lay down some impressive cards or I will have you.*

The fire, when he thought of it in that way, reminded Mitch of Corliss Bilks. And the thought forced him to grimace. He had long known the sort of man Bilks was and what Bilks had always thought of Pap, and so, of Mitch. What an odd time for disgust to come to mind. Yet he knew why he'd thought of Bilks right then—Mitch was locked tight in a situation in which he might well die. Just what Bilks would like.

He gritted his teeth and redoubled his efforts to keep the herd intact. Yet there wasn't a thing he could do to help them, especially riding drag. They didn't need much encouragement from him anyway; the beeves were pounding for all they were worth.

At what point, Mitch wondered, would the urge to outdistance them and save himself and Champ overcome him? He couldn't let that happen. He knew his beeves too well. Heck, he had helped usher a number of them into the world.

He coughed as if there'd never been a time in his life when he hadn't coughed.

It felt impossible to abandon any creature to a fate as horrid as burning alive. And yet that was what they would all soon experience if something miraculous didn't happen.

Then the strange moaning sound he'd heard from ahead rose up again, and he still didn't know what it was. The shout of a man? *Good news, please let it be,* he thought. He tried to stifle his smoky retching, but the effort only made all-but-impossible breathing even worse.

The flames had raced to within fifty feet of them now, and the smoke was black and terrible. Cattle spun as if jerked by unseen ropes, bawling and dropping to their knees. Champ lost his footing once, regained a second time and kept on, but slower, dragging now. The horse's own rasping breaths came harder with each labored lunge. His lather and sweat dissolved in smoke and vapor as soon as it formed.

The unbearable heat cindered all. Mitch felt as if his clothes were set to ignite.

And then they did.

He felt the rush of the worst heat yet along his right side and saw curls of black smoke fed by a rime of orange as his hat brim caught fire. His shirtsleeve did the same, curling and puckering and falling away. He swatted it with his gloved left hand and bent lower, shouting over other weird shouting sounds that had come from somewhere ahead.

Then came a deep groaning from the fire's direction. It was like a sound he'd heard before, years before when Pap had taken him to his beloved Texas coast. It was the pounding, rushing, roaring, bold sound of the never-ending sea rolling to shore, then out again. Only these waves were starved flames, never satisfied as they curled forward on the nimblest of legs, consuming with high greed all in their path. Still he rode on.

So thick was the smoke, Mitch hadn't noticed that the herd had shifted direction westward until he found himself drumming down a slight decline, then sensed something that for a moment felt like trickery—wetness, water flecking up at him, pelting his arms and face. *Can't be,* he thought. *I must be lost in a moment of trickery of the mind.* And then he heard it, splashing. *Splashing?*

He urged Champ onward, half-convinced he was somehow dying and didn't know it. The other half of his mind knew there must be some sort of explanation for the feeling of wetness that persisted, as if rain were falling upward. Then came voices shouting and cattle bellowing around him. And more water, the splashing sound clashing with the roaring flames.

Below him, Mitch saw something that flicked and glinted, something shiny that wasn't fire. It was a river, or at least a creek. And then he was through it, across it, and found himself atop a horse slowing from an all-out run. He weakly tried to urge Champ onward, but the horse would have none of it. Neither did the cattle ahead. They'd slowed to a wobbly lope, the air still thick and gray.

"Ease up, ease up now!"

It was a voice Mitch recognized. "Joe? That you?"

"Mitch? You good? We're safer, but keep walking them, keep 'em moving!"

In another five minutes, the smoke cleared enough that he could see the entire herd ranged wide before him, all still moving at little more than a walk, with riders here and there. And far to the right, there wagged the jostling top of Cook's wagon, singed and smoking, but still rolling, keeping pace with the herd.

Mitch saw Drover Joe along that side of the herd, too, riding toward Cook. Then Sycamore rode up along his left. "Mitch! You made it! Good." His voice was hoarse and low, and he leaned over in a coughing jag once he spoke.

The skinny cowboy was barely recognizable. His hat was scorched, his face and arms were blackened, and the gray hair of his horse, Rascal, was much the same. But when Sycamore smiled, his teeth shone white through the grime.

Mitch reckoned he looked much the same. "Everybody okay?"

"Yeah, seem to be." Sycamore spat, then said, "Look at that." He nodded past Mitch.

Mitch turned and saw what had been at times a

man-high wall of flame was now half the height and pitching low, the line of it little more in places than a smoking, sizzling black zag on the land. And on this side of it coursed a wide shallow stream that looked to Mitch like a gift from above.

"We did it," said Mitch, more to himself and Champ than to anyone else.

But beside him, Sycamore sighed. "You bet we did. We made it."

CHAPTER ELEVEN

MITCHELL NEWLAND SPENT eight years alone on the Twin N, tending his own affairs, minding his own business, and sweating for no man other than himself. At the end of each day, he'd strip down at the washstand and scrub himself raw with a nub of lye soap before broiling a stringy cut of beef from whatever critter had had the bad luck to injure a leg or draw the short stick in the vast games of chance among the powers that spin the earth.

Then he'd collapse on his too-thin wool-stuffed sack mattress, the only thing between his lanky, muscled frame and the sagged ropes of the same narrow bed he'd used most of his life. Then he'd wake before dawn and stride into a new day on the ranch.

Now on the trail, as he once again performed his morning ablutions, Mitch ruminated on the strange, frightening, and downright exciting turns his life had taken in the last month.

He stood at the washbasin, as did all the men in their turn, half-stripped and scrubbing the trail dust and sweat from their faces and hands, each washing with ginger care the various half-healed burns and cuts and singed spots they'd gotten from the hellish prairie fire of two weeks before.

They'd come out of it better than he had thought they might at the time. All in all, they lost six head to the blaze, critters who'd stumbled and either broken a limb or hadn't been able to keep up, and so were consumed by the rushing flames. Mitch had heard their screams—for that's what they were, high-pitched, frenzied screams—as they died, burning alive.

They'd lost no men and no horses, though Rollo had had to put down one fine paint whose lungs had sounded worse with each day that followed the fire. Though Joe had offered, the wrangler refused and did the deed himself. If the men had thought the vaquero had been the quiet type before, he was now wholly silent among them, spending all his time doctoring the horses' burns and tending their various needs.

As to the men, they all suffered from burns and blisters and racking, persistent coughs that a spell of hot, dry days seemed to help. That and Cook's insistence—with Joe's blessing—on dosing each man with a shot of rye whiskey morning and night, "a tonic to begin and end the day with," he said. Nobody argued with that remedy.

Mitch eyed himself in Cook's tiny mirror, raking his whisker-stubbled chin with soapy fingers. It was tricky to see more than a couple of inches at a time of any plot of his face. He wondered if he should let the entire thing go like Cook seemed to be doing.

It'd be simpler, to be sure, than scraping clean every few days, save for the top lip. Now that was worth some thought. He'd been inclined to grow moustaches in the past, but had in the end shaved smooth in deference to Evie's silent yet convincing assessments.

He'd gotten the impression she wasn't certain moustaches were for Mitch, but her preferences weren't high on his list of concerns, at the moment. He would not see her for many months—and even when he did, would she still want him? That last fight had been tough, a judgment that had thumped him hard, as if he'd been kicked, kicked, and kicked again in the breadbasket by an ornery bullock.

A grunt from Cook broke off his thoughts and he turned to see what the cause might be. Drover Joe's horse was recognizable before the man atop it was. The solid, tall buckskin, Trooper, Joe's favored horse for his daily scouting forays, thundered toward camp.

His was a slow, steady, drumming rhythm that grew louder until Joe himself was recognizable, with his usual blue chambray shirt, billowing and wrinkling about his waist as they galloped.

Mitch had not needed to be taught that whenever someone from the drive rode up, or whenever anyone was spotted, stranger or no, he should always be alert and make for the wagon, where the guns were kept.

Other than Joe, when he rode north on his daily scouts, none of the crew had yet found cause to carry a gun, long, revolver, or otherwise. Firearms were near enough at hand in the front of Cook's rolling chuck. This was accepted practice on most trail drives, as the extra weight of revolver and rifles wore man and horse down that much sooner on long days in the saddle. The men who needed to carry guns daily did so—the meat makers and scouts.

There was not much of a cause for concern, said Joe, until they found themselves deeper in unfamiliar terrain. There, he'd said, they'd all go heeled. For no one knew what dangers, in the form of two-legged vermin, might be lurking over a dusty rise, behind a cluster of boulders, atop a jag of sandstone, or hunkered in a dry wash.

"Well, what did you find out?" Cook, not a man for small talk, dried his hands, dripping from the light scrub down he'd given the breakfast dishes. "I got to get on up trail, too much to do before you vultures circle for evening grub."

"Hold your complaining until I give you the news." Joe swung down out of the saddle and stretched his back.

Rollo, the wrangler, happened to be finishing up his own breakfast later than the rest, and nodded toward Drover Joe, who nodded back. Without a word between the two men, the quiet vaquero walked over, accepted the proffered reins, and led Trooper to the remuda to drink, eat, and get a rubdown before they all moved out, northward, ever northward.

The near silent wrangler kept early and late hours, tending his charges as diligently and as kindly as if they were each his own horse. Indeed, for all the care the man lavished on those beasts, and given the very little time he spent in the company of the other men, it was obvious to Mitch that he preferred the company of the steeds to that of his own kind.

He'd heard of such horsemen, of course, but until he'd made Rollo's acquaintance, he'd not met one. To be that close to something other than one's own kind, he decided, was special.

Joe gulped down a dipperful of water from the short barrel lashed to the rear side of Cook's wagon. It was getting low, Mitch could tell, because Joe's arm disappeared inside, the gray enamel tin dipper clunking the soaked-stave sides before withdrawing it for a second go. This one he sipped slowly. Finally he glanced over at Cook, who looked fit to pop.

For his part, Drover Joe Phipps looked to be amused by this. "You might want to raise this buggy up a mite."

"Why?" Cook craned his head forward, squinting. "What d'you mean?"

"High water on the Caliche. Those cloud banks we've been seeing?"

"Yeah?"

"Unseasonable rains north of here. I feared this, a fella back in Cawlins fresh off the trail mentioned it to be one of the hazards of a late start such as ours. Worse the farther north we travel as the season wears on."

Mitch tightened his jaw. It was not intended by Joe as a dig, but it felt like one nonetheless. After all, it had been Mitch who'd forced Bilks' hand, resurrecting the canceled drive, and he carried that as a twinge of guilt every time they encountered a hardship on the trail.

Cook groaned. "How high will it get?"

Mitch walked over to them, drying himself off with his shirt before shaking it and tugging it on once more. It was getting a tad whiffy, as his father used to say of each of them come Saturday evening, also known as bath night. But he hadn't had the chance to wash his spare duds since they'd started the drive. Decent watering holes had been scarce and reserved for drinking by cattle, horses, then men.

Joe's gaze sharpened. "If we don't get there soon, it'll be too high for your wagon to cross safely. At least at the spot I'd like to cross. Other than that, we have three choices, and not a good option among them."

"What are they?" asked Mitch.

"Well." Joe accepted a cup of steaming black coffee from Cook with a nod of thanks and sipped, then smoothed his moustaches. "We can swing the herd west by two, three days. Give the flow time to calm itself— the Caliche is a south vein off the Arkansas River, but it runs roughly east to west, which makes it tricky for us. That way would lose us at least three days, likely four, all told. And I'm not familiar with the terrain we'd meet to get back to our trail once we do cross."

"The second option?"

"Wait it out. Flow like that's bound to shrink and smooth, enough for our purposes anyway, in a day or two."

Mitch pictured sitting riverside, keeping the herd busy on land that had already seen its share of cattle from earlier drives. It was proving to be gnawed down, trampled, and of little use. Their only saving grace so far had been keeping the herd moving, always grazing tender shoots of sparse grasses along the way. "You said we have three options."

"Yeah, he did," said Cook. "And I don't like it, Drover, not one bit!"

Joe shrugged. "Nobody likes it, Cook. But it can't hurt to think about."

"Ha. You ain't the one who'll have to ride that nightmare."

"What nightmare?" Mitch was picturing Cook, soft-looking as he was around the middle, hoisted atop a coal black horse that bucked him to near death.

"We raft the wagon," said Joe. "There's timber enough along the river. A pile of it on both sides, in fact. We wouldn't be the first. There's even something that looks to be a half-built—or half-falling-apart—raft. But if Cook can get there sooner than later, we might stand a chance of crossing the wagon on its own steam before the rain swells the river higher."

Mitch laughed out loud. "Oh, I see," he said, not hiding his smile. "You think because I'm new to the trail that I'll fall for anything, eh?"

But neither Cook nor Joe looked anything close to smiley.

"You're serious? Float the chuck wagon?"

Joe nodded. "Course, maybe we won't have to. Water level looked to be about doable. Likely won't be after the storm. Beeves and horses can swim for it, but a wagon can't."

"How far ahead is it?" Mitch asked.

"I make it six miles."

"Oh, we should make that today, no problem," said Mitch, plunking his hat back on his head.

"Oh, we should, should we?" said Cook. "Ain't anybody ever told you if you want to rile the Almighty, you let Him in on your plans?"

Mitch smiled. "Funny, the way I heard it was if you want to rile Cook, tell him your plans."

The surly keeper of the chuck wagged a wooden spoon at him. "I liked you better when you was ignorant, you whelp."

Mitch and Joe exchanged glances, eyebrows high.

"Laugh all you want," said Cook. "But while you children are yammering amongst yourselves about what a fine day you'll be having, I have to get the rest of this mess packed up and get to that river before another half hour passes me by. Elsewise, come nightfall, you all can eat cold beans and colder coffee and like it! Now get out of my road. I'm busy."

Mitch and Joe did as the gruff cook bade them, suppressing chuckles until they were out of range of that spoon.

CHAPTER TWELVE

I F THE CALICHE River chose to hear Joe's wishes, it was set on ignoring them. From a mile or more off, the flow looked to be sparsely lined with cottonwoods and rabbitbrush, and as it was a sizable flow, there was little doubt that the sooner they crossed, the better off they'd all be.

Mitch and the boys didn't need Joe to tell them that they were in for a long afternoon and night, all hands up and riding. There was still the possibility—at least they hoped so—that they could cross before the rain came. But that mass of black clouds to their northeast was a big one moving with impressive speed toward them.

And then a light rain began pelting down.

"We be able to get across before it hits?" Mitch seemed to be talking more to himself than to anyone in particular.

"Hard to tell," said Joe. "If we can get the wagon across, then the remuda, we can cross the beeves, even if the front of the storm is on us. Crossing'll take some of the starch out of the critters. Less apt to give us trouble should the storm spook them once we get across.

"As far as the wagon goes, be a whole lot better to get it there and across sooner than later, stand a better chance of not needing the raft, which is a whole lot of headache to avoid if we can. Of course, all bets are off if the sky doles out a few shafts of lightning."

"What happens then?" said Mitch.

"For starters, we can't risk having any head in the water. That's an open invite to Mother Nature to have ourselves a river full of dead beeves. Then we need to do all the same things, crossing every critter, but faster. A whole lot faster."

He glanced ahead of them. "Do me a favor and make the rounds, would you? Tell everybody to pull on their slickers and get ready. That dark mess to the northeast won't wait for any of us."

Big raindrops sizzled as they hit, striking the tarpaulin, the dirt, the cowboys' hats and shoulders like flung gravel. The horses and beeves had known it was coming for long minutes and acted as they do—the horses fidgeted and snorted and the cattle grew balky and wary, flexing their nostrils and flicking their ears and ranging their wide eyes all about, looking for what only they knew.

As Mitch nodded and neck-reined Champ back toward the herd, he felt a prickle lace up his backbone, from butt to high up his neck under the hairline. He swung around and saw the last of a jagged yellow finger pinch out to the northeast, far across the river, from the heart of the massive raft of black clouds.

"You feel that?" shouted Joe over his shoulder.

"Yeah!"

"Ain't good. The men will have seen it, too. Tell them to keep the herd moving, but not too tight."

The rain came on hard then, switching from a steady

drizzle into a snapping, pelting rager. Jags of lightning, white-hot steel smelted from on high, whip-cracked downward, lancing the skyline and dancing there as if taunting them, daring them to push onward.

And so they did, pushing toward the river. There was still a chance, they knew, to cross before the water rose too high.

B EFORE REMUS AND Romulus led him to the river, the chuck master had unrolled and lashed down tight his load-top tarpaulin. Mitch helped him finish securing the ropes off all four corners and had spun toggles in them to tighten each until the wagon's boards creaked.

Cook looked up from tying down the last of the barrels. "Don't kill my wagon, boy."

As they worked, Mitch wondered how they might go about lashing together a raft substantial enough to float a wagon.

Joe had said there was ample timber along the river. Perhaps previous storms had carried it downstream. Whatever the reason, Mitch figured they'd be grateful to have it, but hoped they'd not need it.

As they rode, the rain hit harder and faster. With it came the smell, reminding Mitch of summer storms of his youth. Funny, there hadn't seemed to be as many in the last few years. The smell was a clean, stripped scent, like fresh bedding or Evie's just washed hair.

He'd asked her about that scent once, the first time he'd noticed it. She'd blushed and said it was because she'd saved rainwater and cleaned her hair in it. Then she'd said, "So I could come by to see you today, Mitch."

That had been six, seven years before, the day he'd first seen her as somebody other than the half-wild, horse-riding girl in trousers forever challenging him to races that she would always win. But on that day, she'd shown up wearing a dress and a blue ribbon in her chestnut hair that somehow worked magic with her summer green eyes.

Sure, she'd stood close to him before, had helped him birthing calves, fixing corral rails, all manner of jobs. And she'd been plenty useful about the place, too. But that day, she wasn't dressed for work. Even Cherub, her prize bay, had been washed and had a single blue ribbon, matching Evie's, knotted and hanging above the saddle horn in his mane.

Mitch shook his head and blew at the steady run of raindrops sliding off his long nose tip, onto his fledgling lip hair. He had to pay attention. It would not do to lose himself in a daydream in the midst of a storm.

The wagon almost made it to the river before the rain hit hard. Cook had demanded that Mitch give him a hand crossing, and as the burly fellow had looked genuinely frightened, Mitch had agreed.

Now, as they stood looking at the swirling brown flow, Cook's face had leached free of his usual ruddy coloring, and he kept licking his lips and swallowing. "Boy, I can't swim!"

Mitch nodded. This was not a surprise. He'd always taken for granted that because Pap had taught him to swim, most other folks would know how, too. But that hadn't been so among people he knew. Not that he was acquainted with all that many people. Despite Corliss Bilks' efforts to turn it into the heart of worldwide cattle ranching, Mitch was certain Cawlins, Texas, wasn't even on most maps.

"Mitch, you got to make sure I can get across, okay? I don't mind telling you, but not the others, never to them. Oh, I don't like this one bit. If man was meant to swim, the Almighty would have given him fins. Stick with me, boy."

Mitch nodded. He'd already figured on doing that, since Joe and the men would no doubt have the cattle in hand. When he looked southward, Mitch could make out the leading edge of the herd, a moving low mass with taller figures here and there—the men on horseback.

He'd make certain Cook got to the north bank of the river; then he'd head back to help cross the herd.

Mitch had crossed a river twice before on horseback, but each time the horse's hooves never left bottom, never once did the flow so much as nip at his boots in the stirrups. This would be a whole lot different.

Cook looked at Mitch. "You think we can get across without a fool raft?"

Mitch studied the water, not wanting Cook to see any doubt on his face. He was pleased to be asked his opinion, especially on such an important matter, but they had no time to waste and lives were at risk. He swallowed and nodded. "Yeah, I think we can do it. But we have to go now. Right now."

The burly man turned back to the wagon. "Okay, you ride across first and get a guide rope secured around that big bunch of trees there." He pointed at a substantial-looking stand of cottonwood. "And if you have enough, go around that jumble of rocks, too. Should be plenty. I got a lot of rope. I know. I packed it myself."

Within a minute, Mitch was astride Champ once more, with the tag end of a coil of rope tied across his chest, and the rest of it draped over his upstream shoulder. The other end they'd snaked between the mules and tied to an iron ring on the wagon tongue. Mitch would uncoil the rope off his shoulder as they crossed.

Champ was balky as they walked forward. Then with prodding and encouraging words from Mitch, they proceeded into the water with caution. Six feet from shore, he realized the flow was worse, deeper and

more powerful, than they thought. And it looked to be
rising as he watched.

Before him, the Caliche was a wide wash of murky
water, and he couldn't see the bottom. That thought
didn't do much to make him feel better, but they walked
on, aware that time was everything in getting Cook and
the wagon safely across.

From his right, upriver, and yet as if from nowhere,
the carcass of a whole tree bobbed into view and widened Mitch's eyes. It spun like a twig on the brown
surface; its branches, some raked free of leaves, some
sodden with growth, wagged and clawed at the water.

It rolled westward at an alarming clip, and Mitch
found himself squinting upstream through the driving
rain to see if there were others. So far he saw none, but
he couldn't put out of his mind what a bobbing brute
like that could do to a man and horse. Or a dozen
beeves clustered and wide-eyed, frantically swimming
against a devilish current.

The water was cold as it soaked upward over his
boot tops and leached up his trousers. It reached his
saddle and a quick flash of the puckering that blazing
sunlight would do to the leather came to him. Then he
realized he'd welcome the most vicious stabs of sunlight once more, and dug his heels into Champ's already straining body.

"Not as bad as it looks," Mitch mumbled aloud.
Couldn't be; otherwise Joe wouldn't have recommended
crossing now.

As quickly as that solid thought came to him, a wave
slapped into them and soaked his right side clear up to
his armpit, and his mind flip-flopped. *To the devil with
losing days,* he thought. *We're going to die here in this
stinking river of devil's spit. At the very least we'll lose
cows, maybe horses.*

He leaned to his left and looked back to shore, but

could barely make out Cook, and he knew he had to keep on. He looked forward once more and saw that Champ was already rising up, climbing an unseen incline toward the nearing north riverbank.

Overall, the water hadn't gone much above his knees. The chuck wagon and the gear wagon both had good-size wheels, and the river bottom, as far as he could tell, had been largely rubble free, if Champ's lack of stumbling was any indication.

They slopped up out of the river, water sluicing off the big, snorting horse. Mitch held tight to the reins as he shrugged out of the coiled rope and lashed, then tied off the end. It turned out there wasn't enough to also lash about the rock pile as Cook suggested, but the cottonwoods were solid and should do the trick. It was only a guide rope, after all. The wagon should be fine on its own.

He wasn't certain whether he should return back across to the far bank and help the spooked man, but as he watched, Cook made the decision for him. The big Cajun had apparently tossed away his earlier fear and was snapping lines on the backs of his beloved Remus and Romulus.

The brethren mules stomped into the river as if they were born to the task. With each foot forward they gained, Cook appeared to gain in confidence. His snarls of encouragement, if his raw-throated barks could be called encouraging, reached Mitch through the pelting, darkening sky.

Mitch glanced now and again at Cook, who looked suitably serious. Commandeering the wagon had to be more worrisome than Cook made it look. Maybe he was even now coming closer than Mitch thought he might to dumping the wagon. But nothing of the sort happened.

Within two minutes, they were at midstream, and

though the swirling brown water lapped at the floor of the wagon, he didn't think anything that couldn't be dried would get soaked. Cook had lashed all the sacks and casks of meal and flour up high on the load.

M Y WORD, THAT was something!" shouted Mitch as he heaved the last of the rope into a loose pile at the base of the tree. "You made it!"

Cook nodded. "You sound surprised."

"What? Oh, no. I'm relieved, that's all. Aren't you?"

"Sure, yeah. Never doubted it." Cook clacked the lines and urged the mules higher, angling crosswise up the sloping bank to high ground. "Got to get the chuck set up. Boys'll be wanting hot coffee."

Mitch nodded, unsure of what to make of Cook's sudden change in attitude. *That's how he is,* the young man told himself. *Hot one minute, cold the next.* He turned and made for the river, leading Champ alongside.

"Where you headed?" Cook shouted to him from above.

"Going back across to help."

Cook nodded.

Mitch led Champ down the bank.

"Mitch!"

He stopped and looked up. "Yeah, Cook?"

"Thank you." The big man tugged the brim of his rank old derby.

Mitch nodded and Cook and his mules rolled higher. And that was it.

Still, considering whom that thank-you was from, it warmed Mitchell Newland. At least until the river water seized his legs once again.

CHAPTER THIRTEEN

LESS THAN AN hour later, with the rain pelting and lashing in great sheets, there they were, with half the herd in the river, the rest of the herd following suit. Every beef seemed to be bellowing, some among them showing their most ornery selves with violent head-shakes and lunges at one another. They were all balky, knowing what lay before them.

Slowly the men forced them forward, the critters' hesitation obvious as they locked their joints and snorted and bawled, soaked through and dripping as if they'd already been dunked in the swirling flow before them.

"Git up there! Hee-yaa!"

Shouts, whistles, curses, and cracks of quirts and smacks of ropes on wet horse flanks rose as sharp, quick sounds before carrying away as fast on a devilish wind at odds with itself. It whipped torrents of rain one way, only to have a cowboy who'd angled the crown of his sopping beaver topper into it to nearly lose the hat

to a sudden shift in the fickle blow's intentions. Every
man wore his stampede strap cinched tight beneath his
chin.

Mitch tried to seek out Drover Joe. He felt certain
there was more he could do, should do, but the flanks
and the rears of the mass of beasts were buttoned up
by riders. To horn in between a couple of them would
be useless and not right. During long days on the dry
trail, it had not been trouble to do so, and he'd been
able in this way to learn much about the vagaries of
driving cattle, of fetching strays and keeping the rest of
the dust-boiling critters in line.

But then he saw his chance. A trio of cattle had
ranged, slipped away from the herd, and made their
way down to the base of a steep cutbank. He didn't
think the cowboy atop the bank, who faced the bulk of
the herd upstream, had seen the rogues.

Mitch heeled Champ forward, beelining for a spot
ahead of where he thought the wayward beeves might
be located. When he reached the top of the bank and
looked down, he could see that they were still making
downstream, paralleling the river, but not daring to go
in. They looked as if they wanted to give it a go, but
weren't certain how to begin the task.

He switchbacked Champ down the embankment,
steeper there than it had been a few hundred yards
upstream. "Hey, there!"

He whistled and shouted and the cows froze, as he
knew they would when confronted with something unexpected. His experience and skills from running his
ranch had stood him well on the trail, as they did now,
when he approached the three.

He recognized the brands, two of Bilks and one his.
Steers all. It was too much, of course, to think they
had broken from the herd with a plan of sneakiness in
mind, an escape of some sort. They were cows—annoying

and curious and frightened and searching, always searching—for what, he didn't know. Nor at the moment did he care.

He hazed them back toward the herd, keeping them before him and the river, using the roiling flow as a barrier to the left and him and Champ as the guiding force to the right. As he did so, he came to the same conclusion he always did when faced with the back ends of cows. They weren't really dumb. No dumber than any other creature in the world. They were as smart as they needed to be. It was humans who were the dumb ones, spending their days and nights facing the backsides of cattle.

People were the ones to watch with a critical eye. Certainly, he'd come up against a whole lot more odd, dangerous, and even dumb humans than he ever had in cattle.

"Hee-yaa now! Git!" With such encouragement, Mitch managed, clean as you please, to drive them right smack into the herd.

Tully, who'd been atop the rise, shouted down through the sheeting rain to him. "Thanks, Mitch. They got by me!"

Mitch waved and held the spot, as other beeves looked toward the riverbank as a means of escape.

The men managed to drive most of the herd down the long, slow bank of the river. Already the earth at the near edge had become sodden, and mucky close by the water's edge. Chet and Chicken Pete worked them hard from upstream, keeping well clear of the big-horned heads. Any slip at this point and man and horse would be drawn by the roiling waters too close to the massive hooks of the ginger-and-white beasts.

A stout, lightly freckled steer with a sizable horn spread carried himself along the downstream bank, caught up by the spirit of the wild day. Sycamore approached, tried to wave him back, cursing and thrusting his arms into the air, anything to get the ornery critter to amble back to the herd, but it didn't work. It would not do to lose such a solid beast, so he kept at him.

Mitch saw him and wondered if he needed help. But then he heard his name shouted behind him and Sycamore's lone-steer odyssey was forgotten for the moment.

Nor was that steer the only stray. The closer the riders drove them to the river, the more the cattle spread out, and the cows at the far edges seemed to sense a chance at freedom.

Chet and Chicken Pete shouted to each other. "Look out there. See those two?" And "To your left, that skinny one!"

That last comment was directed at Mitch, and through the rain, he saw that the critter in question was one of his own, a rangy steer he'd nearly lost to coyotes when he was born. He didn't much like the comment about it being "skinny," even if it was true.

He loped off after it, and managed to cut Champ in to its west without risking a hooking with a horn. As he turned, he saw one of the boys, the Kid, judging from the slight cut of the man as he sat his horse. He rode far to Mitch's left, downstream, where the land rose in a grassy swell, creating taller banks.

The man rode back upstream slowly, as if he was looking for something. Then Mitch saw ahead of him, but down the bank, to the rider's left, a horned shape emerging. But the cow was not much interested in either crossing the flow or walking back upstream toward the herd.

Mitch looked back toward his skinny beast, but it had already joined the near flank of the last of the herd Sycamore was nudging into the water. He waved an arm to indicate to Mitch that he had that one, not to worry. Mitch waved back and turned to help the Kid. Maybe together they could persuade the other errant steer to get back where it belonged.

"Hey!" shouted Mitch. "Want a hand?"

The Kid looked to the cow, who was down knee-deep in the shallows, standing still and gazing at the water as if it were a pretty view and not a storm-whipped current.

Why didn't the Kid ride down there and drive the fool animal back up the bank and upstream to the herd?

He glanced back at the Kid, who nodded. So Mitch nudged Champ down the bank, the steepest stretch they'd come across so far. They took it at an angle, switchbacking down, sliding in muck. The closer they drew to the critter, the more familiar it became. Then he saw his brand and groaned. Were all the strays from the Twin N?

They were a dozen feet behind the steer when Mitch pulled up. He shouted, smacked his lariat against his slicker-covered leg. Champ dipped his head low and forced up a throaty chuckle.

"I know, boy, but I don't have a choice. Got to get him back to the herd."

He glanced up the bank, but the Kid, while still there, had backed his horse away from the edge and sat there, almost as if he were watching Mitch. *What does that mean? He still sore with me?* thought Mitch.

But he didn't have time to worry about it because the steer was on the move. Mitch didn't let up, and by luck and dumb exhaustion—his, Champ's, and the steer's—he managed to get it back atop the bank, while driving it upriver and back toward the herd. He glanced behind and saw the Kid had followed, but kept away from the river's edge.

"Maybe he doesn't feel well," said Mitch aloud, half-wondering if he'd hurt the Kid with that light beating he'd given him. He didn't much care. But on the trail, he knew frosty terms between hands had to be put aside while they dealt with work. Seems like the Kid would have come down the bank to help. Not, Mitch was pleased to say, that he needed it.

They made it back to the herd as the last two dozen head were funneled in quick fashion into the water by Sycamore and Drover Joe. Splashes and the bawling of cattle blended with the pelting rain and the low, ominous whistle of wind that raked land and water. It felt as if the storm, though raging, hadn't yet reached its full intensity.

Mitch joined Sycamore on the downstream edge and plunged in, whistling and popping quirts, doing anything to keep the cattle focused on stomping in and through the roiling water of the Caliche.

Within a minute, the flowage was chest high on the beeves. By the time they reached midstream, Mitch could tell the cattle, while still finding footing on the river's bottom so far, wouldn't for much longer. Their necks arched forward, snouts up, nostrils flexing, and eyes bulging wide.

Mitch found that if he angled Champ slightly upstream into the flow, the big horse kept his balance better in the constant shove of the rushing brown water.

As Joe predicted, the river seemed to have gained in height, at least a good four inches since Cook crossed the wagon. And since they began crossing the beeves, it had been steady in its creep up the muddied banks. The last of the stock, miraculously, was well in hand.

From the dogged looks on their faces and the lack of cheers of success, the other cowboys were less amazed that they'd done what to Mitch but a couple hours before had seemed all but impossible. Another indication to him that while he might know ranching, trail drives were a whole other creature.

He watched as the last of the beasts sloshed up out of the water on the far shore. He rode Champ up behind them, with other of the men doing the same, strung out at intervals upriver.

Mitch paused, dragged a sopping glove to clear the rain from his eyes, and looked back across to where they'd come from, checking for any stragglers they'd left behind. That's when he saw a lone rider sitting atop the far riverbank, skylined against the lashing purple rage of the storm.

He squinted, certain he was seeing an apparition. Surely all the men had made it. He'd been part of the last cow crossing, after all. But as he thumbed the water once more from his eyes and squinted into the lashing gloom, he saw the rider move, angling downstream. And then he knew by the slight stature who it was.

The Kid. What was he playing at, joking around at a time like this?

"Hey!" Mitch shouted, and waved an arm. "Hey!" He knew full well the Kid couldn't hear him from that distance, but he might see him waving. Mitch's shouts attracted the attention of the man closest to him, Drover Joe Phipps.

"What's wrong?" Then the big man followed Mitch's pointing arm.

By then Sycamore had ridden over. "Hey, ain't that the Kid? What all's he doing?"

Mitch looked at Joe, saw the man's face settle into a mask of concentration, the rain dripping off his long moustaches. He looked old to Mitch, older than he'd ever looked in the brief time Mitch had come to know him. A darn sight older than the ten or so years he had on Mitch.

"My word," said Joe.

Mitch looked back to the Kid, saw him riding back and forth along the bank slightly downstream of them.

"I'll wager he can't swim, boss. I've seen it before in a hand," said Sycamore. "What's more, I expect he's afraid of the water."

Joe nodded, then looked at Sycamore. "Get back to the herd, Sycamore. I need you there. We'll figure this out."

Mitch followed as Joe rode, paralleling the Kid downstream. All the while the Kid rode slowly, holding his horse back, reined tight, creeping crosswise down the bank, nibbling closer to the water.

Joe halted his mount and cupped his hands to his mouth. "Cross, Kid! Now! Come across! It's not that bad yet!" But even as he finished bellowing, Joe knew the Kid heard only the sound of shouting, no words.

Still, Joe hollered to him. "Ease into the water! Then slide off and grab hold of the horse's tail, son! The tail! Let the horse do the work. . . ." Drover watched a moment, then shook his head and cursed, the first time Mitch had heard him do so.

The Kid glanced over at them once then with a suddenness that made Mitch and Joe jerk back. The Kid sank heels hard, his arms flying up as his hat slipped off his head, dangling down his back by the strap. And the horse lunged into the river.

"Oh, no," said Mitch.

They watched as the weight of the big dun slammed hard into the flow, shoving a surge of spray higher than a man's height into the air. Then the horse lost its footing and slopped on its downstream side, bucking and thrashing, doing anything to save itself from its bizarre situation.

When it righted, no rider could be seen.

Joe kicked his horse into a lurch and bolted downstream, Mitch right behind. They caught sight of the Kid's flailing arms and head above the surface and then gone, up high, gone again. This happened three, four times, and still he managed to rise each time to the surface, arms flailing.

The Kid's horse bobbed twice, its thrashing head, wild eyes, and flying mane enough to show them it was still in the fight. Then it found purchase on the river bottom and made for their side of the flow, the water shoving it with each lunge farther downstream.

It reached the shore and dug hard up the bank on shaky legs, saddle hanging and reins dragging, before pausing to blow and catch its breath atop the slope.

Downstream of the Kid, a bankside cottonwood whose roots had long ago been undermined had flopped into the water, though still tethered to land by the last of its gnarled clot of roots. It jutted a dozen feet into the water, wagging and bobbing with the violent current. The distance between the Kid and the dead tree lessened with each second, as the hotheaded Kid thrashed and flailed in the water.

Mitch could not imagine the raw horror the young man must be feeling—to be so petrified of crossing water that he couldn't tell anyone of it, and yet couldn't fake confidence enough to do the job. And now to find himself in the mouth of the thing that struck an agony of terror in him.

They saw the Kid slam into the tree, fetch up, water spraying up about his head for the length of time it takes to breathe out—and then he slipped from sight. Mitch and Joe dropped from their saddles and, holding their reins, stomped downstream, into the river's edge. They held their breath, hoping to see the Kid fighting, thrashing, doing his best to beat this new foe with all his usual pent-up rage.

But no, he was not floating downstream. He was still

fetched in the tree, this time on the far side of the tree's trunk, jutting halfway between the bank and midriver, angled downstream. The black shape didn't move for a moment; then an arm rose up, as if the Kid was weak and barely able to beckon to them.

"He won't last. I've got to go after him," said Joe, not taking his eyes off the small, fetched, bobbing black mass hugging the wagging log. Mitch protested, but Joe shook his head with violence. "Leave me be— the boy needs help or he'll be in real trouble!"

Mitch jammed his left boot in the stirrup and swung aboard Champ. "Not you, Joe. We both know it can't be you!" He looked down at the older man.

The unspoken was enough—Joe was needed, indeed was vital to the drive, whereas Mitch, should the worst come to him, was far less experienced in the matters of a cattle drive than any of the men, and so, less important. A hard truth, but there it was.

By then Mitch noted three other men had gathered, all looking between him and Drover Joe and the Kid. As to Mitch's offer, none of the other men stepped forward. They all knew Mitch was the one for the job.

"Here!" Sycamore handed up an end of sodden rope. "Tie that about your waist until you get to him. If it all goes to hell, at least we can drag you back!"

Mitch nodded. Typical Sycamore, good, clear thinking, even in a trying moment.

Mitch made the rope fast about him with a large simple knot, easy to free once he got to the Kid; then he worked Champ back into the water.

"Mitch!"

He paused once more. It was Joe.

"Come onto him from the high side. You'll never fight your way upstream to him."

Mitch nodded, said, "Okay!" and rode back in.

Champ's powerful, wide chest forded the oncoming water, parting it like the prow of a solid river steamer as they cut upstream.

Though the rain had been cold earlier, the river's lapping depth felt oddly warm as it seeped up his legs once more. Mitch figured he was either getting used to it or losing all the sense he was born with. Likely a combination.

He appreciated Joe's concern, though it was advice he didn't need, and Joe knew it. But the man looked desperate, as if he were sending Mitch out onto a battlefield unarmed.

"Maybe he is," muttered Mitch to himself, to Champ, to the river, to the storm itself. "But he's forgetting—maybe he doesn't really know—that I've run the Twin N for eight years on my own. We've been in worse scrapes than this, eh, boy?" Mitch patted Champ's neck once, then refastened his grip on the reins.

They were halfway across and Mitch could still see the snag bobbing. With each downward wag, he spied something darker, irregular, what he hoped were the arms, shoulders, and head of the Kid.

His upstream angle gave him a vantage point that shifted with each step they took, with the tree now blocking much of what he'd seen from shore. "Hang on, Kid. Hang on!" He shouted this, giving himself scant but needed confidence that what he was doing was wise.

Mitch knew the Kid's life was in a dire spot, but his own raw survival instinct gnawed at him to quit this fool's errand, save himself, and to hell with the Kid, the biggest burr under Mitch's saddle he'd felt for a whole long time. Maybe ever.

No, there was that young drifter his father had taken on for a season to help with a great and unexpected boon in calves that year. Randolph had been his name, and though he'd only been maybe eighteen years old to Mitch's eleven, he quickly got the read of the place, like how Pap would drink himself snoozy every day after the midday meal.

That's when Randolph would tease Mitch, then goad him into fighting. And if he refused, the muscled drifter would cuff him and trip him and slap him until he lashed out. Then he'd welcome the fight and lay into Mitch with a hard flurry of hits, always below the face. Mitch came to understand that was the way with Randolph, sneaky and safe.

"And if you tell a soul," he'd say, "I will claim you are a liar and that it is your own drunkard of a father who beats you senseless. And you know what they do to such men. Why, they run them off and farm his kids out as free labor elsewhere."

Then he'd smile and bruise Mitch with a few more hits. His father never knew. Mitch kept the twinges of pain from him, claiming he had been thrown from a pony and landed hard.

One day, Randolph up and left. Along with the silvered picture frame that held a photogravure of Pap and Mama.

If Pap ever cared to know where the frame had gotten to, he never asked. It occurred to Mitch much later, years down the road, that perhaps Pap had thought he had himself sold it in a drunken spell to pay for more booze. Like everything else in the past, it was too late now to do much other than learn from it.

Mitch made it across the river, noting with surprise that it had swelled to an even greater height than it had been minutes before. Still fifty feet downriver of him, the great angled girth of the tree was fast becoming engulfed, awash in the boiling might of the river.

From his changing perspective, Mitch spied the dark form that he hoped was the Kid's sodden slicker. The Kid's arms were still hooked over the top of the tree, gripped tight to withstand the rush of water made more powerful by the tree's battle with the flow.

"I'm coming, Kid!" Mitch and Champ thundered down the bank, assessing the situation as they approached. He had to angle closer, close enough to get the rope to the Kid, somehow loop it around him. What if the Kid was unable to tie it around himself? Could he drape enough of a loop about him to tug him free? Might be that would only result in ripping him loose from the tree before being lost downriver.

For good or ill, that blasted tree was the only thing keeping the Kid from washing away in the storm like the lengths of other logs and branches and brush that bobbed by, over-ending and spinning downstream.

He urged Champ into the water about ten feet north of the tree. He could see the Kid clearly now, saw his arms still snatched tight and holding on for life. He looked up at Mitch.

Mitch had never in his life seen such terror on another person's face. "Hang on, Kid! I've got a rope." He struggled with the knot while Champ fidgeted and tried to turn upstream to get back to the near bank.

"Knock it off, horse!" growled Mitch as he finally broke the back of the knot and pried it apart. His fingers had begun to go numb and he felt a shiver working its way upward, from his legs and backside.

He slipped the rope from around his waist, aware that if he dropped it, all would be lost—he'd lose the lifeline to the shore. That could not happen. Gripping the thick rope tight in his right hand, Mitch gritted his teeth and squinted his eyes hard, opened them, and repeated this in vain hopes it would clear the rain from clouding his sight and annoying him further. He kept his white-gray mask of a face turned upward, brown water parting about his lightly whiskered chin.

He looks like a child, thought Mitch. *Nothing more than a scared child. I have to save him.* Seeing the Kid staring up at him, his eyes barely blinking through the gush of water slopping over him and his mouth parted, then pursed shut as if he were trying to speak, drove Mitch to tie a loop faster, wide enough to drape over the Kid. It was the only way.

"Grab this loop!" he shouted. "Get it around yourself! You hear me, Kid? You hear me?"

He thought for sure he saw the Kid nod about the same time he finished tying the knot. He hauled more rope toward himself, glanced back across the river toward the far bank at Joe and the boys. There were more of them gathered there, lining the bank, standing stiff and waiting in their slickers, watching him.

The rain sheeted down, and he was thankful there had been no sign of lightning since they'd seen those dancing jags of it on the horizon earlier.

He tossed the loop, and the Kid tried to reach up with one arm, but as soon as he let go his white-knuckled grip with the right hand, his body swung away from the log, pivoting on his clawed left hand. The loop splashed into the water, out of the Kid's reach.

Mitch had hoped the Kid was standing on the river bottom, but now he wondered if maybe there was a deep pool scooped out on the downstream edge of that tree by the constant wash of water over and around the big impediment.

He dragged the rope back to him. "Okay!" he shouted. "We'll get it this time!"

He glanced around and saw that Champ had kept his distance from the ominous, pulsing bulk of the dead tree, so he urged the horse closer. The horse hesitated but Mitch did not relent and they stepped closer, sidelong to the tree. He let Champ choose his own way with care, and the horse seemed in little rush. Though it took just a few seconds, it felt an hour to Mitch. He could only guess that to the Kid, it was a lifetime.

"Raise that arm again," he shouted, hoisting the loop.

The Kid shook his head, and his mouth pulsed open once, twice, forced impossibly wide by the water sluicing in and furrowing up over his face.

"It's the only way—the water's coming up faster!"

The Kid tried to shake his head again, but his right arm came loose, and he flailed.

That was the moment, had to be. Mitch shot the loop straight and true, snagging once on the Kid's upraised arm, only because the Kid pawed the air in a frantic bid to once more grasp the tree trunk.

Mitch tugged the loop to his right and it settled over the Kid's neck. But too late, the motion jerked the Kid and he lost his grip on the log with his left hand.

Mitch saw the hand come away with something more than air. He leaned far to his left, yanking. The effort worked and the rope cinched tighter under the Kid's armpit, but over his head, settling on his neck. He held as the rope jerked and sang in his hands, then pulled right out of them.

Only then did he realize he was on the wrong side of the tree, for the slack he'd pulled had snagged on the upstream fingers of long-dead branches. If the rope settled into any of them too deep, the men would pull and drag the Kid back into the tree, maybe killing him, surely preventing them from getting him to shore.

Mitch glanced at the far bank. The men were poised, holding the end of the long rope, fighting the pull of the current, straining the rope, making of it a long arc on the surface that rose up, water sizzling off it and steaming away into the pelting air. They were waiting for Mitch to give the high wave, an indication that all was clear and ready for them to pull hard and fast.

He had to try to free that rope, but how? Snap the branches with something. He leaned to his left, toward the tree, and held on to the saddle horn with his right hand. With his left he freed his big hip knife. It had once been his father's, and he was loath to lose it. There was a leather thong dangling from its butt, but in that moment he had no way of cinching it about his wrist.

The first branch resisted one, two hacking blows before giving way, leaving a stub the rope might pass over.

"Hang on!" he shouted, as much for himself as for the tumbling, gasping Kid. Champ stood firm, rock-like, the water ripping into and around his stony legs.

Second, third, and fourth branches snapped with more ease than Mitch expected, and he jerked himself upright into the saddle once more, not daring to breathe relief yet. The Kid still twisted like a sack of bait at the end of a line. The water slamming him, tumbling him over and over, snagged as he was.

As soon as he was upright in the saddle once more, Mitch waved an arm high and the men ashore yanked on that rope until it snugged, zinging tight inches above the blowing surface of the river.

The Kid moved, dragging toward the log. One moment his head broke the water's surface; another it was thrashing, plowing the current. He rose up and gasped once more, a sound Mitch heard even over the roiling river.

"Hang on, Kid!"

The rope snagged, popped, snagged again on each successive nub Mitch had created by slashing at the branches. The stubs thus far proved no match for the tight rope, except for the very last one.

A jag of small branch jutted sideways along a finger

length of branch nub, and there the rope stayed, tight, the Kid gagging and flailing two feet from the tree. Mitch pulled out the knife once more, leaning down and lunging with the knife. If he cut the rope, all was lost. But he had to try.

Then the jag of branch broke and the rope snapped and pulled tight with a zinging sound once more. The men on the far shore shouted a loud, unified bellow of effort, and the Kid plowed through the river at a speed far faster than any man could swim.

"Haul him fast, boys," said Mitch, breathing shaky breaths and following the Kid's progress through the rising water. "Haul him hard and fast. Otherwise, with that big mouth of his, he's liable to swallow the river dry."

And as if they'd heard him, that's what they did. As they overhanded that sopping thick rope, the Kid disappeared behind a white spire of rushing spray. He'd not be able to breathe in it, but at that rate, Mitch reckoned the Kid would reach the far shore soon enough.

The force of the pouring water carried the Kid downstream, but the men hauled him ever closer to them. Soon as he hit the shallows, he was surrounded by the swarm of men. They dragged him farther up the low mudbank where they unbound him and made certain he was alive. They hoisted him and drained his lungs until he began to flail his arms.

Several of them bore his sagging body up to the top of the rise, to the homey safety of Cook's high-if-not-quite-dry camp. Smoke pulsed from beneath a vast tarp Cook had managed to erect, with an array of ropes and poles, over a cookfire and the butt end of the chuck wagon.

Mitch worked to ease Champ back away from the bobbing mass of the big dead tree. It would not do for the big horse to falter and slam into that ominous timber. His eyes flashed back to the trunk, and there was a ragged patch of exposed tree flesh where before there had been bark. The Kid had gripped tight to the tree, clawing to stay above the water.

If only someone had taught the Kid when he truly was still a kid not to be afraid of the water. *Respect it,* Mitch's father had told him, *like you do a gun, but don't fear it. Fear is no way to live a life, son.* Pap's words, if not the particular sound of his voice, still clung to him all these years later.

When he eased away from the tree, intending to angle across and upstream once more, Mitch realized it would be better to get away from that bobbing beast first. Downstream looked clearer, and if it could be said of anything about the river, it appeared more forgiving in that direction.

Mitch paralleled the river, guiding Champ downstream along the southern bank until he found a spot still upstream of where the rest of the men had gathered, waiting to see if they needed to rescue the rescuer.

He focused his efforts on the river itself. It felt as though it had risen another foot since he'd last crossed. Then he struck in again, leaning forward. "I'm sorry, pal. One more crossing, then we'll call it good on rivers. At least for a few days."

The horse responded by gamely striking for the far shore, as if he knew that cutting straight across would get him west of there, downstream, and with luck, about right where they wanted to scramble ashore once more.

Thankfully the day's dismal light hadn't yet left them, though it was grayer with each passing moment. The air, too, felt thicker, as if the storm was now beginning its efforts to swell the river.

Their crossing was as simple as Mitch could have hoped for, and when the big horse stepped onto the low, muddy, hoof-pocked bank, four men were right there, guiding them up, hands patting Champ's quivering neck, slapping Mitch's rain-slick chaps.

He slid down out of the saddle and Rollo grabbed the reins. Mitch shook his head. "No, that's okay, Rollo. I've got him."

"No, no, I take him." Rollo smiled. "*Bueno*, boss."

As he stood there wondering if he really had seen the normally stone-faced vaquero smile, a big hand clapped on his shoulder.

"By God, Mitch. Well done. Well done. That was solid."

It was Drover, and while he wasn't smiling, he did look a whole lot more relieved than he had earlier.

"Thanks." Mitch shrugged. "Had to be done. Is the Kid okay?"

Joe nodded once and walked up the muddy bank. Two others followed him. Sycamore, with the rope coiled across his chest bandolier-style, walked beside Mitch as they slid and stomped their way, switchbacking up the riverbank.

"He's as cold as he'll ever be, at least until he meets his end. Which wasn't today, thanks to you." Sycamore smiled. "Worst he'll get is a case of sniffles. Especially once Cook gets through with him."

He leaned toward Mitch. "Word to the wise, don't cough or sneeze around that crazy Cajun. He'll wrap you in some god-awful mustard plasters and seal you up in places I don't care to mention. Uses pepper and goose grease, he does. Claims it's something his mama used. Which to my mind explains a whole lot." He nodded with a long, solemn face that Mitch found difficult to not answer with a laugh.

Mitch turned away and rubbed the rain from his face. "Thanks. I'll keep that in mind, for sure."

"Yes, sir, you do that."

* * *

THEY MADE IT up to Cook's camp and the Cajun bustled over to Mitch. "Heard what you did. Good for you. Damn foolish thing to volunteer for, but okay, then." He leaned close, eyeing Mitch closely. "You coming down with something? Touch of ague? I seen the signs, you know. That nose is red-red."

Mitch backed up and shook his head. "No, sir, Cook. I'm fine. A little wet, but I feel good." He patted himself. His gloved hands smacked his wet-through slicker.

Cook narrowed his eyes and grunted, then wagged a finger. "Got me remedies. You come to Cook should you feel poorly. Time-tested by my own sainted mama herself."

Mitch nodded. "Yes, sir. I'll do that," he said, echoing Sycamore from moments before.

Cook lumbered back to the wagon and Mitch turned his wide eyes on Sycamore, who looked equally alarmed. Then Sycamore touched his nose, nodded, and walked away.

Mitch sought out the fire and there was the Kid, huddled and shivering beneath two wool blankets. They were up over his head like he was an old woman afraid of the coming night. The other men nearby cleared back and found other things to do, though all within earshot, Mitch noticed.

The blankets shifted and the Kid looked over toward Mitch, then up at him. Mitch could see half the Kid's still white-gray face. The lips bore a purple tinge, but with Cook's help, one way or another, he suspected the Kid would soon be in the pink once more.

The blankets shuddered and the Kid turned his head back to the fire. Mitch leaned over and fetched a cup someone had set on a rock, then poured himself a cup of hot coffee.

"Appreciate . . ." the Kid spoke low, coughed, and spoke again. "I appreciate it, Newland."

Mitch was about to say that it was nothing, anybody would have done it, but somehow that felt as if it would cheapen the Kid's life, make him seem less than worth fetching from the snapping jaws of a wet death. "Well, that's all right, Kid. I'm . . . well, I'm glad it worked out."

The Kid offered a low, quick chuckle. "Yeah, me, too."

Mitch sipped his coffee and the Kid sat and shivered. Finally he stuck a pair of withered white hands out from beneath the blankets and held them toward the flames. "My name's Edward. Edward Stokes. You could call me Ed, if you like."

"Well, all right, Ed. That's good. And I generally go by Mitch. The Newland part only comes into play when I sign things that folks want money for."

The blankets bobbed in a nod and Mitch sipped his coffee. It was bitter and strong and hot. And it sure tasted good.

Some of the men drifted back to the campfire, some walked off reluctantly to tend the herd, trading places with others.

The rain lashed downward as night draped over them. The cattle, to a beast, were as far from stampeding as they ever would be. Most of the men, save for three night riders, were huddled about the guttering but welcome fire. Then Drover Joe Phipps emerged from out of the wet, dark gloom.

He kept his distance, but they could tell he was not himself. He stalked a circle about the campfire like an agitated wolf, glaring at no one in particular, but his steely gaze dragged over each of them as he walked.

Then he stopped, filled his coffee cup, and the men almost seemed to sigh. Maybe he was finally simmering down.

As they had begun to relax once more, Joe barked a question: "What was that about, Stokes?" Joe's voice was steel on steel, and his fingers gripped the tin cup so tight his knuckles whitened.

"Hmm? You don't think we should have known you can't swim a lick? Nothing to be ashamed of. But dying? And for no reason? That is truly shameful." He stomped away, lashing out the last of his coffee on the ground, and muttered, "Damn kid."

Nobody said a thing. The dead-quiet scene was somber and tense, the only movement the guttering flames and the random shiver from the wool-wrapped Stokes. The smoke hugged the scene before escaping around the edges of the low tarpaulin.

Then Joe spun back on them and stood outside the tarp, as he had before. "Anybody else keeping a tight, cute little secret? Anything we all ought to know so we don't have a repeat performance of this mess? Huh?"

Nobody said anything for long moments.

Drover Joe pulled in a deep breath, and when he next spoke, his voice was lower, more measured, though it still bore that hard edge. "Hear me now: Beeves we can stand to lose, but not men. Never that." Then he walked off once more.

No one spoke for a long, long time.

O H, GOD, COOK, no more, please! I feel fine!" Stokes backed up and clunked into the side of the wagon, his arms outstretched before him in an effort to fend off the big man with the deep spoon. It brimmed with a milky, thick tincture that reeked of onion and meat gone off in the heat.

"Course you do! That's the power of Mama's tonic! Now open your whiny mouth and take this dose."

"Do the job, son. Take it like a man. Need you fit for

work." Drover Joe turned and hid a smile behind his coffee cup.

The other men did the same, wincing a little as they heard the Kid gag down yet another spoonful of Cook's vicious tincture.

"There now," said the big man. "You see if you don't come back and thank ol' Cook for saving you from the brink of a long, lingering sickness." He walked back to the wagon and sniffed the bottle before stoppering it with the cork. He wrinkled his nose and shook his head. "Powerful stuff."

Mitch noticed that Cook's eyes were watering, either from the memory of his sainted mama or from his own encounters with the woman's brutal tonic. Likely both.

CHAPTER FOURTEEN

I 'BOUT HAD enough of beans and biscuits, followed
with biscuits and beans. Oh, and don't forget beans
and beans with a couple biscuits on top." Tully, the
pock-face cowboy with the strange patchy black hair,
spat and worked his backside on his saddle.

"And that's another thing. This here dust. It ain't
right that a man should have to ride behind something
stupid as a cow, let alone a herd of them as they stomp
and bawl and drag their cursed hooves and raise what?
Dust, dust, and nothing but more dust. What I don't
take in of a day as beans, bread, biscuits, or burnt coffee, I take in as dust. I've puzzled on this some and I'll
tell you a thing right now."

Tully snorted through his nose, making that peculiar clicking sound from his nostrils that the other men
found unsettling. Sycamore in particular didn't care
for it, enough so that when he found himself seated
next to Tully, he would cobble together any excuse to

change seats. If Tully knew or cared, he never let on. He was normally a quiet fellow. Just not when he was alone.

"I tell you a thing right now, horse, and it is this: Dust used to be dirt. Dirt and, I'd guess, a fair bit of dung, to boot. So that means I am working for money I won't see for months, but I am being paid to eat burned food and dirt and cow dung. This ain't right. Somewhere along the line I made a poor choice."

"And here I thought I was odd for talking to myself."

Tully spun, his face pulsing instant red. There sat Mitch Newland, the man on the drive the others quietly called "the greenhorn," and such. Trouble with that, as Tully understood it, was that Newland knew his way around the herd, owned a goodly portion of it, and, if Sycamore was to be trusted, Tully learned that Newland owned his own ranch and had run it since he was little more than a child.

But now here he was, prowling in the daylight and coming up on a man unawares. That gave Tully the skin creep. He normally liked to keep his voice and own thoughts to himself. They were his, after all. Why scatter them about like seeds in a windstorm? He only spoke out loud when he was certain he was alone.

"I . . . I did not know you would be there. Behind me." Tully looked at his right knee.

"I came to spell you." Mitch nudged his big mount forward and the horses stood, some feet apart, facing the herd.

For long moments neither man spoke, the only constants the late-morning sun's peening heat and the dust and the bawling as the herd crawled forward. *Nope,* thought Mitch. *I can't disagree with a thing Tully said.*

As if privy to his thoughts, the pocked cowboy offered that clicking sound from somewhere in his nose and spoke. "I . . . I was only bemoaning my plight to myself and my horse, is all, Mr. Newland. Didn't mean nothing by it."

Mitch nodded. "You didn't give voice to a thing I haven't thought myself, Tully. I understand. I expect every man on this drive feels the same way. I'd be surprised if they don't all do the same thing—shouting to the wind, that is—when they find themselves alone. In fact, I think it's a healthy thing to do."

He stole a glance at Tully and saw what he perceived as relief on the man's face. Then Tully spoke again. "That true what you said about talking to yourself, Mr. Newland?"

Mitch nodded. "It is. My pap said it was a good thing to do, as I would meet interesting folks that way. So far, I'd say he was right. And the name's Mitch."

"Oh, okay. Though I'm not so certain how interesting I am. I been called worse, so I'll take it as a kindness, of sorts, from your pap to me. Funny little trail that notion took, now, isn't it?"

Mitch smiled and watched the odd Tully ride off through the dust. He liked the idea that Pap was with him even now, on the trail. He also vowed to remind himself to tell Joe they ought to give thought to butchering a steer. It had been many days since Joe had brought back any deer meat. He knew it cut into their profits. If Joe objected, he'd tell him to make certain it was one of the Twin N beeves.

An hour later, Drover Joe rode up on him, catching him almost as unawares as he had Tully. Not quite, though, for he'd seen the tall figure making his way around the perimeter of the herd long minutes before, but a couple of steers butting heads caught his attention, and by the time he'd interfered in their mischief making, Joe had ridden up behind him.

"Nicely done."

"Hey there, Joe." But that was all he had time to say, for the older cowboy wore a grave look.

"Trouble ahead, Mitch. Been making the rounds, warning the boys. Everyone's getting heeled. Figured you'd better, too."

"What is it?"

"Indians. Apache from the looks."

"What do they want?"

"Don't know yet, but I expect they'll claim this is their land and want payment for us riding across it."

"Are they right?"

Joe shrugged. "Hard to tell. It belongs more to them than to any whites." He looked northward, toward where they were headed.

Mitch saw nothing but more of the same rolling land, browned in a wide stretch where previous herds had stomped through, grazing the grass down to its nub. Too many head and too little time between herds, combined with the summer's bold heat, didn't give the grass much of a chance to green up once more.

But Joe wasn't looking at that. He was looking beyond that, toward this new danger.

"Didn't look like more than a dozen of them, but that doesn't mean they haven't split up and are cutting wide, more coming up on us from the east and west." He nodded his head to each side of them.

"What do we do?"

"Not much we can do except meet them head-on. They know we're coming. Heck, they know we know they're there. Let it play out. We have to keep the boys cool. You hold the herd and I'll see if I can talk us through it. If that tactic looks like it's being taken poorly by them, I'll shake my head no. Easy enough for them to decipher, but they won't know what I mean by it. That'll also be the point where you and the boys best get comfy with the idea we might get rousted by them."

"You mean gunplay?"

"Bound to come to it at some point, Mitch. I'll do my best to avoid it."

Mitch had a sudden thought. "What about Cook?"

Joe nodded. "He's all right. Got a late start, so he wasn't that far ahead. I rode up and told him. He turned and is keeping pace with the front of the herd. You'll see him in a few minutes, cresting that rise yonder."

The situation unrolled as Drover Joe said it likely would, with a line of Indians waiting for them. They were not what Mitch expected, once he finally rode close enough to get a look at them.

The boys had worked, in the short distance they had and given the size of the herd, to bunch the beeves without crowding them too hard. It helped them to keep two men riding drag, and two more as outriders on the east flank. That left Mitch to float along the west edge with Sycamore. Cook was a good shot, so he'd help defend the east flank. Joe rode point and they slowed the herd considerably, which, given its normal moseying pace, was saying something.

Joe kept his revolver untied and his repeater lying across his lap. Several of the men also carried rifles. Mitch regretted his was in the chuck wagon, but he was a fair hand, if he did say so himself, with Pap's revolver from the war. It was sizable, but Mitch was no daisy, and the polished walnut grips had in recent years felt as though they had been made for his large left hand.

"Come what may," he told himself, surprised to hear the phrase pinch out of his mouth. It was a phrase Evie had said at times, a remark he wasn't certain she had been aware she'd spoken.

He'd asked her about it once, a couple of years ago, and she'd said, "Oh, I think it was something I heard my old maiden aunt Tillinghast—Father's aunt, really—say once when she visited us for a time when I was younger. She never did again. Claimed the landscape and the sun had what she said were 'deleterious effects' on her skin and that she would instead write long letters. And she did. I still have them. She was an interesting old bird. Spent her whole life in Boston, except for that one trip to see us. Odd."

Why that memory came to Mitch at that moment, he could only guess. He supposed it was because Evie was never far from his mind, and now that trouble was rearing its head, he wished to think of her. Once more he regretted their parting on such poor terms.

A volley of quick whistles, as if a bird was trying to draw attention to itself, told him Sycamore was where he needed to be. That meant the herd was as secure as they might make it. All was set. Now they had to wait for the Indians, whoever they were, whatever tribe they were, to decide how they all might finish their day in peace.

Sycamore broke rank and rode over to him. "Got told by Tully that Drover wants you up front with him."

"Oh" was all Mitch could think to say. But sure, why not? He was part owner of the herd, the boss of the drive—in title anyway—and Mitch thought he should be there. He'd originally assumed that his lack of experience took it out of consideration. But now it was.

"Right. You'll be here?"

Sycamore nodded. "Yep, you bet. We're covered. Got Rollo holding the far west, ahead of the rear. His horses ain't too happy about it, but Drover said to keep them in check."

Mitch nodded. "Okay, then. See you later."

"Don't worry, Mitch," said Sycamore to his back. "Enough of us have been through this before, and it always comes out all right. They're likely hungry, want a few head to eat, is all."

Mitch nodded. He hoped his Southern friend was right.

As he rode to the front, he saw in plain view what Drover Joe had described. Arrayed on the long east-west ridge before them stood eleven riders. Why eleven? He wondered at the oddness of the number, then at why it should strike him as odd. *Why not eleven, Mitch?* They were Indians, after all, and the notion of a dozen of something might not mean anything to them.

Joe beckoned him up to stand beside him. Champ fidgeted.

"Should have brought you up before. I was thinking of other things." It was Joe's way of apologizing, Mitch guessed. As if the seasoned cowboy had offended him in some way.

Mitch shrugged. "That's fine, Joe."

Joe nodded. "That one in the white tunic. He's the leader. I half-think I've run up against him before, maybe the whole gang of them, though I bet not. Fanciful thinking. I'm guessing they want to cut out a few head of stock, feed their kin."

"They look rough, all right. Like they haven't eaten in a long while."

"Yeah, well, don't let your sympathies get too far ahead of you. They can as likely be crafty. The truth sits somewhere in the middle."

"What happens now?"

"Now we're on their time. They'll sweat us out, figure the longer we hold here, the more desperate we'll be to strike a deal."

Mitch nodded. "That's not far off the mark."

"Yeah, but they don't know for certain. You don't play much poker, do you?"

Mitch shook his head. "My cash comes too dear. I'm saving up to marry . . ." He left off, not wanting to say her name.

Joe nodded. "I know."

"You do?"

"Sure, half the boys know and the other half likely do, too. You're the envy of them."

"I am?"

Joe looked at him. "Don't act so shocked, Mitch. Evelyn Bilks is a fine girl. Smart and knows her mind." He looked back at the men ahead and jerked his chin in their direction. "Now, let's see if we can't give her something worth waiting for."

The ride forward to meet the Indians was the longest in Mitch's life. "You said before there might be more of them."

"Yep, likely to both sides of us. Or this could be it. Closer we get, the more pathetic they look. My guess is they're in tough straits. Good for us. That means they want a few head. Then they'll skedaddle."

Joe and Mitch halted. "It's a dance. And I hate dancing," said Joe. "Not natural."

"Me, too."

"That's because you're a man. Goes against our grain. Here he comes now."

And Joe was right. The one in the white tunic, Mitch now saw, was riding forward. He held a rifle balanced before him on his paint's shoulders. His bare feet bounced lightly against the horse's belly below a frayed orange, blue, and black blanket. He was followed closely by two more riders, one from each side, who rode side by side.

They halted twenty feet before the two cowboys. The man in white was a wrinkle-faced fellow, older than Mitch thought he'd be. The lines on his face were deep, all grooves and cracks and crevices as though his skin were mesquite bark, puckered, popped, and split by sun and time.

The others were much the same, though their faces

somehow were younger. They all wore leggings of broadcloth, blue at one time, thickly gathered and ill fitting. Their feet were bare, horned with calluses, the toenails gnarled and worn at the yellowed ends.

On none of the faces did Mitch see a hint of kindness. No smiles, nothing of the sort. Hard lines carved by years of squinting and watching for enemies, he guessed. *And here we are. Wouldn't it be nice to let them know somehow that they have nothing to fear from the drive?*

They were used to whites spreading slowly into their lands and their lives, as a spill did into a cloth laid atop it. It was not the first time he'd seen Indians, up close, but it was the first time he'd seen them in such a rough state.

Joe held up a hand and nodded. "Howdy. We're traveling through with our herd." He spoke evenly, never taking his eyes from the face of the man in the once white tunic.

The man to whom he spoke responded in kind with his own level gaze. When he spoke, the high pitch of his voice startled Mitch.

"This is our land. You are not wanted here."

He sounded as though he had not spoken in a long time. As though it were an act foreign to him and his voice a mechanism that required lubrication, the soothing effects of grease. It was a moment longer before Mitch realized the man spoke in English.

Joe let the comment settle like a blanket, drifting down on the little group. "Like I said, we're passing through. We won't trouble you for long."

The man shook his head.

Mitch worried what might happen should they flat-out refuse to let them pass through. Would they have to cut wide west, toward the mountains he could not yet see but knew they were there waiting for them?

"You are not wanted."

Joe nodded. His voice was even and his face looked unbothered. "We must pass through. Then we will trouble you no more."

There was a sound as though one of them might spit. Mitch wasn't certain which man it came from.

"You must pay. Or we will kill you."

Hard, sudden terror gripped Mitch's innards and squeezed. The man had said this as though he were telling how he'd seen a sizable buck deer.

"How much?" said Joe, as if he hadn't heard the killing part.

The man waited for a moment, then said, "Half."

Joe snorted and shook his head. "That will not do. You can have three head of beef." He held up his right hand, not the one, Mitch noticed, that rested on his cocked rifle. Three fingers stood upright. "Three head."

The man regarded the fingers, then Joe's face. "This many." He held up his hands, the palms facing them, and pulsed the digits twice, three times.

"Nope," said Joe. "Three head."

The old Indian shook his head and said something in his native tongue.

It went on like that for another few minutes, each time with Joe standing solid and the tribesman shaking his head, sometimes offering a death threat. Finally, he held up two hands, ten fingers raised.

Joe shook his head. "Three," he said, offering three fingers in the air.

Again it went like this some time; then the man held up one hand all fingers in the air.

"Give him five, Joe," said Mitch in a low voice.

He saw Joe's jaw muscles tighten and flex as though he were chewing gristle. "Okay, five. We choose." Joe turned to Mitch, his eyes sharp, and his voice low. "You and Sycamore cut out five. Two of yours, three of Bilks'.

Drive them off northwest. I expect his men will relieve you of them soon enough."

Minutes later, Sycamore shouted, "How many we giving them?" as Mitch rode up.

"Five. Three from Bilks, two of mine."

"That don't hardly seem a fair ratio," said Sycamore, already rounding on the nearest flank. "The state of the grasses hereabouts, they should be paying us."

Mitch smiled at the man's thinking. He couldn't disagree, at least where grass was concerned. They knew they'd be left with little enough on this stretch of the drive.

Sycamore nodded. "Those five look like they'll do the trick?"

Mitch looked them over. For two-year-olds, their condition was north of fair. He nodded, but felt a twinge as he and Sycamore hazed the beeves out away from the body of the herd, cutting the little group northwestward toward the waiting cluster of sullen Indians sitting their horses, unblinking and scowling, like wind- and time-stripped rocky spires they'd passed in a vast, rocky canyon to their east a week before.

Once they watched the eleven haggard Indians herd the cows into the distance, Joe reined up close to Mitch. He glanced around and in a low voice said, "Don't you ever do that again."

"Do what?"

"Step on my toes like that."

"What's two more, when we have nearly eight hundred head anyway?"

The man bit back a remark, sat a moment, then said, "You do that once, word gets out we're a soft touch. It also makes it tougher on the next herd coming up the trail. This isn't the last time we'll be in this spot. Way you deal, it'll get mighty spendy."

Drover Joe's words lingered in the air as he turned and rode off.

Despite the tongue-lashing, Mitch wasn't so certain they hadn't solved the situation the right way. The Indians were half-starved, after all, and none of the men on the drive was in danger of fainting from lack of vittles.

CHAPTER FIFTEEN

THEY HAD RIDDEN past a wide, rocky canyon the week before that looked as if nothing that ever figured out a way in would ever again find a way out. And anything unlucky enough to be birthed in its deep, shadowed, rocky crevices wasn't anything Mitch nor any of the boys, they'd all agreed, would want to come across in their travels.

That night, as he'd dished up plates heaped with a thick stew of cubed beef, red beans, and potato chunks, all seasoned with chiles, Cook joined in on the palaver about the spooky low wasteland they'd thankfully left behind earlier that afternoon.

"Heard tell there's whole tribes living down in places such as that all over the country hereabouts. They been scratching around down there since time began and I expect there will never be a day when no respectable person would ever trek down in there, least not in his right mind."

Mitch had had his fill of thinking about that dire

place, and asked Joe instead about the alternative trails he was leading them toward. If they didn't get the herd onto steady grass, while still making at least a dozen miles a day, they'd wind up with a handful of ribby beeves by the time they arrived in Montana. But slowing down any more was not a consideration.

"We'll be in taller feed once we get back to the mountain-hugging trail." Joe wiped his moustaches with the back of his hand, and set his plate down on the one bare patch of space left on Cook's work surface. None of the hands would dare do that, but being the foreman—and the highest-paid man on the drive— came with liberties. Annoying Cook was one of the few he indulged in.

"The new trail comes with good and bad. The good is we should have it to ourselves, no herds nudging into us, nor fear we'll be stuck behind some other gang. That happens more than you'd think out here in May, June. The trails suffer from greed. You take some of those bigger herds: They strip the land faster than the biggest herd of bison on the move ever could, which has been the way out here since bison were invented."

Cook lumbered back to the wagon from the fire and eyed Joe's empty plate. "You planning on more?"

"I'm planning on thinking about it. When I get to the thinking part, I'll let you know."

"Uh-huh. You do that. Me, I'll be over here, waiting for the water to hot up so I can continue with my workday. Unlike some around these parts, my work ain't never over with because it's dark and I feel tired. You show me a cook who has time to enjoy himself and I'll show you a man who ain't been born yet."

Joe and Mitch moved over toward the fire, and left Cook muttering and clanging pots and spoons and plates.

"Any louder, we'll have a stampede on our hands." But Joe said it lightly.

The surly cook and the foreman had worked together for several years now. As far as Mitch knew, this was their third or fourth shared drive.

When talking with the boys, Cook was quick to defend Joe, should he hear grumbling about the day's hours being long and grueling, and the fact that a man had better be made of stern stuff to keep up with Joe and the ungodly demands he put on a cowhand.

"He ain't going to ask you to do nothing he wouldn't himself do, and do it better and faster . . . and quieter." Cook would usually end the sentence with a wag from his dripping bean spoon.

Over by the fire, sipping renewed cups of chicory-dosed hot coffee, Joe resumed talking about the upcoming trail. Mitch enjoyed these quiet times and regarded the fact that as partial owner, he was provided the privilege of conversation with a man he regarded highly.

"Some of the trails suffer in high-trail-drive season because everybody wants an early start come April so they can get first crack at the new spring grasses and decent water. That's when mountain freshets run fulsome, supplying downcountry flows such as we've been using to water the stock. We should have better water closer to the peaks and the farther northward we go."

Later, Mitch found himself alone on the southern flank on night-riding duty. Despite Mitch's fool moment with the Indians, Joe hadn't let it color their work or, what Mitch hoped to call it, friendship. That night, in fact, Joe had acted as though no peppery words had been spoken, and Mitch had not brought it up, though he'd been tempted to offer another apology. He sensed, though, that a man such as Drover Joe Phipps might take it wrong.

Mitch sighed. "Champ, I ever tell you that Pap used to say that too much is too much? No? Well, he did. Wise man, was Pap. He also used to say that a man had to know when to stop a thing in life and when to start the next thing." Mitch leaned forward and patted the horse's neck. "Too bad he didn't take his own advice."

The cattle didn't seem to mind Mitch's one-sided conversations with the dark. It had been a quiet night with little restlessness among the weather, the critters, and so, the boys—a good night for Mitch to think. And as he knew they would, his thoughts turned with their usual frequency to Evie.

After their heated words at his cabin, he thought he'd lost her for sure, and the ache in his head and arms and belly and, yes, lower, too, was unbearable. But though he'd gone several times to the Bar B as preparations for the drive fevered up, he saw no sign of her.

"Twice I went to the ranch house's back door. You know the one, Carmelita's kitchen."

Champ twitched an ear and Mitch continued. "I knocked as I always did on that half-door's pie-cooling shelf. And I looked into the kitchen and down that long hallway beyond. But no Evie in sight."

He recalled that Carmelita had pulled a sad face, no slight trick as her plump cheeks were red from work and her brown eyes wrinkled at the corners from laughter. "She has told me not to talk with you, Meetchell."

Then she'd smiled. "She will be fine—you will see. I know her like no other. She is up to something, though. She won't tell me what."

Carmelita had leaned forward then, her ample bosom filling the pie shelf, and in a low voice said, "But I know her, and I will find out."

She'd looked over her shoulder to see if she was still alone in her kitchen, then patted his hand. "Meetchell, you look so sad. But this is the lovers' quarrel you must have in order to be together for life, like the swans. Okay?"

Mitch nodded. "You know what I did, Champ? I bobbed my head like the one swan in the history of all the earth that went without a mate—a young, stupid male swan destined for some farmer's stewpot, or the belly of a coyote, his feathers lining its den, forgotten and gone."

In truth, Carmelita's words had of late provided him with comfort, however slight, and he thought about them, hoping his feverish mind wasn't pushing and pulling meaning from them that wasn't there. He needed truth on this matter.

But the thing that offered him the most hope was finally seeing Evie. "I got a glimpse of her, though, on the morning we left. She looked so pretty, standing by the big corral. She was skylined in the morning light, standing bold in her boots and split suede riding skirts, one hand on her hip, the other holding that post. Never wished so hard in all my days that I was a fence post."

Mitch looked up at the night sky and closed his eyes. "Oh, but she was wearing that pretty shirt with the little bit of lace at the collar, tiny pink flowers all over the cloth as if she'd just rolled in a garden. I wish she'd rolled with me in a garden."

He'd told her once or twice before that she looked pretty in that shirt, and so he noticed she'd worn it more frequently after that.

He'd tugged Champ around and faced her. After a moment he raised a hand, then waved it once, twice and waited, holding there, his hand high. She didn't move. He let it drop and had almost turned back when her hand went up, the one holding the corral post.

"I turned back to face her again, but she'd already dropped that hand, Champ. Dropped it and walked back toward the barn."

There in the dark, with the cattle making soft sounds all about him, Mitch recalled watching Evie turn away and walk back toward the barn, out of the sun's slant, back into shadow.

CHAPTER SIXTEEN

ONCE THEY MADE for Joe's alternate route, which would take them westward, closer to the eastern slope of the Rockies, the drover promised there would be grass aplenty. "A different way for a bit, then we join up with the trail again. It takes in stretches of two other trails, the Driscoll and the Southy. By then we'll have the Laramie range to our east. There's a town there, Bellerton, where Cook can restock. I haven't decided if we can afford a day off so the boys can hoorah before moving on. Time's tight on this one."

By then it should have been old hat, but Mitch still felt a twitch of annoyance on hearing Drover Joe's plans, all made without him. He trusted Joe's judgment on all matters concerning the drive. Yet he was part owner of the herd, and felt he should be consulted about taking a day off.

Mitch wasn't even certain what a full-bore hoorah might be, but it sounded enticing, especially because when he'd said it, Joe offered a wink and a wry grin—at least that's what Mitch guessed was hiding beneath those voluminous moustaches of his.

They had made their way west, then northwest onto the Driscoll Trail. There was sign aplenty of previous herds. Chet, a likable if boastful sort, made a show of determining details of the most recent herd. He had, by his own telling, spent time scouting for none other than the Boy General himself, ol' Custer, a fact he related once more as he dropped down out of his saddle.

Chet indulged in an odd flourish that involved him whipping off his hat and smoothing his annoyingly long tresses. Then he crouched low enough that Sycamore was about to ask him if he had taken ill. One mention of a gut ache and Cook would be at the ready with his mama's tonic.

Chet said something about how a trained fellow could tell much by the smell and feel of cow pies. And yes, he nodded with a solemn look that dared any of the boys to challenge him, even the merest of tastes was required for a full assessment. He performed these self-appointed tasks while Drover Joe, Cook, Mitch, and Tully looked on with open mouths and high eyebrows.

The rest of the boys would hear of it soon enough. Chet rose, smacked the dust from his chaps, and declared that the pies left behind by the last drive were nigh on a month old. He nodded once, climbed aboard his buckskin mare, and rode back to take up his spot on drag.

"Was that helpful?" Mitch asked Joe later in a low voice.

"Nope," said the cowboy as he rode ramrod straight in the saddle, eyes roving the skyline and the foothills to their west. He glanced at Mitch. "But it was one of the more amusing things I have seen in quite a spell."

* * *

THERE WAS MORE than a mild whiff of discontent among the boys once Joe's decision circulated. They were, it turned out, not going to be swinging close to Bellerton, a town a couple of them had visited in the past. The rest, having heard from their fellows of its varied and delectable treats—from women to whiskey, faro to filling meals not containing biscuits and beans— were sorely disappointed.

"I was all set to have a time on the town. Been a long while since I have whooped it up," said Sycamore.

The rest of the men thought he was going to say more, but he sat in silence, staring at the cold beans on his plate. And so it went, with the men moping and turning surly stares at Mitch and Drover when they weren't looking.

At least until Cook returned from being gone with the wagon on a northeastward overnight trip. He rolled back into sight the next day, his wagon freighted once more.

That noonday meal was a somber affair, with Cook doling out slablike cold beef sandwiches. He and Joe were strangely quiet throughout the quick feed. Then Cook packed up and rolled north of them, out of sight to set up.

They pushed on, making their way slowly into a vast, rolling grassy plain with a stream north of them and the foothills of the coming Rockies to their west.

Well before they had to stop for the day, they spotted Cook's wagon—turned out, he didn't get that far— atop a vast grassy rise in the distance, tarpaulins staked, his grub station all set up, and his cook fire looked to be working double hard.

Mitch was on his way to switch out with Chet riding

flank when he saw Joe ahead and trotted over. "What's Cook doing, Joe?"

Drover rubbed his head, then resettled his big hat. "I reckon the cat'll be out of the bag soon enough anyway." He glanced left and right as if any of the others might hear him. They were all far enough away they were likely to hear nothing more than the usual complaining cows and cicadas buzzing in the heat.

"Cook stocked at a trading post northeast of here. Took a gamble sending him there, as I haven't been near that place in a few years. Turns out, it's still there. He was able to buy what he was scraping bottom on. I also asked him to lay in a small barrel of something the boys might find tasty, considering they've been denied a whoop-up in Bellerton."

"Whiskey?" said Mitch, not certain how he felt about this.

"Well, that was the idea. But the only thing he could get was brandy. So it'll be a quiet affair. But Cook has promised me he was laying out a special feed to go with it."

Mitch's gut rumbled at the thought. "You think he'll make a pie or some such?"

"It's likely." Joe turned Trooper and made for the front of the herd. "Time to let the men know we'll be settling the herd on the flat this side of the creek, below Cook. You want to go that way, work around to Rollo? I'll take this side."

"Sounds good," said Mitch, not bothering to hide a smile.

"Oh, and, Mitch?"

"Yeah, Joe?"

"Keep the cat's head in the bag a bit longer, eh?"

Mitch grinned and touched his hat brim before riding to tell the boys they'd be stopping early, without telling them why.

* * *

THE MEAL WAS prime, and Cook accepted the many and repeated compliments from the men without a trace of modesty. He'd prepared slow-cooked beef roast with thick, dark gravy, roasted potatoes, carrots, and some sort of toothsome greens he'd found and uprooted along the way. He'd also made a platter of ham steaks, sizzling and juicy and succulent.

And while the brandy washed it all down nicely, it was the four deep-dish Dutch oven pies—one of mixed berries, two of apple and currants, and another of some sort of mystery custard Cook refused to explain—that topped the meal and reminded them all how fine a cook ol' Cook was.

Each man was spelled in turn and a skeletal crew rotated every few hours to watch the herd. Joe insisted on working double shifts himself. Mitch quickly understood and followed suit. And it was Cook his own self who rode out to deliver to each of them a hearty slab of pie and a modest stoppered bottle of brandy.

"To prevent the ague," said Cook, winking as he handed it over to Mitch.

The rest of the afternoon and early evening went on much the same, slow and lazy and contented beneath a high blue sky. A soft breeze added an air of further pleasantness that even the cattle seemed to enjoy. They grazed and lazed and drank from the stream and lolled as much as did the boys. Sycamore, Tully, and Chet frolicked upstream in the creek, and most of the men took the opportunity to launder certain articles of their clothing.

"Thank the Lord," said Cook. "You men wasn't fit to be around."

Nobody mentioned to the big Cajun that he was only fit company from his upwind side.

Later, as night fell, Joe said, "Morning will be the same as all the rest. Have to push on in if we want to beat the snows."

"Snow?" said the Kid. "You seen the sky today, Drover Joe?"

The foreman chuckled. "Matter of fact, I have. And while I enjoy it a whole lot, I don't buy it for one thin minute. Weather's a fickle friend."

"Aw, come on," said Tully with a grin. "I can't imagine there's snow inside of a couple of months of here."

Joe shrugged. "Think what you want to, Tully. I know what I know. We'd best keep tight. You never know what's coming next."

CHAPTER SEVENTEEN

FOR THE SECOND time in as many days, Joe halted the herd at midday. Mitch saw no reason for the lanky cowboy's abrupt stop. He followed the foreman's gaze across the near slopes to the mouth of a vast mile-long funneling landscape.

The hills squatted close in and far off. Some with surprising height, owing this to the nearness of the vast, stunning, rock-shafted mountains immediately to their west. They'd been slow to come up alongside the peaks that had seemed to beckon for days before revealing themselves to the drive.

Joe had taken obvious pleasure in showing this to them all. The cowboys had shaken their heads in disbelief all day that first day, and much of the second whenever they remembered to look up from pushing the herd along the vast grassy sward before them.

Even Rollo broke off his perpetual fussing over the loose assemblage of horses that minded him like no beasts Mitch had ever seen mind a man. He admired this, despite the quiet Mexican's taciturnity. Tully, of all the men, seemed mildly perturbed by the vaquero's silence. But then the self-proclaimed "reformed preacher" never did seem to settle a kind word on anyone.

"I never did see the like," Tully had said as if personally offended, more than once at night when Rollo would kindly accept with a head nod a heaped tin plate of steaming food—arranged with extra care, Mitch noted, by Cook—before walking quietly back to his charges, close by whom he'd spend each and every night of the drive.

But on this day, it wasn't the vast, raw-rock presence of the mountains, nor the visual pleasure of a vast vista of grass, still a day ahead, but theirs for the grazing, that had halted the herd into momentary silence. Even the cattle seemed to feel something odd was in the offing, as if something in the air were about to reveal itself.

"What is it, Joe?" Mitch said, alongside the foreman.

Joe said nothing, but continued to gaze northwestward toward a rocky hillock a half mile or more off.

"Hope I'm wrong," he finally said as if to himself. "Hope, though"—he glanced at Mitch, then back to the raw, rocky knob—"never got a man a thing but heartache and an empty belly."

He reached back to his saddlebag, unfastened the brass buckles without looking, first one, then the second, and snaked a gloved hand inside. He pulled out a cloth-wrapped spyglass. Mitch knew what it was, had seen it twice before, and had even been allowed to use it once to spy on a mother grizzly bear and two cubs cuffing each other and frolicking while their ma flipped rocks and snacked on grubs and a vast quantity of little fluttering things.

"Moths," Joe had said, answering Mitch's question before he knew he was going to ask it. "You wouldn't think a critter as big as a bear could eat enough of those tiny things to make a difference, but they do. I've watched them eat moths for hours."

But Joe's face and deliberate movements told Mitch that on this day, they wouldn't be watching anything so interesting as bears foraging.

"Hope you're wrong about what, Joe?" Mitch's voice sounded pinched and old to him.

Again, Joe was slow to reply. But when he did, the two words he spoke were filled at once with menace and curious intrigue. He twisted the spyglass and uttered a low grunt. "Range pirates."

"Pirates?"

"Yep."

Mitch squinted but couldn't see a thing except rock and here and there the black smudges of pines. "How many?"

"Too many."

"Could they take the herd?"

Joe nodded. "If they want to."

"That many? I still don't see them."

"That's the point. But they're there."

"All around us? We could change direction." Mitch knew the suggestion was at best a solution a child would come up with. He looked to the northeast and thought he saw something on the lower yet still substantial hills there. "There," he said.

Joe looked. "No, there."

Mitch began to raise an arm to point, then as if he might be seen, jerked it down and nodded. But what he was seeing was more obvious than whatever Joe had seen.

"I'll be damned." Joe twisted the knurled ring on the telescope. "That explains a whole lot."

"What?"

In reply, Joe handed Mitch the brass tube. It took

Mitch a moment to align, then pull into view what the tall man beside him had seen—a staggered line of war ponies skylining the ridge, lances and rifles stippling the sky, and in their midst, a white-shirted figure.

"Aren't they . . . ?"

"Yep. Same ones. And more. Those Apaches were the advance guard, the scouts. They weren't looking for free food so much as looking to count the head and the men. Likely more of them behind those we can see. Same with the rascals on the west slope. The two groups are working together. And we're caught in the middle."

He looked at Mitch. "I won't dip this rank bone in sugar and call it tasty. We're in trouble, Mitch. Now they know what we're about, how many of us there are. Best go warn the others. I'll hold the front. Tell Cook first. He's solid. Then send the Kid around the perimeter. Tell them we're stopping and for each man to ride to the gear wagon one at a time, gun up, then get back to their spot. Nobody panic, but tell the boys we might be in for a fight. They're a solid crew. There's not a man among us who'll balk."

As he nodded, then rode off, Mitch realized the word "solid" was about as good as you could get in Drover Joe Phipps' estimation. Mitch wondered if he himself was the solid sort. He looked back but still didn't see the pirates Joe spoke of. Maybe they weren't there. Maybe he was mistaken. The thought flared, then pinched out, like the head of a struck sulfur match.

Of course he was right. Mitch had not known, nor heard of, Drover Joe to be wrong about anything. He was careful, and so, he was right. And he'd be right about this.

"Range pirates," he muttered as he and Champ galloped to the chuck wagon. The words made him think of the stories of swashbucklers his father had told him, tales before his time as a deckhand on the high seas, when foul men bent on foul deeds pillaged the goods and lives of others for personal gain.

"It's business, son," Pap had said. "It ain't legal, nor is it the moral thing to do, but it's still business. Like the tycoons are doing back East. Won't be long before the entire country's run by crooks, son. Mark my words."

"I guess it's come to pass, Pap," said Mitch as he reined up beside the chuck wagon.

Even before he climbed down, Cook rounded the back corner, thumbing a massive revolver he had strapped about his waist. "Trouble, I guess."

"Yep," said Mitch, and told Cook as quickly as he could what they'd seen, who they were, and what Joe wanted of the men.

"Yeah, guns are ready. Ammunition, too. I'll stay put long as I should, no sense me riding off with the wagon. Only get separated anyhow."

Mitch strapped on his own gun, hefted his rifle, and climbed back into the saddle.

"Mitchell boy," said Cook, "don't get risky. Could be we can pick 'em off. Got a few hands who are good shots. I ain't among them, but the Kid is. And Joe can core a bean at fifty paces. Sycamore, he's got the goods, too."

Mitch nodded. "Yeah, Joe said we're all solid."

That made Cook smile. It was the last nice thing Mitch would see for a long, long time.

CHAPTER EIGHTEEN

The first bullet whistled in and thunked into the horse's neck. It sounded to Tully like an open hand smacking water. He watched in wonder the sudden ooze of hot red blood bubbling from his beast's sweat-sheened hide, not but a hand's reach up on the left side of the horse's neck. Blood dribbled from beneath the wispy fringe of black mane.

He never heard the echoing crack from the second shot that cored Tully's left temple, burrowing like a giant weevil into that tender spot behind his eye. It was a spot he'd rubbed a thousand-thousand times as he fought off the demons of too much drink of a night before, or the confusion over what to do about the woman—a girl, really—he'd left behind some years ago in a cabin along the Sabine, a woman he knew had borne him a child. A child he'd never made an effort to meet.

And now, in a finger snap of time, a stranger had poked away all such concerns. A stranger Tully would never see, a stranger who went by the name of Mandrake Simms. A man who sported oiled and curled moustaches, a dry laugh beneath mirthless gray eyes, and a withered stick of a pinkie on his right hand.

He'd carried the hideous deformity since birth, concealed in a black leather glove, a freakish thing he thought a half dozen times a day about hacking off with his own horn-handled fleshing knife. That he hadn't yet been able to do it, not even while drunk, told him much about himself.

He lowered the rifle, a Bosworthy with telescopic sights that the man he'd relieved of it had, after three generous drinks from Mandrake Simms' bottle of the finest Tennessee sour mash, divulged that the rifle was a bespoke piece, made for him by a man who built one piece every year.

Each had to be ordered from an English gunsmith two years in advance of receipt. The rifle cost no less than a thousand dollars when new; though the money had been dear to him, it had been worth every cent.

Now, when Mandrake fired it, he had to agree with that unfortunate man, whose neck he'd snapped before a fourth drink was poured. The rifle was exquisite, and that was a word he'd only used twice before in his entire life. Once had been when recalling to himself aloud his dalliance with a whore in St. Louis. She'd refused to act the coquette like the others in the bordello and had instead, without uttering a word, relieved Mandrake of every inhibition he'd ever held in all his thirty-four years. In his mind, that evening had never ended.

His second encounter with the exquisite had been on sipping from a bottle of fine Scotch whisky he'd acquired from a Scotsman in a Conestoga bound for Oregon Territory. The man had squirreled away the bottle in a locked box deep within his wagon. Mandrake had sniffed it out and then stomped the man to paste for not divulging its location sooner.

The boys of Simms' band of filthy compatriots had fought like the inbred curs they were over the spoils of the rolling find—money, weapons, food, and, of course, the sobbing mother and screaming daughter. And finally, dear dead daddy's boots.

The bottle had, alas, been nursed, then drained over time, but the succulence of the memory, as with his time with the whore, remained.

And so the bullet from his exquisite rifle had performed as he had grown accustomed to—it burrowed deep into the head of the horse, and then another deeper into the head of the man, one among many on this latest cattle drive bound for points north.

In truth, he'd all but given up on any other drives coming along this route this late in the season. A herd of any size—and this one had to contain well more than five hundred, though fewer than a thousand head—should have branched eastward at the Arkansas River many miles before. That they hadn't told Mandrake they were likely making for Montana Territory to sell their beeves for a tidy profit to the wealthy, beef-starved miners.

The crew and herd should have passed through this range a month and more earlier in order to make Montana's mountains before imminent snows swept in and choked life in the north for far too many months of the year.

When one of his men had related the news, passed from the Apaches in his employ, of a solid-size herd traveling through, Mandrake had altered his plans. These involved driving the last and smallest of their plundered herds north to the gold towns of Montana Territory. He'd done this twice earlier in the season, but had nearly given up hope of being able to do so again before snow pinched off the opportunity.

Despite the success of the venture, he vowed this

would be his first and last season appropriating herds of cattle from their drovers. It had been, pound for pound, most profitable. It had also been the dirtiest, smelliest, most distasteful work he'd ever undertaken. It was a good idea he would gladly leave behind, along with his crew. He'd grown bored with them as well, with their drunken hooting and fights night upon night for months now.

Mandrake longed for a lengthy cruise along the California coast in a side-wheel steamer, gambling and enjoying the finest of whatever money could afford him, for he would have plenty of it. One last herd, and a month of travel, first to Montana Territory ushering the filthy beasts, another two weeks, perhaps three, to make the coast, and his desires would be within reach. *Endure,* he told himself. *Endure the hardship for it will pay most handsomely soon enough.*

Mandrake Simms sighed and raised the rifle to his shoulder once more. *Soon,* he thought, and almost smiled as another cowboy rode into view, faster now, inspecting his friend's collapse. *Soon.*

His smile widened. He was about to pick off yet another bowlegged, simp-minded cowboy atop a plodding, tick-riddled nag. He pulled the trigger.

CHAPTER NINETEEN

Bᴇ ᴛʜᴇ ᴛɪᴍᴇ Ed Stokes, aka the Kid, the last man to retrieve his revolver and rifle from the wagon, circled back to his post far back along the east flank, Tully was dead, and so was his horse.

That's how it began. And that's how it kept on for what seemed like hours to the boys of the drive. But the lion's share of the trouble dished out to them was heaped on their heads within minutes of that first pair of shots.

Chet and Sycamore, toward the rear of the west flank, spun and looked to each other for answers. Chet saw past Sycamore and jerked his chin toward the rock hills beyond them, to the west. Then his eyes flew wide as a shot's echo reached their ears.

Sycamore saw Chet's throat flower into a grisly rose of meat, as if he were being savaged by an unseen wolf. The man whipped backward, his head rapping hard against the horse's rump. The horse, a spirited bay in the best of times that required Chet's constant reassuring tones and steadying hand and legs, was now given free rein to buck wild. And she did.

Chet's right boot was still in the stirrup and stayed that way even as his dying body jerked with each hop and slam until he flopped out of the saddle. Sycamore watched as his pal drove face-first at the ground, slammed against it as if he were dining on rock and gravel and tufts of the bristly clots of grass they'd been traveling through for days.

Chet's leg stayed in the stirrup, but the weight of his body twisted the leg into an unnatural shape. Sycamore heard the bones pop, split, and crack.

The rank, flighty horse bucked and thrashed, and soon enough Chet's foot slid out of its boot. The horse skedaddled away and Chet lay facedown in the dirt, his legs mangled in a sticklike heap.

Sycamore watched all this take place in a matter of moments, two breaths' worth, before it occurred to him that this was no playacting, Chet had been shot in the throat. Sycamore's breakfast of beans and bread and coffee and the three slices of dried apple rings he filched from the burlap sack Cook kept for such purposes—knowing the boys liked to think they were getting away with something—geysered up and out of his throat and left him gagging.

This is really happening, he thought. *All the drives I've been on, nothing worse than a broken bone here and there, a stampede or two, a snake-struck beef, but now here it is. Ma always said chickens come home to roost eventually. People are getting shot and I might well be the very next one.*

Sycamore sunk spur, and as Rascal jumped at the rowel's digging pain, he hammered his boots hard against the big body. He had no idea where to go or what to do; he only knew he had to get away from whoever had shot Chet. This prompted the young Tennessean to look behind him, and he almost wished he hadn't.

Six, no, seven, no . . . eight riders were bent low, thundering at him from the hills to his right, the west. They rode far apart from one another, widening their distances as they dug hooves and raised dust.

They looked to still be a quarter mile off, but as Sycamore knew, it would only take them less than a minute to make it to him. And then what? "Then, Sycamore, my boy," he said to himself, "in that case, you ride faster! Keep 'er running hard, and don't look back."

He took his own feeble advice and cut south, keeping the herd right to his left, and hoped he would outrun the demons. *Have to be rustlers,* he thought. *Of course there would be rustlers out there. There always are.* He bent low, smelled Rascal's fear mingle with his summery, sweaty musk, and it gave Sycamore an extra edge of nerve, knowing his horse's survival depended on him, and his on the horse's. He could—no, he had to make certain they lived this thing through. Whatever this thing was.

He passed the spot where the herd of horses, Rollo's remuda, had been but a few minutes before.

MUCH LIKE HIS charges, the horses of the drive that made up the remuda, Rollo was always ready to move. He was a creature of instinct as much as they. Moments before, he'd seen a far-off dust cloud drawing close. Then it became two, then four, until the riders had spread apart farther, and then he knew they were about to be ambushed.

He saw others from the east, and though it was too far to see beyond the length of the herd, he guessed riders were making for them from the north as well.

That left the south still open, and Rollo knew what he had to do.

He circled back, whistled his call, and drove the perk-eared gang of drive horses in a thundering swarm of whinnying beasts southward. They pounded hard and he rode with them, hoo-raahing them from their midst before a vicious pain stiffened him.

It felt as if *el diablo* himself had reached into his back and snatched his spine tight in a fist of flame. Rollo's body sizzled and snapped and his breath wheezed out from something he no longer recognized, the body of a stranger to him forevermore.

He made it far enough to see his beloved horses disappear in a fast-moving boil of dust before he looked skyward. He could not seem to force his eyes down.

His horse, Amigo, beloved Amigo, hammered the grassy plain as his beloved rider no longer behaved as though it was an honor to carry him. He acted poorly, a sack of wet meal atop the saddle.

Then Amigo's burden dropped to the earth and the great horse, freed, pounded hard to catch up with his brethren, already far in the distance, running southward, making for a canyon where grass was forever green, where water flowed pure, and where no two-legged creatures bothered them any longer.

EDWARD "THE KID" Stokes saw the remuda break, with Rollo driving them hard southward, and knew whatever trouble it was Mitch had yammered about earlier had finally visited them.

He looked west, past the herd, toward the rocky hills and beyond to the mountains. He saw riders, a dozen or more, maybe as many as twenty, pounding toward them, then breaking and scattering apart, riding in all directions at once, everywhere but where they'd come from, out of the hills. So how many raiders were there? A pile of them. He recalled something Mitch said about those beef-mooching Apaches working with the rustlers, too.

The drive was a small one, only had nine hands, including Cook, which was far fewer than the number of raiders the Kid was already seeing. He knew that the shot he heard moments before had taken at least one of the men, Chet, who'd been riding the west flank with Sycamore.

Where was that big Tennessee galoot now? And Mitch and Joe? "Drover Joe, my foot," Stokes cursed as he pulled his horse left, then right a few paces. "Man should have known better than to lead us into a trap."

He knew even as he said it that he was talking foolish, said it only because trouble had fallen on them. Thing to do was deal with it. He checked the wheel on his revolver, palmed the hideout gun he always kept on him, tucked under his left side, under the vest. He was sure most of the men knew he had it, but nobody'd said anything to him about it, so he didn't, either.

His sheath knife was there, on his right side, ready should it come to that. And his long gun, a Winchester, his last purchase before the drive, was laid across the saddle.

Nothing more to do but hold his spot. "Be a damn cold day before I run." And he knew in his heart he wasn't blowing smoke. He felt that way, and it made him feel good to know that about himself.

Call him whatever anybody wanted to, and some of those names were well earned in the past—sure, he could be prickly—but he was no quitter. Agree to do a thing for a man, especially on a handshake, and you'd best own up to it, or live with yourself as a no-account all the long days of your life.

As he held his fidgeting horse at the rear of the increasingly rowdy herd of bellowing cattle, Edward Stokes' thoughts turned to his aunt Matilda, who'd raised him. And on the day he left home, in a huff, as usual, she had cried and begged him to at least not pursue a line of work that required him to wear a gun.

"I tried, Aunt Mattie," he'd said. Sort of.

And then the first rustler rode into view.

IT ALL HAPPENED quicker than Joe Phipps expected it would. He'd been in two other rustling attempts on past drives, one on the Hunter-Missouri Trail, when they'd been ambushed by a half dozen men covering their faces with tugged-up bandannas.

They had looked thin, their horses ganted, and their abilities with a gun equally as pathetic. Likewise was the force behind their growled threats. A quavering edge to their voices gave them away as cowards, desperate men who should have stayed at their diggings or behind their plows. That raid had not ended well for any of them.

Two died of bullet wounds in the melee, one succumbed a week later to the stomping he'd received from the fluster of beeves they'd been trying to appropriate, and the remaining three were tried and hanged. By then Joe was long gone on a crew returning to Texas, by way of Abilene, to deliver another herd to a different railhead.

Joe's second run-in with rustlers came two years before this drive. He'd been foreman on that crew, too. They'd fared poorly: One of his men had died, and a dozen head of cattle had been made off with. Considering the size of the crew that had hit them, Joe figured it could have ended worse.

As far as he knew, none of the thieves was ever run

to ground, save for the one they caught who ended up dying before his trial. The deputy marshal was eager to prove himself worthy of the job his boss would soon be retiring from, and he'd used a rough hand too often on his unarmed prisoner.

But none of those crews had involved two bunches of owlhoots at once: the first, the ragged band of Apaches he'd mistaken for beef moochers a week before; the other, a gang of range pirates he felt in his bones made up a vast number, likely north of a dozen men.

The second shot had already done its job by the time Joe heard its far-off crack. They were a fair piece away, a distance he'd never thought a man might shoot, and the gunman had dropped Tully and mortally wounded the former preacher's horse, to boot. That was both impressive and frightening.

If the man wanted, he could pick off everyone on the drive, without any of them being able to do much more than ride south, away from the herd. And that thought was what drove Joe to ride like hell's very own hounds were snapping toothy furrows in his bootheels. He thundered back toward the closest of his men, Chicken Pete, who stiffened impossibly straight in his saddle before Joe hammered up.

Oh, no, thought the drover even as he leapt down in time to catch Pete as the man slumped forward, then pitched sideways and limp into Joe's arms.

"Damn it!" barked the foreman, lowering the still-breathing man. Pete's horse, already keyed up, danced like a dervish, nearly stomping the men.

The big cowboy did his best to stay on the herd side of the horse, but that soon proved fruitless. His own horse, Trooper, jerked away, vexed by the dancing steed beside him.

As he laid down his charge, Joe heard a slamming thunk as another slug drove like a tiny fist into Pete's horse's brain. The big beast swayed, wobbled, and dropped to its front knees before slopping sideways.

Fortunately it fell away from Joe by a couple of feet. Under cover of the dust it raised as it dropped, Joe dragged Pete closer to the barely flinching beast. The big legs trembled and stilled, and would prove no further danger to the dying man.

Joe heard a harsh, raspy breathing and lowered his ear to Pete's chest. He heard nothing from within. Pete's time had come. And yet there was breathing, echoing in the cowboy's ears. Then Drover Joe realized it was his own.

As the dust cloud teased apart, Joe watched Trooper shy away, bucking, then bolt southward along the edge of the herd. Mitch, riding hard up the west flank, further spooked the riled horse, and Trooper bolted to his right, westward, in high terror for the foothills.

Sight of the horse caught Mitch off guard; then he realized it was Joe's big buckskin, riderless, and he reined up, confused.

"Get your head down, Mitch!" Joe growled out the words and poked his own head up to peer over the dead horse's belly. Nothing parted his hair nor shot off his hat.

Mitch slid from his saddle, leaping over the horse between them, and crept up low. So far no more shots had been fired.

"Keep down. You're here. Might as well make yourself useful." Joe nodded toward the horse's rear legs. "Drag those back and make room for Pete. He can flank the end."

"What? Use Pete's body?"

"He's beyond caring. Unless you'd rather do it yourself?"

Mitch gulped and tugged on Pete's legs while Joe shoved the dead man's shoulders. The bulwark made of two dead bodies, man and his horse, was a grim edifice, but suited Joe's temporary purpose. He didn't plan on being there long. They had to get back around to Cook and the others on the east flank and get them out of there. Had to get the boys safe. No herd was worth dying for.

"Mitch, I need you to cut through the herd. Lead your horse, but let him go if you have to. Get to Rollo and the boys. Tell whoever you can to hightail it south. I think it's our only chance. They're closing in on us from the west, north, and east."

Mitch swallowed and nodded. "What about you?"

"I'm going to try to hold them off here. Pick off who I can. Hell, this is a mess. We were surrounded before I even knew it. Never scouted this morning. I thought we were in tall cotton. Oh, hell."

"No, Joe. Don't blame yourself," said Mitch, eyeing the terrain, seeing trace of killers behind every snag of sage, every stray rock. "This isn't anything—"

"Go! And for God's sake, keep down!"

CHAPTER TWENTY

MANDRAKE SIMMS PARTED the air with another rifle shot that drove forward like a tiny battering ram.

He remained watching through the long brass tube sight, eyeing the air as if he could see the little lead missile travel its entire deadly route. He sucked in another breath through his nostrils and barely noted a shift in the barrel's aim as he pulled the trigger once more.

Man and horse, rider and mount, dropped. The horse thrashed and squirmed its last, hoofing at the earth, churning in efforts beyond its abilities. The man, however, gave up his ghost with suddenness.

This always impressed Simms, and not in an incredulous way. He found it sad and unfortunate each time he dealt a fellow a well-placed shot that men gave it all away so readily. The most valuable thing they will ever have, their lives, and yet they drop, often with not so much as a twitch or a kick. Drop and gone.

Of course it's not the shootee's fault, he told himself.

He's acting his part in the stage play. What it really meant was that Mandrake himself was a heck of a good shot. He knew it, and polished the notion in his head, over and over, that should he want to, he could trade bullets with the best of the gunhands going.

Of course, a lot of those did their business with a revolver, sort of freehand, whereas Simms relied on his fancy long gun to do his best work. Fine by him, as in the end, dead was dead and he could slide the thing back in its scabbard and let the horse lug it around. He did wear his pearl-handled revolver on his person, but only when he was out on the trail.

In towns, between bouts of what he liked to call his "work"—the tasks he thought up to make money—he wore another pearl-handled weapon: a two-shot nickel-plate honey of a hideout gun that tucked neat as you please in his jacket.

He'd not had to use it because whilst in civilization he had not put himself in a situation where he would need to rely on a gun. At least not if he could help it.

He paused between reloading the rifle and glanced down at the flat below. His men, all two dozen of them, thundered from the west, spreading apart as they rode, like fingers flexing on an outstretched hand, toward the dusty, seething mass of the herd that would soon be his. All his.

He still found it incredible that the men would believe him when he promised the flat fee of five hundred dollars per man for each drive they hijacked, all payable in a lump sum at the end of the season. The fees were tallied and kept in an official record book, which he made damn certain they all saw. It impressed them, as he knew it would.

Each man was paid a fifty-dollar gold piece after each job, an amount that went against what he said would be their "final earnings." The paltry amount kept them in booze and tobacco and prostitutes when in the northern mine camps and, most important, kept them quiet and satisfied. He did not wish to raise the ire of a group of men kicking up a fuss over money owed. Not yet anyway.

Long ago, as a younger man working for a squat, bald, wily, and not overly scrupulous attorney in Chicago named Dorling Fagin, Simms had learned much about the savage natures of men, their base selves, and how to bend this to suit his needs.

"Figure out how to do that," said Fagin. "Then do it over and over again, and you'll never want for finery or amusement in your life, Mandrake."

That advice stuck to the young trainee like paint to a sign, and it had proven to be true over and over again.

The majority of his men were never going to receive their big payday. Simms had already chosen the most trusted three, who would, when the time came, help him dispatch the grunt laborers. In exchange for what he would assure them would be a substantial payout.

Of course, before he doled out that money, those three men would each meet much the same grisly end as had the men they'd each dispatched. This would leave Mandrake Simms with the entire pile of his earnings, or rather his takings, to enjoy as he saw fit. And the plan would work because he had perfected it by honing it four times now with various schemes over previous years.

This, however, would be his biggest, most audacious scheme yet, involving four herds over five months. It required a base camp, a dozen men with the sole task of overseeing the camp itself, tending the herds, and feeding the men.

Periodically he rode north into various mining towns—Crescent, Jute Flats, Hercules, and Placer City. He'd been making his presence known, learning of the people who purchased beef for the masses of hungry men—and a few women—in each bustling burg. In this manner, he'd sold most of the animals from previous filched herds, save for a number of head kept in the valley for one last push, less those needed to feed the men.

"One last herd," he muttered. He could practically taste the oysters and braised breast of duck in San Francisco. He grunted and cleared away such premature pleasures from his mind to concentrate once more on the task at hand.

He judged that this herd, which he and the men had been watching for more than a week, about eight hundred strong, had come from Texas, from the look of the beeves and the dress of some of the cowhands. The animals appeared to be well tended and driven with care, lest they walk the tallow off their ornery longhorn hides.

Simms looked to his left, northward, and spied the frayed band of ragtag Apaches he employed as scouts, a ruse that had served them all well.

The Indians were able to procure free meat for their respective families at their encampment to the northeast, along the Willow River. They also gave Simms the lowdown on the herd's size, how many men were present, the level of orneriness among the trail hands, and how well armed they appeared.

The Apaches had proven surprising in their abilities and had even willingly participated in the rustling, something Simms was only too happy to allow. Beyond giving them more meat animals, they would not be compensated for their efforts, however.

There they were, in the distance, fanning out, armed and riding. Rather than making straight for the herd, they showed skill by holding back, picking routes down the long hills. They let Simms' band of idiots ride hard and fast into the waiting guns of the cowboys, who had by now armed themselves and were shooting back, out of desperation in a thin hope for survival.

Simms didn't bother to predict the behavior of men. He rarely was surprised anymore. Being the first to ride into battle, hard at the gaping maw of a waiting gun, brought little more than the expected result—a quick, painful death. Much the same result was had by being the first person to bid at an auction—responsible for an amount painful to the coin purse. And yet, at the outset of each auction, each battle, there were men who could not restrain themselves.

Let them be the fools, then, Simms told himself as he watched the first wave of his men plow through the grass and trade bullets with the cowboys surrounding the herd. Some of his men fell—fine with him, as he no longer needed their idiotic services. He needed only enough of them to drive the herd back to the canyon.

He watched his idiots overpower the few cowboys tending the herd. They'd been given orders to kill them all but the trail drive's cook and any other men who looked to be of use in driving the herd. But that number, including the cook, should not exceed three. Too many men were too many men.

CHAPTER TWENTY-ONE

Cook snapped the lines hard on the backs of Romulus and Remus, his two long-suffering, much-loved, mostly deaf mules. They were so alike they could be brothers, and Cook considered them such. In his more whimsical moments, Cook imagined he was their papa, keeping the docile pair on the narrow path.

He rarely laid on the lash, but on this day, trouble had raked up a furrow around the herd, and unless Drover Joe was mistaken, they were all in for a hellish time.

"Snap to, lads! We need to make it down off this rise and into that gulley yonder. Keep you boys safe while we see what's what."

The gulley in question was a hard, quick ride to the east, and within a half minute Cook had found a way in. The depth wasn't enough to hide his boys and the wagon within, nor did he think anyone had seen him drive down there, but he hoped it would afford some protection.

From there he intended to set up a position of defense to pop as many of the invaders in the head as he could. He also thought the other boys might find the gulley of use should they become overrun—looking to be a likely possibility.

He'd scarcely set the brake and was reaching for his scattergun when a sliver of a shadow passed over his hand.

"Curse me for a fool," growled Cook as he looked up, swinging his gun into play, and saw a dark face with a wide, leering smile, black gaps where teeth once jutted. Those left were green stumps. The eyes above them were narrowed, dark, and fierce.

The attacker held no weapon, but it didn't matter, for in that eyeblink of time it took Cook to see all this, he knew he'd made a terrible blunder.

He didn't get a chance to turn around, but saw in the leering Indian's narrow eyes that he would soon be laid low. A hot wash of pain flowered along the right side of his head and his vision bloomed wide. Dots of light like blizzard snow pelting down through a night sky filled Cook's sight before his eyes pinched shut. The big Cajun collapsed with a groan and a grunt.

His mules flicked an ear each, then champed and stomped in place.

The man who'd hit Cook in the side of the head toed the victim's ample left side. The fat man didn't move. The clubber grunted and motioned to the other one to help him load the big unconscious man into the wagon. Somehow. He was big.

They managed to lay him across the boot well below the wagon's seat. Then while the clubber drove the wagon up and out of the gulley, his partner, the leering man, bound the big unconscious man's wrists tight with a rawhide thong.

The chief of the whites, Simms, would pay well today, for this was the one who prepared the meals, like a woman. Who knew why whites acted as they did? Simms wanted this fat man, and they guessed that his wagon would bring extra money.

The clubber drove the wagon in a long, wide arc north, then westward, toward the narrow green valley where Simms and his men kept the cattle to fatten them before they drove them north again. The leering man climbed over the seat and rummaged in the wagon compartments he could reach. He found little of use. Mostly bundles of dried foods that tasted terrible, something grainy that smelled nutty but tasted like sand. He threw it to the ground.

Again and again he did this with bundles and crocks of goods that made his tongue hurt and his eyes fill with water and made him weep like a woman even though he was not sad. It was shameful and he did not turn to look at his friend driving the wagon.

They had been lucky to have seen the fat man driving his cooking wagon away from the herd. They had raced to it and crept closer, closer. The mules did not give them away. Sometimes mules will betray you in this way. But not this time. The men had moved closer, crawling, and still the fat cooking man did not hear them. Until it was too late for him.

Now they would not have to risk fighting with the cowboys who were protecting their herd. The cowboys would all die, of course, because Simms' men were hard men who cared nothing for other lives. They only cared for liquor and white man's money.

The leering man, known to the others of his band as Tail of the Wind, because he had been a swift runner in his youth, could understand part of what the whites liked so well. He pawed open the compartments of the wagon, hanging off the side as his friend Vulture Feather drove through the worst of the holes—Tail of the Wind knew it was Vulture Feather's cruel plan to knock him free and leave him afoot—on the flat leading to the hills that led to Simms' valley.

And then Tail of the Wind found what he wanted, and he could not help it: He let loose with a yip and a yi-yi-yi! For his gnarled, bony fingers closed around the slender neck of a bottle that was mostly filled with the liquid that looks like sunlight and burns like it, too. He picked the little cork from the mouth of the bottle with two of his five teeth and spat it to the earth.

His first swig was as it always was, hateful and pained. He let it soak into him, down his throat to his guts. It sat there, warming him from inside, as if he had swallowed glowing cook-fire coals.

Vulture Feather cursed him and beckoned him with his left hand, and so Tail of the Wind made his way slowly forward to the wagon's seat, the bottle in one hand, a smile on his wide, leering face. When he reached the seat, he handed the bottle to his friend, jammed his feet on the back of the unconscious fat man below him, and waited for the bottle to return to him.

CHAPTER TWENTY-TWO

Mandrake Simms had a long-abiding passion for finely cooked food. That Mr. Horton-Wu, the half-Chinese range cook who had fallen into his employ, had been a source of equal parts pleasure and pain, happiness and grief, vexation and sublimity.

The aforementioned Horton-Wu could one day concoct a delectable feast from the scantest of supplies: a flank steak skirted with a moat of mushroomed gravy ringed with small potatoes of the whitest flesh in a buttery soak. This would be accompanied with a crisp, cold salad of fresh greens topped with cheese crumbles and crushed macadamia nuts and dusted with a proprietary seasoning that reminded the eater of only the happiest of childhood moments, yet the taste remained aloof and elusive, the eater unable to quite put a finger on the particular flavor and thus was cheated, too, of the specific memory it so powerfully evoked.

That Horton-Wu was able to do this was a wonder

to Simms, whose own childhood was anything but inducing of pleasant smiles.

The next day, however, Horton-Wu could boil the head of a goat and hack off rubbery hunks, which he'd serve in shallow bowls. It was a stew fit for pigs, he'd mutter, and sulk his way back into his kitchen tent. For long months, the only thing that kept Simms from gutting the audacious artist like a fresh-caught trout was the pervasive memories of the man's better meals.

His patience, of late, however, had burned low. Horton-Wu had spent more time inside a bottle than not, and his erratic inconsistencies had dwindled to the point that he was uncaring and unwilling to attempt to create anything close to his glory dishes of days past.

And so Mandrake Simms, with a genuine ache in his heart, had shot the half-drunk disappointment behind the left ear. He'd made certain they were well away from the camp proper. He also knew they were being watched by no fewer than thirty-seven men. Not that he would care should any of them object. He also didn't think anybody had trouble with this decision. Horton-Wu had sufficiently disappointed and insulted each of them throughout the months of his career with Simms.

To Simms' men, the only downside in the killing was knowing who was going to be the next cook—Craven. That was the fellow's name. It made Simms' skin prickle when he thought of saying the word. And when he actually spoke it, he winced.

Craven was not a trait he admired in any creature, and the new cook was the model for such behavior. He also couldn't conjure a meal to save his backside, though he was game to cook, the only one of all the several dozen men in the loose employ of Mandrake Simms who showed any interest in boiling water. Craven's very keenness in the task at hand put them all, not least of whom was Simms, in a tight spot.

Craven's beans were perpetually undercooked and contained too many pebbles. His coffee stank of fly-blown meat, and his meat tasted of burned-over coffee. No one knew how or why this was possible. There wasn't a day that slipped by that summer that Mandrake Simms didn't regret his folly of shooting the one cook he had ever met in all his days who had elevated cookery to a level worthy of high praise.

But as he liked to cook for himself even less than he did in partaking of the mealtime efforts of Craven, he kept his peace and tapped his finger on the hammer of his pearl-handled revolver, something he was adept at using.

On Simms, the quick draw was a smooth procedure, slick as deer guts on a pump handle, as the old man who'd taught him the move once told him, before Simms cored the gray buck's chest with a close-in shot one day when he figured he'd learned all he could from the man. Didn't help that the old man had been riding him, digging, really, about why he put up with that odd withered finger of his.

The way Mandrake saw it, a man's body was his own business, not that of anyone else. Over the years, he'd buttoned up the eyes of two whores who'd giggled about it.

Now he'd filled his summer with poorly prepared food and close quarters with too many men, a number of whom were mix-breed drifters. They were uncouth and vicious in their dealings, from sunup to sunset, even in sleep, sawing away in drunken slumbers, rippling the canvas of the tents that served as bunkhouses in their vast canyon stronghold.

He'd had enough of their drunken raging, their belching and farting and spitting and shouting and fisticuffs and tiny tortures of one another, let alone the poor bastards he'd allowed them to drag back to camp.

The female captives fared the worst, if only because

they lived longer. He wasn't opposed to such shenanigans, but drew the line when their screams woke him. This summer was not about having fun—well, not much anyway. It was, however, about making money any way he could, preferably lots of it at one time, and then cutting loose from this raft of fools and going his own way until the money he'd earned dwindled to enough to set himself up in some sort of venture once more.

It was a recipe that had worked for him in the past, to much effect. This was the first time, however, that it involved cattle.

He'd been all set to somehow bleed dry the knob-headed rock hounds pounding and digging and rooting away their vital years in the snake-infested dirt in Montana Territory in their blind grope for gold. That itself would be a goal worthy enough of his efforts. But then he'd heard a phrase he swore he heard before, yet for some reason it hadn't stuck to him. This time it did.

A scrimy old spinster who ran a bordello had told him that the folks who made the money in mine camps were those who mined the miners. *Think about that,* she said.

There's cash money waiting for someone with balls enough to soak the dirt grubbers for every little thing they need up there in the mountains, where bears and deer and snakes and lions provide the only source of entertainment. That is, until the whores roll into town. They bring with them booze and a faro table, and then guess who's making all the money in a town such as that. She winked and took his money.

Thought about it, he had.

Her words had given Mandrake the nudge he needed. Why risk having his neck stretched again and again? He didn't doubt his abilities where evasion was required, but such a life was getting tiresome. Why not set up shop in a town such as Placer City or Garnet and . . . what?

He had no interest in selling alcohol or women to knuckle-face Swedes for a buck a throw. No. So what else did miners need to do their job? They needed tools. Gah, selling hardware interested him less than wrangling a gaggle of screechy whores.

He'd been mulling over this problem in the midst of a particularly fine morning meal at a hotel in San Francisco, overlooking a sunny blue sky on the Pacific. He'd been chewing slowly and gently so as to prolong the experience. He was enjoying a concoction he'd not known existed before then, which the waiter referred to as eggs Benedict, when he'd paused in midchew.

Food, Mandrake. Of course. It was the one thing all miners needed more than a pickax or a shot of red-eye rye or a roll in a lice-riddled corn-shuck mattress with a cranky whore. They needed to eat. Beefsteak, and lots of it. And that's when the notion of a cattle drive, or a summer's worth of them, came to him. Why not?

He'd finished his meal quicker than he'd intended, but this time he could forgive himself. He had a grand notion and much planning to get up to before the drive season began in earnest.

And that was how Mandrake Simms had occasion to find himself, a mere five months after that epiphany of a moment, perched atop a jut of granite in the foothills of the Rocky Mountains in Wyoming Territory, eyeing with a satisfied smile a scene far below of utter chaos and madness, a scene that he had orchestrated.

Simms was confident this situation had provided a solution to the problem of that damnable unskilled mess that was Craven. Should the trail drive's cook prove satisfactory, then he could kill the weasel with full knowledge he was doing the right thing.

As he smoothed his waxed moustaches and licked his lips at the possibilities, Simms allowed himself a quiet grunt of satisfaction.

CHAPTER TWENTY-THREE

Mitch threaded Champ back through the middle of the herd as fast as he could, hoping for some magical idea to come together in his head, something that would save the men, the herd, the day. It struck him how unprepared they had been for such an attack. How most herds who'd traveled this or any trail route before must have been the same, so vulnerable.

They had nine men, drovers at best by occupation and inclination, whose job it was to usher a mass of unruly, stringy, bleating, bawling, bellowing Texas longhorn cattle from one place northward for two thousand miles to another place where other men would buy the animals, kill them, and eat them. Surely there was a problem with such a plan.

Yes, he told himself. There was a big one. To begin with they didn't have enough men to fend off an attack by range pirates. And when the attack came, they were laid low, decimated.

Mitch nudged Champ forward, and broke through

the middle of the east flank of the herd. He was still hunched low in the saddle, and turtled his head forward. There sat Ed Stokes, the Kid, facing north.

He saw Mitch, tensed, and pulled his rifle to his shoulder, its snout aimed at Mitch, who did the same with his revolver. They were some yards apart and each twitching on the trigger when mutual recognition eased the moment. Mitch jerked his chin, nodding toward Stokes, who lowered his rifle.

"Okay?"

Mitch nodded. "Stay low. Joe said to head southward, get anybody else you can."

His was a whisper-shout as he rode slowly toward Stokes, pivoting his head to all sides. With the noise and uncommon commotion, and without constant tending, the beeves were ranging apart. Mitch's instinct was to gather them, prevent any from straying too far, but then he thought, *Why not let them spread out? Why not let them stampede? Heck, why not make them stampede?*

"I ain't leaving your herd, boss. No, sir, I signed on for the haul and I'm in it."

"I figured," said Mitch. But visions of Tully, of Joe, the invaders riding in hard from the west and, if Joe was right, from most every other direction, too, meant they'd soon be overrun. "And I appreciate it, Ed. But we don't have a chance. There are too many of them."

As he rode closer, he saw something slip on the young man's face. Behind those hard gray eyes, doubt poked through. He rode up and paused alongside, facing south.

"How many?"

"Couple dozen, maybe more. Plus those Apache."

The Kid grunted. "We have to try to fight, don't we? I mean, I can't run, knowing you and the others was . . ."

Mitch turned to where Ed was looking. His mouth went drier. A rising cloud of dust boiled up from the cob-grass flat, a stretch between the herd and the larger foothills that offered, even at this point in the season, hummocks of browning brittle grasses cattle rarely found toothsome. Between the hummocks grew the low, painful cacti that man and beast did well to leave alone.

The cloud boiled up from this, making straight for the herd. Mitch and Stokes and some of the beeves heard a thumping, drumming rhythm that soon gave way to its cause. The cloud parted low at the forefront to reveal a cluster of a dozen or more men, in addition to the couple dozen already closing in on the herd, pestering the cattle and trading shots with other of the boys.

This fresh group took on a more definite shape the closer they drew. Mitch saw a tall, lean man in a sugar-loaf hat and a long, narrow black beard trailing off his chin, bony cheeks bare, dark eyes hidden beneath a wide, low-pulled brim. Crisscrossing his chest, double bandoliers of ammunition bounced. He rode with his mouth pulled in a wide grin, as if he were enjoying himself more than any man ought.

Then that smiling mouth moved, perhaps barking vicious words to his close-following compadres, and his smile widened, for he seemed to look over the narrowing herd right at Mitch. He jammed the reins in his teeth and filled each of his big, bony hands with a weighty-looking revolver.

The group of men emerging from the dust cloud looked to be a dozen in number, and they rode hard and fast, led by the bearded smiler, right toward the stomping, milling herd of spooked beeves, seemingly heedless of the certain pain the clashing animals' horns promised.

The herd split apart like water before a fast-moving ship, sending a ripple through the mass of animals that the previous frenzied minutes had not. The beasts re-

formed their milling mass behind the advancing group
of pirates, but the herd kept moving, running faster
and jerking like a flock of crazed, ground-bound birds
sharing a single thought: run at all costs. Flight as an
instinct became all to the cattle. This did not concern
nor slow the advancing rogues.

Throughout all this, Mitch and Stokes swung hard
for the southern end of the herd, not trying to turn the
riled beeves, but to escape the oncoming wrath of the
killing pirates.

A sudden cry from the Kid jerked Mitch's gaze to
his right in time to see Stokes stiffen and jerk upright
in the saddle. The Kid turned to face Mitch, surprise
drawing his eyes wide. He looked about to speak, but
blood spumed red and bright where words should have
been.

Then something whistled by Mitch's skull and he
crouched even lower in the saddle and jerked the reins
hard, angling back into the herd. He didn't know if it
was a wise direction in which to ride. He was beyond
thinking such things. He was rabbiting, he knew, out of
raw fear and self-preservation. *Anywhere,* his beast
brain told him. *Go anywhere, and go there fast. And
keep low while you're doing it.*

He hoped he wouldn't be shot in the back, the front,
or the sides. He hoped the riled longhorns wouldn't
sink a hook into Champ. Most of all, Mitchell Newland
hoped he was going to live through the next couple of
minutes.

But hope, he knew, was a fickle, fleeting thing, and
as he nudged Champ deeper into the bawling, dust-
clouded herd, he wasn't feeling particularly hopeful.

CHAPTER TWENTY-FOUR

MITCH MADE IT halfway back through the herd before the beeves began disappearing away from
him, as if he'd repelled them somehow. *Maybe it's the
stink of fear washing off me,* he thought as he tried to
swallow back the hard knot lodged in his throat. Sweat
snaked down into his eyes and stung, making it difficult to see.

Not that he could see much in the boil of dust, a
cloud that hung among and above the herd as the beasts
lunged and stamped and fought. He was too far in and
far too surrounded by madness, of the beeves and the
pirates, to do anything but move with the beasts.

Champ whickered low and menacing, and kept up
in a near constant utterance of annoyed and threat-
ened sounds as they moved forward, in what felt to
Mitch like one ill-chosen step at a time.

Then he heard whistles and shouts, close-up, some
far off, some curses and other words that sounded Spanish, none from voices he recognized, and he knew the

herd was being driven off. Very soon he'd be seen, caught in the open, blinking from the dust and not knowing where to look. He reached to draw his revolver but found he already held it. One, two more steps, and the horse grunted. The dust parted, peeled apart, drifted off with what he could see was the herd.

He guessed that somehow he'd still not been seen. It could not last. And it didn't—a rifle cracked to his right, down low, and he heard a familiar voice shout, "Devils!"

Mitch slid from the saddle and crouched low, trying to hold Champ's head low. It didn't work. "Joe?"

More gunfire from somewhere ahead. He heard a groan, again from his right.

Moments passed; then he heard a stifled growl.

"Joe? That you?"

The last tatters of dust blew away as the herd humped it westward. Mitch saw several mounted figures hazing the beeves. He heard shouts and whistles. The sound of shots lessened.

"Mitch! Get out of here! I'm surrounded! Man alive, get out of here! Ride south!"

He continued to low walk, not certain what to do. Southward was where he'd seen men shot. Here, at least, Joe was alive. But for how long? "Joe, you hit?"

He heard breath being sucked in. "Yeah. In the leg. I'll live."

The words hung, then dropped to the dusty earth as if shot. Mitch inched forward, saw the browned land before him, northward, dip low. A gulley? His knee knocked into something hard. He glanced down quickly. A boulder. "Joe? You in that gulley?"

Champ reared back, whinnying, and jerked the reins from Mitch's hand, then bolted as a massive knife whipped wide before him. He had but a moment to see a wavery version of his own face in the blade as it sliced the air.

He rolled to his left as the blade sought him out. It was keener than any slab of polished metal Mitch had ever seen, its thinned edge razoring again and again at the diminishing gap between him and an enemy who'd appeared as if conjured, as if he'd grown out of the dusty soil itself.

The wielder, an Apache, lurched at him as he rolled in the dirt. The attacker's bony leer wore a pronounced mass of square white teeth that gnashed in counterpoint with each swing and lunge of his muscle-corded arm. It was as if he were relishing the very taste of the terror he was causing, supping on the flavor of Mitch's horror as he advanced.

Mitch smelled him, the raw animal stink of him, a thousand-thousand days and nights of unwashed feral sweat clouding off him in waves. It was as if Mitch was being pinned to the low rock, held by nothing more than the brute's hard gaze and flexing nostrils, oily with meat sweat.

"Mitch! Roll to your right! Now!"

The voice, of course, was Drover Joe's. Mitch's reverie of fear ended within a finger snap of time and he heeded the order even as the brute lunged. While Mitch drove himself low, ramming his right kneecap square on a head-size rock, his trembling fingers searched for his revolver. He no longer held it, nor was it in his holster. He snatched for his own knife and freed it from its sheath.

He kept rolling, spun, and saw his savage attacker had followed his own lunge with a growl of anger and scooted to the far side of a low half-buried slab of rock. Mitch saw the grease-gleaming black curve of the man's head skulking low. *But not low enough,* he thought, crouching with haste behind a bare berm of earth.

Mitch would not be where the man hoped by the time he emerged to Mitch's left. He shoved to his right, wary of stepping too far off the sloped edge, and pitching backward into a shallow draw. The route was littered with small prickly pear cacti that would leave a man pus riddled, sore, and aching for days. But it beat being pierced by a skinning blade.

He tried to keep low, mimicking his attacker's stance and approach, as he made his way behind another slight rise, six feet to his right. His knee was still in disagreement with him after slamming into the rock and balked, much like Champ would do over most anything, depending on how he'd slept. *Champ, curse that horse,* he thought. *He ran off with my rifle.* Mitch glanced about him quickly, but did not spy his dropped revolver.

The knee twinged and Mitch gritted his teeth, half shoving with his bootheel, bulling through the sudden minor affliction. *No weakness or whining, boy,* he thought as he wheezed, barely a whisper, low down beyond a close-by rock slab.

He tugged his legs up tight, squatted, and wiped the palm of his knife hand on his trouser leg. The grit and sweat made his hand sticky once more and he repositioned his fingers, wrapped tight about the horn handle of his hip skinner.

He'd never had to stab a man with it, nor with any other blade in his life, but that didn't mean he was incapable of it. To defend his own life, he'd damn sure kill. That much he knew about himself. He only hoped he'd have no more of those foolish moments of seizing in place, too stunned by fear to defend himself.

If that happened, none of it—not his childhood, not his father's sloppy, misguided kindness, not the ranch he so loved, not the horses and the cattle, and most of all not Evie—would matter if he let himself be gutted to death on this vicious plain by a rogue Apache who looked to be half-coyote, half-starved, and all mean, as Sycamore might have said. No, he would not let that happen.

Mitch ran his tongue tip across his top lip, tasted the sting of salty sweat, felt the prickle of bristly whiskers, and waited in the new silence that had descended on this little tableau. Were the other men fighting the same? How had Drover Joe seen him but not been able to help? Was he in the midst of his own fight to the death with another silent, savage attack?

All this took place within moments, yet it felt to Mitch like a lifetime of lifetimes. The heat of the sun, relentless in its hot-skillet fury, baked down. Seconds ticked by. Then he heard a rustle, as a bird's wing might make. Mitch risked a quick look, prairie-dogging up but a moment. . . .

"Stay down, Mitch!"

Instinct forced him to jerk to his left, but not far enough.

Mitch did not see the second Apache, this one wearing a soiled white tunic, emerge from a dip in the landscape some distance to his right. He did not see the man pull his arm back, teeth set tight behind his stretched lips, then thrust his arm forward, sending a tomahawk whipping in from the east, end over end.

It sliced the air before slamming into the young rancher's skull, behind his left ear. And Mitchell Newland knew no more.

CHAPTER TWENTY-FIVE

JOE PHIPPS SWALLOWED hard, and wondered for the fifth time in as many minutes if this was the way he was going to go out on his run of all-too-brief days. Was he destined to die in this shallow divot in the dirt plain of . . . Where were they in now? Wyoming Territory? Yes, that's right. He was becoming addlepated from all this fighting—had to be the reason he couldn't think straight.

Joe squinted across the rolling stubbled plain. He saw nothing but waves of heat and lumps that moved now and again. Horses? Men? Cattle?

He remembered then that he was not alone in his shallow hidey-hole, and looked to his left. Yes, there was Mitch. He'd dragged him over after the Apache who'd attacked him had run off, deviled by shots from Joe. He didn't think he'd gotten the bastard, though.

Through a haze of heat and pain, Joe regarded the boy. For that's how he'd thought of Mitchell Newland, a boy, a pup. He was a good one, but still wagging his tucked tail, eager to please, despite the fact he was a young man, marrying age and all. And born into a ranch, to boot.

Admittedly it wasn't much of a spread, but it had water and some promise. As much promise as anybody in Cawlins, Texas, might aspire to anyway. At the best of times, that entire region was little more than a hard-scrabble hiccup on an unforgiving landscape. But Mitch was to be commended for sticking with it as he had. Most kids, when losing the last of their folks, would sell up and move away.

Not Mitch Newland. He'd stuck with it, and now it was paying off. Or it had been until the killers and thieves struck. Lord, but the trail crew had been woe-fully undermanned. Even if he'd hired on double the number of men, they still would not have stood a chance of resisting the pirates. Not that Corliss Bilks would have agreed to fund a bigger crew. He'd fought Joe on the ones he'd chosen, whining that Joe could do the job with fewer men.

"Wouldn't have mattered," he whispered.

Joe looked left and right, and though he was tempted to shift himself sideways, he dragged his legs alongside the crater's edge against which he lay; he knew bet-ter than to move. Best to wait it out a while longer. Maybe the last of the raiders—the ones left behind to lay low any moaning, twitchy survivors—would finally grow bored and lie to their captains back at whatever hellish hole they'd slid out of earlier.

Nothing but death awaited him—he was sure of it—should he try to rise and make his way over to the boy. The range pirates were still out there, waiting to pick off anything that moved. He'd already heard three shots that had done that; two had earned gasping groans as the men who'd been shot had finally had their last hopes ripped away.

Joe took stock of what he had—a hip knife, his rifle, and a revolver. He'd managed to keep his hat, a boon out here now that the sun was showing off, a far-up bright thing pinned in the eternal blue of the sky. What bullets he had were in his gun belt, which was half filled.

He had all that and a heck of a leg wound. He'd need to tighten his bandanna soon or risk bleeding out sooner than he might. He also had Mitch, the boy, not far away, flopped on his back, head bent forward, his own hat also blocking the sun.

He'd managed to grab Mitch's knife and pistol, both in the dirt near him, and dragged him back to the shallow gouge in the earth where they were now trapped. Then someone from the north began pounding shots at him. That had been hours ago, but he didn't trust the man wasn't still out there, keeping an eye.

Given the kid's position, Joe could not tell if Mitch was still breathing. Even though Mitch was six or eight feet away, the heat rippled and danced off everything, obscuring his vision.

Then the trigger finger on Mitch's near hand twitched. It rose up and trembled in the air before dropping to the sandy earth.

"Mitch!" Joe waited a few seconds for a response. Nothing. "Mitchell! Mitchell Newland!" He growled it and glanced once more up at the crater's rim across from him, a good twenty feet away. How close were the snipers? Would they hear him? Would they see movement if he dragged his legs backward and inched toward the boy?

"Mitch, it's Joe Phipps!" His voice was a hoarse whisper.

The finger, then the hand, jerked, spasmed as if smacked, caught filching from Cook's jar of sweetmeats. He kept on whispering in low tones. "Come on now, Mitch," he said. "Wake up. Need your help."

That seemed to do it. *Clean living,* thought Joe with a wry grin. *Leave it to Mitch to respond to someone looking for a hand.* Mitch moved his head side to side slowly, his hat bobbing, and Joe saw the danger they'd both be in within a few short seconds if he didn't scoot over there and ease the boy into wakefulness, and keep him from moving about.

"Take her slow now, Mitch," he said, holding his breath against the pain from his wound and dragging his legs back out of potential view of whoever was out there, armed and interested in picking him off.

That's when Mitch came to with a jerk and a shout. He worked his legs as if he were trying to run, kicking up sandy dirt at the same time his left arm whipped wide. He shouted, "N-n-n-no! No!"

"Hush now," growled Joe louder than he had before. He'd already jerked his legs close in and held off screaming himself, so raw was the bullet wound in his leg. Wouldn't do to keep dragging it in the dirt. He had to believe there was a way out of this yet.

"Joe?" The kid's voice was softer as if he were lost in the dark.

"Yeah, it's me, Mitch. Stay still now."

"Oh." He shook his head slowly like an old man, as if he were disagreeing with Joe. "My head, oh . . ."

"You took a hard knock to the bean, that's for certain. But you're okay. Going to be okay now, Mitch. I need you not to move. Hear me? Do not move."

"Okay, Joe. You always know the right thing. . . ."

If Mitch had meant it as a sarcastic dig, it couldn't have stung worse. But Mitch didn't have it in him. Didn't mean Joe wasn't filled to the brim with shame and rage and guilt over what happened scant hours before. And he couldn't help reliving the day in his head, gritting his teeth tight at every wrong choice that had led to this.

They'd all awakened—except the night riders—to another pretty blue day on the trail, with the added excitement in the air, for men and horses and cattle, of reaching the greener grass and mountain streams nearly visible ahead. Might even have reached them by the end of the day. One last sunbaked flat to cross, then they would be in better shape for the rest of the drive to Montana Territory.

Drover Joe's scouting trip of the day before had turned up nothing but promising terrain ahead. He'd not seen sign of others out there sharing the same trail. Certainly not of dozens of thieving killers. But then again he hadn't ventured west, northwest, or northeast, for he was confident of the trail they were on. He'd been on it but two years prior. They only had to follow it and they might make their destination before any hard weather dropped on their heads.

"Joe . . ."

"Yeah, Mitch, right here." He was within reach of the young man now and set a reassuring hand on Mitch's right arm, gave it a squeeze. "Sit tight. We'll be okay."

Mitch didn't respond, but Joe saw his chest working slowly and did his best to ease himself back against the sloped edge of the hole. If he had more strength and knew for certain he wouldn't be seen, he'd scoop into the earth behind them, give themselves a few more inches of protection from sniping eyes. But he wasn't confident his arms wouldn't be seen from a distance.

He did not want to attract any attention to them. He wanted whoever was out there to think nobody was in that shallow crater. And if they thought it might be occupied, since Mitch and he weren't moving, they must be good and dead.

"Wait them out," he muttered, biting the inside of his cheek to keep awake. It wouldn't do to doze and have Mitch come around again, thrashing and yelping.

Or worse, wake up to see the working end of a gun barrel about to spit leaden fire in his face.

Despite his efforts, Drover Joe Phipps lost his fight with consciousness. The sizzling sun hammered at him with the same relentlessness he himself had always shown a task. No breeze rolled through to ease the day, even for a moment. When he woke, for several confusing, peaceful moments, he did not remember what had happened. And then he did. And the weight of his guilt made him wish he hadn't awakened.

A quiet voice beside him said, "Joe? You okay? You alive, Joe?"

Alive, yeah, he guessed so. What else could this be? Hell? Not hot enough for the likes of him. Joe slid his swelling tongue out over his cracked, peeling lips.

"Yeah." His voice sounded thin, fragile. "Still here."

CHAPTER TWENTY-SIX

J OE SUCKED AIR hard through his tight-set teeth. "Went right through the meat of my leg. It smarts."

"Smarts?" whispered Mitch. "You have a knack for understatement, Joe." He tugged his shirttails free of his waist and, glancing up toward the rim of the pit, pulled his sheath knife and slit down low on his shirt. His hands shook.

"Easy, Mitch. No need for you to end up bleeding, too."

"Too late," he said.

"What? Your head, right."

Mitch nodded and winced as he tore a strip of cloth off his shirt bottom.

"Pinned down in a snake pit. Curse me for a fool," said Joe.

"Why?" Mitch leaned back, looking westward once more. He saw nothing save a dust devil tiring itself out.

"I should have seen it, should have known sooner."

"Known what?" said Mitch, looking at Joe now. He thought maybe the man was beginning to turn feverish.

"That devil with the conchos on his vest. He was with that tribe looking for tribute payment last week. He hung back. Should have known then. He had a half-breed look about him, and all curly wolf."

"Are you sure?"

Joe nodded. "Yeah. Likely been scouting us for days. I've heard of this. A rogue band will take what they can get. Then they'll wait you out and help a gang of owlhoots to pick your carcass clean later on down the trail." He groaned. "Oh, I should have known."

"Who are the range pirates, then?" said Mitch, hoping to steer Joe from blaming himself.

Joe tried to shift his weight to the other side of his backside and winced. Once he got his breath back, he said, "Don't know. Not seen them before. But they're a mixed bunch: Mexicans, half-breeds, whites. I saw one wearing a kepi and another swaggering around with a skinny sword. Might mean there's a campaigner or two among them. More than likely it means they stole them off some poor soldier they butchered for his coin purse."

Mitch knew Joe was right; none of it mattered much now. They were here, pinned down in a snake-infested wasteland, each a wounded man. They were both nearly out of ammunition, and the only water they had was what was left in a canteen that lay thirty feet beyond the rim of their crater, tantalizing them.

What felt to Mitch like a year, but was more likely an hour, passed before he spoke again. "You think they're gone?"

Joe's eyelids fluttered; then he squinted. "No, no way. They'll wait us out. Might even venture closer after dark. Best thing we can do is be ready, knife them when they lean in." He licked his crusty lips.

Mitch thought perhaps he'd gone back to sleep when Joe spoke once more. "How's the head?"

"I'll survive." He regretted saying it right away, since he guessed Joe's wound was far worse than it looked, and it looked plenty rough. "What I meant was—"

"I know what you meant. But we'll both survive. I don't plan on cashing in yet. At least not until I do for those who did this to us . . . and to the boys." He perked up a little then. "Any sign of them? Any of the boys moving out there?"

Mitch risked another glance up above the slight berm, a ridge of crusted rock formed at the northern edge of the crater that sat nearly over their heads.

Joe squinted up with one eye, crushing his hat's brim back for a moment. "This jut of sandstone above us. I bet it runs deep. Deep enough anyway."

"For what?"

"For us to dig under. Provide us with shade, shelter. Might buy us a few seconds when those bastards come sniffing at sundown."

Mitch liked the idea and swiped a couple of paws full of gravel with his ratty-gloved hands. "Easy digging. If you can shift to your right, I'll give it a go."

"No, we both will. Do me good instead of sitting here wondering what's happening up there on the flat."

Mitch flipped over, and though he tried to hug the rim, a slicing shot whistled in, pocking the dirt a couple of inches from his left bootheel.

"Get your legs tucked in!" growled Joe. "And keep that butt down."

"Sorry."

"You will be when they shoot you. Now they know we're alive. At least one of us."

"You think they had doubts?"

"Yep. Aw, don't worry about it. Let's them know we aren't easy. They'll have to work for us."

"How many you think there are?"

Joe shrugged. "Could be the one. I don't aim to test my guess, however. Now let's get digging. We could use the space. Tell you what. You dig the hole. I'll drag the dirt out, shove it with my good foot. That way we can make a hollow. I'll rim it with some of these rocks. Might slow the snakes down."

"You weren't kidding, then?"

"Kidding?" said Joe. "At a time like this? What would I be kidding about, Mitch?"

"The snakes."

"I might josh a man now and then, but never about snakes."

Mitch groaned and set to digging. Careful lest he unearth one. Or more than one. He'd seen plenty of the cursed things growing up on the ranch, and then there was that vicious thing that laid his steer low. The picture in his mind of its swollen muzzle, enormous and freakish, was horrible. He'd never forget that as long as he lived. Which, he hoped, was a whole lot longer than one more night.

"I'm not keen on spending a night in a snake pit, Joe."

"Nor am I, but here's where we're at. How's your head feeling?"

Mitch shrugged. "Like a stone that's splitting open from the inside out. I'm still seeing about four of everything. How's your leg?"

Joe laughed. "Like it's being prodded clean through with a cherry-hot steel rod." He chuckled.

"What's funny?"

"We're a pair, eh? Laid up, left to broil and die in the sun, and all we can think to talk of is how awful we feel. Comparing our ailments like a couple of old biddies after church."

They both knew there was much to talk about, too much. Perhaps they would never get around to it. The way they each felt at that moment, it would be all right if the horrors they'd lived through, the guilt they felt in surviving the attack were never talked of, never dragged to the surface and held to the light.

"Like old-timers on Trundleson's front porch," said Mitch.

Joe closed his eyes and nodded. Old, yes, that's how he felt. Old and tired and past his time.

Neither spoke after that. In the nighttime hours, the coolness of the air caught them unprepared, settling over them with its teeth-chattering cold.

Mitch woke to morning light and to Joe attacking him with his long gun.

Except Joe wasn't whomping on him. He was . . . What was he doing? Then Mitch saw something move across the crater.

Joe shouldered the gun and held his finger on the trigger. The effort soon weighed on him, his hands, then arms shook as if he were palsied, and he lowered the gun.

The thing he'd thrown with the gun barrel—for that's what Mitch now saw had happened—moved away with a jerky ease, seeming to slide one way, then another, staying in the early shadow caused by the ragged lip of overhanging gravel before disappearing into a darker shadow, a crack in the earth.

"What was that? A snake?"

Joe nodded as Mitch looked at him. The older man looked awful. Worse than the day before.

"Woke to see it coiled on your belly. Likely for warmth. Was afraid if you woke and saw it, you'd flinch, scare it. Might have bit you."

They were quiet a time; then Mitch said, "It was a monster."

"Big enough," said Joe.

"For what?"

"Huh?"

"You said it was big enough." Each word took effort Mitch felt he did not have. "Big enough . . . for what?"

"Oh. To kill you."

Hours later—Mitch knew it to be hours only by the angle of the sun, with its relentless brightness and heat—he traced his tongue tip along the inside of his mouth. His tongue alarmed him by how thick it felt. As if a cow's tongue had been stuffed into his mouth, a cow's tongue made of sand.

"Joe."

Nothing. He said it again, then turned his head. The effort felt as if he'd been at it all day, and it left him spent. "Joe."

"Huh?" The cowboy's voice was a hoarse whisper.

"Joe, we must get out, away . . . before . . ."

"Yeah," said the older man. "Away . . ."

That was all either man had effort for. As Mitch dwindled into a vicious, hot sleep in which he pictured himself baking to death, drying out like an old washrag left out in the sun, he thought that, at long last, Corliss Bilks was going to get what he always wanted. He was going to own the Twin N, because Mitchell Newland was about dead.

And then he thought about the two people in all his days who meant the very most to him. Pap, dear old Pap, who couldn't get out of his own way enough to let himself live a long and good life. And then Mitch thought of young, pretty Evie. Whom he would never again see.

And she was the daughter of Corliss Bilks, a man who hated him and his father and who cared not one whit who knew it, nor did he care about anyone or anything other than himself, it seemed, maybe not even his own daughter. That she was Bilks' child mattered not at all to Mitch. He loved her for who she was and because she loved him; that much he knew was certain.

And with that dusted-up mess of thoughts roiling and swirling in his mind, young Mitchell Newland, of Cawlins, Texas, and then of somewhere in Wyoming Territory, let slip the final length of rope tying him to his wakeful life and allowed himself to drift on the vague black sea of oblivion.

CHAPTER TWENTY-SEVEN

THERE WAS LITTLE in the world that Bakar imagined he had not seen. After all, he had been born on a mountain in the wonderful Basque country. Yet after much warring and vicious treatment by neighbors, those who had once been friends and who now were either no more of this earth or enemies still living, Bakar had been compelled to flee the beautiful, peerless land of his birth.

Since then he had roamed the vastness of America and found, if not peace within himself, a distinct lack of the presence of other people. People were the very creatures he had learned through a lifetime of many hard lessons were the least trustworthy of all animals. No other beast he had encountered in his travels, from sharks in oceans to fish in small mountain freshets, from a ship's mousing cat to a mountain lion yowling from within its dark den, and hundreds of others, besides, could convince Bakar otherwise. Man was the most vicious beast to have ever roamed the world.

He was ruminating on this fact, a worn topic of much comfort he favored, as he rolled westward from the east, helming his little sheep wagon. One of his companions was Pep, an ancient one-eye, tail-free cur he had found some years before, shivering during a brutal snowstorm outside Dewlap, Idaho Territory. Since then he and the dog had been traveling companions, and the fact that the dog was likely ignorant of either English or Basque, between which Bakar volleyed with no regard as to his coherence on any particular subject, seemed not to matter to the dog, who slept much of the time these days.

But the little stout mule that tugged them along, now that was a beast of a different matter. King Louis, as Bakar called him, snorted and brayed at the right moments in Bakar's expansive discourses.

And so it was that Pep, King Louis, and Bakar found themselves slowly trudging up a winding path among hummocks of harsh grasses, brittle in summer's heat, before cresting a rise.

Bakar saw King Louis' grand ears flick forward as if he were hearing a far-off brass band. In that moment, Bakar thought perhaps he, too, heard a burst of ragged sounds, as if someone dragged a crosscut saw blade over a broad flat stone; then it would stop. Within moments he saw for himself what had drawn the beast's attentions.

The plain below, a last vast stretch before the mighty east flank of the lower Rockies, was not as Bakar had last seen it some years before. No, that time, there had been bison and pronghorn and grasses more green because it had been earlier in the season.

It did not have today's scatter of bodies of men and horses and cattle, though mostly men and horses. All were bloated in the hot sun, a few had burst their fetid offerings, and even as he watched, another—a horse—

reached its limit and succumbed to a ragged rupture caused by the very things King Louis and Bakar had heard, the draggers of the crosscut saw blades: vultures.

Only three or four of the dead were not fully covered by the squawking, flapping feasters. Most of the bodies were aswarm with a mass of squabbling, glistening black bodies, constantly unsettled, then clawing and beaking their way back into the midst of a clot of their kind. There they gorged on whatever unfortunate dead beast lay beneath, jostling slowly with each tear and tug.

That there was so very much for the vultures to dine on explained why Bakar had not seen any of them circling high above in the clear blue of the otherwise pretty day. They need not circle and work scouting for their food, for there was enough below on this plain of death to keep what seemed to be every vulture fed from fifty to one hundred miles away.

A light breeze flowed toward them from below, and the stink was the next thing Bakar noticed. He looked to his right at his companion, Pep, now gone nearly blind, though his milky old eyes seemed to follow his twitching black-and-pink mottled nose. Even his bent left ear, a haggard thing on the best of days, appeared perked at half height, partaking in this sensual wonder.

"What is this, what is this, what is this . . . ?" Bakar repeated this many times as they sat eyeing the vast, vicious mural below. Bakar, since childhood, had enjoyed riddles, especially of the spoken sort, formations of thought given voice that performed a trickery. It was clear to Bakar that the riddle of what had happened and how and why surely needed to be worked out.

He swigged from his canteen, dumped a little into a tin bowl. After the dog had licked up what he wished, Bakar climbed down from the seat and dumped more water into the bowl and held it out for King Louis. The mule sipped and flicked an ear.

The mule and the dog both seemed focused, still ruminating on the scene below. Bakar climbed back into his seat, tugged the brim of his wide straw hat low over his eyes, and joined his friends in assessing the gruesome vista.

"There, you see," he muttered, holding forth, westward, an old crooked finger the color and texture of puckered buckskin.

"That horse flopped atop that rider, the one beyond that one I know you are looking at, Pep. Yes, that one. They were running away, trying to run far from this madness. Whatever this madness was. No disease could have done this. And I see no arrows sticking up like the arms of dead pines in the high dry places. No." Bakar shook his head, conviction turning it into a vigorous, lengthy nod. "This is the hand of men. Badmen, to be sure. This is a place of much death brought about by much evil of man."

They sat for long minutes watching the great, awkward vultures accost the dead and one another, rattling their guttural squawks into the tainted air above. A thin breeze carried the rank sweetness upslope once more. Only the dog seemed interested in exploring this new snatch of information. He raised his old gray muzzle skyward and worked his nose as it passed, gleaning of it information Bakar might only guess at.

"We shall go from this place and forever more we will not cast our shadow on this plain."

There was no reason to venture down the long, low slope and roll among the dead. He was old and so was the dog and so was the mule, for that matter. Even the wagon had seen its better days many years before. Why tempt the winged death merchants?

He was relieved to have made that decision. As he

tugged the lines to guide King Louis along the ridgetop northward, and so to cut a wide circle about the edges of this field of madness, Pep jerked his snout down once more and perked his ears forward, as much as they were able. His brows tightened as if he was seeing something in the distance, far below, that incensed him. A growl, rusted from lack of use, worked up the old mutt's throat and burbled out his whiskered lips.

Bakar paused, the lines dangling from his hands. "I see I must remind you, Pep, that you are nearly blind with age. What is this all about?"

Still the dog growled and would not look at him, so filled with concentration was he on a single spot below.

Bakar held a hand over his eyes and leaned forward in time to see a buzzard drop into a wide, sandy pock hole and walk jerk-legged, wings wide, raw knob of a head bobbing, over to the legs of another dead man. It pecked, and then stumbled and flapped backward as if struck.

Far above, Bakar heard grating sounds boil up from its angry body, and it approached the dead man once more. Again it lurched backward as if struck. Or kicked . . .

"Pep, I now wish I had figured out how to spend the money on the brass telescope I once saw for sale in that street market in Mexico City. Then it would give me the sight I need at this moment. The vendor said it had belonged to a mighty sea captain who had traded people for sugar and sugar for people. Can you imagine? On second thought, I do not think I would want anything such a person would have likely coveted. It would no doubt be tainted with his evil ways."

The dog growled again.

"Yes, yes, I think you are correct. King Louis, are you certain you, too? Would like to participate in this investigation? Oh, but I am afraid I will have to insist.

It is too far for me to walk and then walk back if there is nothing to it. And then if there is something to it, I shall need your help. And yours, too, Pep. Of course." He thumbed the top of the dog's head. Pep continued to watch and growl.

The mule chuckled deep down in his chest and then snorted as if a blowfly had tickled his velvety muzzle.

"Very well, I shall consider that as a sign we are all in agreement." Bakar sighed once more, and after tying a ragged blue bandanna about his face and tucking the bottom into his buttoned collar, he tugged the lines and the trio switchbacked their way down the slope toward the sad plain below.

CHAPTER TWENTY-EIGHT

MITCH DID NOT envision the face of God to look quite like the one that hovered before him. He'd always pictured a lot more hair, maybe a big beard. And not wearing a floppy old straw topper.

He tried to speak, to say, "Hello there," but the only thing that croaked out was something that sounded like "Hell . . ." *Even dead,* thought Mitch, *I have managed to offend the Almighty.*

Then God chuckled. "You are not there yet, fellow. But from what I have heard, this place is pretty close."

This didn't make any sense to Mitch. He forced his eyes open wider and tried to speak another word, but he heard nothing from himself. Something cool touched his mouth and he flinched.

"Water, nothing more. Now let it do its job, eh?" The voice drizzled more of the soothing liquid on and in his mouth.

Mitch sighed and his eyelids fluttered closed. The water leaked in between his swollen lips and he coughed once more, but some of the water made it farther down his gullet.

Mitch opened his eyes again and willed them to stay open. "What . . . ?"

"What am I doing here, huh? Is that what you were about to ask?"

"Joe," muttered Mitch. He tried to turn his head but it seemed that something inside burned like the devil himself was probing there with a pair of hot tongs.

The man who might be God, might not, glanced toward where Mitch had been trying to look and nodded his head. "He is next. Now drink."

He drizzled more of the water into the young cowboy's mouth and Mitch closed his eyes and tried to swallow. It went easier. When he opened his eyes, the man was gone. As he guessed. It was a mirage, nothing more.

Then he heard murmuring, one voice, the same one that had spoken to him. He opened his eyes again and tilted his head to his right and squinted. There was the man—with a halo behind his head? No, it looked like a hat brim. Yes, the man wore a straw hat. Okay, maybe he wasn't dead, then.

"Joe?" That time, Mitch heard himself, heard the word he'd said.

"Yes, yes, he is here, and he is alive. It was his legs we saw. Isn't that right, Pep?"

Mitch heard coughing, then a mumbling, moaning sound he didn't think belonged to the man who wasn't God. But what did he know? Maybe God was a mumbler, a man prone to coughing.

That was all Mitch thought, and all he heard, for he slipped away once more. But instead of death, this time he was thinking of a mountain stream, thin, to be sure, but a stream of pure clear, cold water. And how lucky he was to have found it.

* * *

Mitch's eyes fluttered as vivid memories burst into his mind—the bawling herd, the dust, the flooded river, the Kid, the smoke and flame of a prairie fire, gunshots, screaming, snakes, whipping and snapping, fang-gnashing snakes, and the sun, so much sunlight, beating down on him, boring into him with a hot, blazing eye, and . . . Joe! Drover Joe Phipps! Where was he? It was all too much and it came back to him all at once, with the force of a hammerblow.

Mitchell Newland gasped and jerked forward. He found himself seated not in sunlight on hot sand, but on blankets, alongside a crackling campfire, leaning up against . . . a wagon wheel?

"What's . . . what's going on here?" He looked, shook his head, but it hurt like thunder inside. He held up a hand to it and remembered. . . . Joe had dragged him to safety. "Joe!"

"Right here, Mitch. Good of you to join us again."

The young man looked to his left, saw his friend and savior, Drover Joe, leaning against a wooden crate, his wounded leg propped on a saddle.

"Joe, you're alive?" Mitch's voice was hoarse, his throat sore. "We're alive?"

"Yep," said Joe with a grin. "Thanks to that man right there." He pointed across the fire.

Silhouetted by dancing flames sat what looked like an old man, though it was hard to tell in the firelight. He wore a big hat—straw, from the look.

It sparked a fresh memory. "Hey," said Mitch. "You're God!"

Joe and the old man laughed. "Oh, I have been called many things in my life, young fellow, but I could never measure up to that one."

Mitch felt his face redden, and the old man spoke

again. "If there is any thanks owed, it is not to me, for I was in the act of turning my back on such an unholy place as this. But Pep here"—he stroked the back of an old dog stretched out by his left leg—"he deserves the praise. And maybe King Louis, too."

Mitch hadn't seen the dog before. And he wasn't certain what a king had to do with anything.

"Pep stayed my hand as surely as if he had laid a paw on my arm and said, 'Hold, brother, for there is something else, something among the dead we have yet to learn.' And so we traveled down from on high, you might say." He grinned again at the thought of being mistaken for God. "And that is why we are here helping you two men."

Mitch drew his legs up and held his head in both hands. It was confusing. He still felt as though it was a dream of some sort, as if he could not wake fully. As if at any moment the horrors of fire and snake and gunshots and screams would visit him once more, and this time would not let him be.

"Mitch," said Joe. "You're all right now. We're alive. It's real."

Mitch looked up at his friend. "Okay, then. If you say so, Joe. That'll work for me." For a few moments no one spoke; then Mitch said, "The others?"

The look on Joe's face told him it was a question he should not have asked. The foreman dragged a hand down his stubbled face. Even in the firelight he looked rough, sunken cheeks and puckered, dark bags beneath his eyes. But the eyes themselves were sharp and clear. Mitch wondered if he himself would ever feel that way again.

CHAPTER TWENTY-NINE

The next morning, Mitch insisted on helping the old man and his mule in fetching the dead. The night before, they had all agreed they had to do something with the men. Mitch didn't want old Bakar to feel as though he needed to help. He and Joe had vowed that somehow they would bury their own.

It was a difficult conversation that Joe barely participated in, save for head nods and frequent rasping of his stubbled jaw with a big hand. Mitch didn't need to pry to know what it was the big cowboy was feeling.

But Bakar had insisted and said he would deny them any more of his help and supplies should they try to exclude him from the retrieval efforts. "Besides," he said, "young Joe here is suffering terribly from a wound in his leg. He would only hinder our progress."

He'd said this, in fact, only after Mitch insisted his throbbing skull was not nearly as bad as it felt. In truth, he was certain his bean, as Joe called it, was little more than a stone that had been slammed with a sledge and split in two.

Once they had set up Joe in the lee of the small wagon, his rifle at hand, and with Pep by his side—the dog had taken a matter-of-fact interest in Drover Joe—Bakar and Mitch followed King Louis the mule, towing a wooden pallet they'd cobbled together from the tailgate of Bakar's wagon. It would do to ferry the dead.

Where they were going to drag them had been a brief topic raised the evening before as well. The sunken hole, what Joe guessed was an old buffalo wallow, where Mitch and Joe had taken refuge, and where they had expected to die, would be ideal. They agreed to lay out the men within half of it, leaving room between each to scoop out the sandy soil to cover them with.

Once they had walked a dozen slow yards from the campsite, making for the farthest of the bodies—Bakar knew where they lay because he had visited each while Mitch and Joe were still unconscious—Bakar tapped his long, high-arched nose and winked. "You fool no one with your bravery, young Mitchell."

"I don't know what you mean, Bakar," said the young man, half in sincerity. Did the old fellow think he was somehow guilty of such an act? Surely not, and yet the notion lingered in his mind like the stink of ill-cooked fish.

"No," said Bakar, offering a slight smile that helped the barest bit to buoy Mitch's low-flagged spirit due to their unfortunate task. "Your head pains you, no?"

"Well, yes. But it's not that bad."

"Bah. I see it in your eyes. They are squinted and pinched as if you might be able to keep out light and the boom-boom-boom of each step we take. It will get better for you. Each morning will take care of that."

It was gruesome work, and though each of them

wore a bandanna, beneath which rode a liberal dab of axle grease smeared with peppermint oil beneath their noses, the retrieval of the bodies of Mitch's pards was terrible work.

The body farthest from their camp turned out to be that of Rollo, the silent wrangler vaquero. He'd been shot in the back and much savaged, as each of the men had, by night creatures and the vile vultures. Chasing away the latter required a goodly amount of cursing and threats from Bakar, neither of which deterred the winged brutes for long.

Mitch and Bakar slipped a blanket beneath Rollo, then dragged him up onto the tailgate travois. Mitch was relieved to be able to cover Rollo's stretched, cracked face with his slicker. Though his friend, the wrangler was nearly unbearable to look upon, his body burst in places from savagings by the scavengers until bone and purple puckerings of meat hung out.

"I reckon I should, well, you know . . . go through their gear and pockets, see if there isn't something we should bring back for their families." Mitch said this but couldn't bring himself to look at the dead men, laid out like splits of firewood.

"I'll do it." Joe's voice was low, hoarse.

"Joe, I can do it. It's okay."

The big cowboy turned red-rimmed eyes on him and shouted, "I said I'll do it, damn it! This mess is all my fault. Least I can do." He turned away, but not before Mitch saw tears welling in the cowboy's eyes.

"Joe, I . . ."

Bakar laid a firm hand on Mitch's arm and shook his head. He held the young man's ragged sleeve and led him off to follow King Louis the mule, making their way to another fallen man.

And so the morning ground on. It was the most difficult day in Mitch's life, a day he would gladly have traded with anyone. Man after man, five in all were loaded and dragged to the gulley.

The entire time, he wondered why he had been spared and they had been chosen to die. Again, as if he'd read Mitch's mind, Bakar said, "There is no way a man can make sense of something such as this. No way, unless he decides to make up a reason and believes in it. And then he will surely lose himself forever inside his head."

He tapped the side of his old gray-haired skull. "Do not let that happen, Mitchell. You are far too young for madness." He let that hang between them for a few moments while they trudged to the next dead man. "Now, when you reach my age, well"—he shrugged—"a little madness is not so bad a thing, eh?" He smiled.

Though he could not return the smile, Mitch appreciated Bakar's efforts to lighten the moment.

It took them hours to bring back the men. Mitch was confident he knew who each was, though two of them he had to identify by their horses and gear, not their clothes or hair color. Few of their faces were recognizable.

By the time they unfastened the travois from the traces, Joe had managed to lay out a small pile of possessions atop the edge of the gulley. He moved slowly and had to sit down frequently, so hard did his leg wound pain him. Mitch didn't ask how he knew which item belonged to which man.

It was Mitch who broke the silence first. "Joe, that's all of them. I can't find Cook or Sycamore."

"Well." Joe's voice was that same low, hoarse sound, a rusted hinge called into service once more. "Yeah. Cook I wondered about, as nothing of the chuck wagon is in sight. I reckon somehow he made his escape. Maybe ol' Sycamore Jim got away, too."

"Hope so." But they both knew it was more than

likely they were on the far side of some low rise that he and Bakar hadn't looked beyond yet.

"I only found one of their number, Joe. Should we—"

"No," said Joe, his eyes lidded low. "Leave him for the buzzards. It's the least he deserves."

Mitch didn't disagree. And that was all that was said on that matter.

Joe and Mitch insisted together that they should be the ones to bury their friends. Bakar backed away with a gracious nod, but looked relieved. With the help of the old man's shovel, the two cowboys covered their pards with as deep a layer of earth as they were able.

Finally, after several hours of slow going, Bakar said, "It is time we eat. There will be time enough in coming days for you to bury them deeper. You both need to heal and recover. This day has been hard on your bodies, your wounds, and"—he tapped his head—"on your minds."

They did not argue.

At the campfire, Bakar heated a thin soup and passed out a biscuit to each man. "I wish I had more to offer you." He shrugged.

"This is fine, fine. I thank you for . . . well, for finding us." Joe's voice trailed off.

Mitch looked at Bakar and nodded, his throat choked with the heavy emotion of the day's undertakings and with the gratitude he felt toward the old man, his mule, even the old dog.

Bakar was too kind to make little of what he'd done for them. Instead, he changed the subject. "Yes, yes, the wind will do what it wishes, but out here, fortunate for us, it wishes to stay away from our tiny camp, eh?" He shrugged. "For some reason it is not interested in making us suffer from the smells of this place. And who am I to question this?"

He stretched out his long legs and yawned. "I have

learned in my seventy-seven years alive in this world to take the kindnesses as they come to me. A pretty morning's sun, sometimes rainfall. Even the cold snows of winter are their own beauty, eh?"

Nobody said anything, as Mitch and Joe were still mired in their peculiar blend of gratefulness and grief. They nodded and continued to slowly eat.

Long after, while each man stared at the fire, lost in his thoughts, Bakar spoke. "Tomorrow I will ride King Louis toward the west. I have seen tracks of horses. Perhaps we will have luck."

And that is how they ended their hardest day yet on the trail.

CHAPTER THIRTY

"I SHOULD HAVE done yesterday's work on my own,"
said the old man, holding a cup of water to Mitch's
mouth.

The young man's hands shook as if he were more
ancient than Bakar and afflicted with the palsy of an
old-timer not long for the world of the living.

"No, no," he said, but his voice was little more than
a whisper. He tried to shake his head and dark, heavy
thuds of pain drove down on him like a cannonade, the
imagined sound bursting his skull from the inside,
clods of flesh and sod. . . .

"Mitch." Something prodded his shoulder. "Hey,
Mitch?"

The young man opened his eyes. It was Joe. "Sorry.
Must have dozed off."

Joe stared at him, but it was the old man who spoke.
"I am worried for you, young man. Your friend Joe
here is beginning to heal, but you will need to stay low
here at the wagon and heal yourself. It will take some

days. The gash on your head is healing on the outside, but I am not so sure of it on the inside."

Though Mitch heard the old man's words, and he knew them to be correct, the thudding in his head prevented him from doing much more than nodding. *Fine,* he thought. With effort he leaned back and reached for his hat once more. As he had with Joe in the pit, he covered his eyes to prevent the killing sun from finishing him off.

He heard the two men talking, sometimes about him, their voices low, not whispers, but loud enough. He wanted to tell them to pipe down, but he hadn't the strength. Instead he listened, hoped for sleep, but it wasn't his to catch yet. Then he heard the old man saying he was heading out, as he'd said the night before, to look for sign of horses. Joe sounded displeased but defeated, and the man left camp.

Some time later Mitch woke, his thirst mighty, and made the mistake of opening his eyes and sliding his hat back on his head. The sun peeked in and tormented him afresh. He fought down a pulse of sickness rising up his gorge, then spoke. "The old man, he okay?"

"Yeah," said Joe. "But he's more stubborn than—"

"You?"

"Well, sir, I'm not so sure anybody's that stubborn. But he runs a close second."

There was a pause. Then Joe said, "I am concerned for him. Those bastards who attacked us could come back anytime."

Mitch nodded slowly, agreeing. "But he's been out roving the world a good long time, so he says. That has to mean something."

No more was spoken for some time. Mitch dozed again, giving him powerful relief from his head wound. He awoke to Joe saying, "Here comes somebody." Joe's rifle clicked, a smooth metallic sound.

Mitch felt a whole lot better than he had earlier. "How many?"

"Just the one." Joe squinted into the distance. "And this dog isn't of much use save for holding down this particular patch of earth."

"But he's doing it well," said Mitch, pulling out his six-gun.

"Well, I am pleased to hear you're not so far gone you are afraid of cracking wise with me." Joe leaned farther forward, still staring at the approaching rider. "My word, if that isn't the old buck. And it looks as though he has something in tow."

The closer Bakar rode, the more Joe shook his head. "You won't believe it, Mitch."

They both watched, Mitch shading his eyes to keep the cursed sun from causing him further grief. "Did he actually find horses?" He wondered if Champ might be out there somewhere. He'd not seen him among the many dead horses about them.

"I believe he did. A stout-looking brown—not certain yet whose it was or even if it was one of ours—and right behind it looks like Cloudy, my old mare. Oh, my word, my word . . ."

There was a genuine cause for celebration that evening among the two men, the first time they'd felt anything but misery in what seemed like a year. It had only been, to the best of their knowledge, less than a week since the attack. They'd purposely not talked much about it, the wounds of burying their pards being so fresh.

It took another couple of days before they were able to consider what they should do.

"You come along with me," said the old man. "Together we will all ride north to one of the mining towns. We will seek out the law there."

The old man's suggestion was appreciated, but it

didn't sit well with Mitch. He looked at Joe, but the drover only shrugged.

Bakar smiled and changed the subject. "I am thinking we should have camped by the flow, no matter that it is little more than a trickle. I widened it for the horses to drink." He also had skill with snares and caught enough rabbits to keep them all fed.

His modest wagon, when he wasn't burdened by two banged-up cowboys, served as his rolling home. It was a small version of a sheep camp wagon Mitch had seen some years before when a sheepherder had spent a couple of months outside Cawlins. Joe was familiar with them, having seen many on his trail-drive travels.

In order to make a comfortable spot for them, Bakar had dismantled the wagon's ribs and dragged much of the wagon's innards outside, setting up a cozy, useful camp for them all.

"We appreciate this, Bakar," said Mitch. "Everything you've done for us."

Bakar had only shrugged. "You would do the same."

"Are we keeping you from being somewhere?"

"No," said Bakar. "Me and Pep and King Louis, we are seekers. There is much to see in this world."

"But how do you . . . ?" Mitch realized what he was asking was none of his business.

Bakar smiled. "There is very little that we require that we cannot find out here." He waved a hand wide as if the vast plain, the blue sky, the mountains beyond were all his own private mercantile. "When we do need a little something, oh, say, spices to make our meals tasty, I stay in a town for a day, sometimes two, and trade my labors. So far"—he smacked his chest lightly with an open hand—"my body has not failed me."

"I admire that, Bakar," said Joe. "I have often wondered what it would be like to live in much the same way, not beholden to a boss, relying on myself."

"It is not for all, but for me, it is fine." They sat quietly and sipped a weak but tasty tea the old man brewed from flowers and dried grasses he'd gathered in his travels.

After a while, Bakar said, "You men are thinking of what to do next with yourselves."

It was not a question, but Mitch spoke. "I am. I can't speak for Joe, but I . . . I have to find the men who did this. I have to try. For the men who died. For their sakes."

Joe sat a moment, not moving; then he nodded. "Yes, it's only right."

IS IT VENGEANCE you are after?" said the old man two days later when Mitch and Joe were saddled and loaded up.

They had pulled together a meager mixture of their own possessions and gear salvaged from the men. It was not a pleasant task to sort through, but it would do no one any good rotting away on the flat. They had also divided up the few personal effects they'd taken from the bodies before burying them.

"God willing," Mitch had said at the time, "one day we might be able to find their families."

Joe didn't answer Bakar, but tugged the cinch and double-checked everything he'd already checked. Finally, he turned from Cloudy. "I wish we could give you something more for your troubles, Bakar. When this is all through with, when we make it back to a town with the herd, I would like to know how to find you so we can thank you properly."

The old man's brows drew together. "I don't understand. Did I not do what you would have done for me if I had been the one found?"

Mitch and Joe nodded. Couldn't disagree there.

"Then we are well, you and I. I am happy to have been able to help you. You are better than you were. We can part in peace, each with a good feeling about our fellows."

They'd spent the morning helping him put his wagon back together. He, too, would be moving on, but he would make straight for the north. He had a friend, Old Dollar, he'd heard was in a mining camp Bakar wished to visit before snow closed the region and prevented him from coming or going with his usual ease.

Joe shook the old man's hand, then pressed his brass-and-leather telescope into Bakar's horned old palm, along with a small buckskin pouch. "It's not much, but it should keep you in spices for a time."

Instead of trying to return the present, Bakar stared at the spyglass with wide eyes and nodded, running a thumb over the worn brass tube. "Oh, but I thank you, Joe. I will think of you both as I watch the hawks soar high above." He held the coin purse and grinned. "And when I make my special peppered rabbit, eh?"

Joe bent down and stroked Pep on his old head. The dog turned a milk-eyed face up to Joe and wagged his stub tail. "Good boy, Pep," said Joe. "I reckon I'll miss you most of all."

It was Mitch's turn, and he, too, shook Bakar's hand. "I cannot thank you properly, but please know I am and will be forever grateful that you saved us."

"Oh, Mitch, you are a smart young man. You would have found a way to save yourself. I only helped a little."

They both knew that was hogwash, but it was kind of Bakar to have said. Mitch stroked the dog's head, patted King Louis' neck, and mounted up on the brown horse.

They looked back once, but the old man was already seated and wheeling north.

"I slipped what money I had in his tea tin. I expect he'll find it before long," said Mitch.

Joe smiled. "Bakar was right. You are a smart young man. Now, what say we use those brains to follow the trail our herd left behind?"

Mitch nodded and they resumed their journey, this time angling westward, two dead men hoping to raise holy hell.

CHAPTER THIRTY-ONE

THEY TOOK THEIR time riding west, cutting the easy-to-follow trail left by their herd. Several times early in their trek they found evidence, in the form of dung and tracks, of cattle having moved through the same region earlier than their herd.

"What do you make of that?" Mitch slid gently down out of the saddle. His head was healing, but anytime he jarred it, his vision blurred and a dull pain filled his skull.

"If I were a betting man, and I'm not usually, I'd say ours wasn't the first herd to pass this way." Joe scouted some more, bent low now and again, then stood upright and hopped on his shot-up leg. He pulled a frown and sucked in air through tight teeth a few times until the pain passed.

The old man had doctored him up in fine shape, but the wound was slow to heal. It was on its way, but it sure was taking its time.

"You think somebody made a habit of ambushing herds on this stretch?"

Joe nodded. "Seems like it. Though I imagine we were as much a surprise to them as they were to us. Being so late in the season and all. Damn, but I wish I hadn't chosen this route."

"But we did. Nobody could have known. So now it's up to us to make it as right as we can. Somehow."

The rest of the afternoon was spent with one man riding low, scouting sign, while the other rode with his eyes swiveling across the foothills before them.

That night they camped in a declivity that was well hidden from anyone who might be on the scout from westward. They kept their horses close and their weapons closer.

They were each outfitted with a rifle and two revolvers, plus a long hip knife and ammunition enough to open a situation. The extra gear they carried had belonged to their friends, and they still felt odd about it, no matter the reasoning they fed themselves.

Mitch sipped the cup of hot tea brewed from the leaves the old man had given them. They'd grown accustomed to its mild flavor, though both sorely missed Cook's thick-as-tar coffee, ideal for waking up a man and keeping him that way, especially on night rider duty.

"I thought for a time there that I was done." Joe looked up at the sudden words, and Mitch continued. "Even after Bakar found us, I thought for certain my days were few. But I realized I was wrong. I'm not done, not by a long shot. And what's more, I've nothing in the world to lose and everything to gain."

Joe nodded, sipped his tea. "I hear you, Mitch. But you're dead wrong when you say you have nothing to lose."

"Huh?"

"You have Evie Bilks, Mitch. Don't discount the love of a good woman. I did once, a long time ago, and I've regretted it mightily since."

Mitch didn't say anything. He knew Joe was right, but he wasn't certain he really still had Evie in his life—that is, if Evie would still have him in her life.

As he settled into sleep—Joe insisted on taking first watch—Mitch continued pondering how she was doing down there on her father's ranch in Cawlins. He wondered how the Twin N was faring, and if he'd ever make it back there, to see his own spread once again.

Before sleep quieted his aching head for a few hours, he tried to chase Evie Bilks out of his mind, tried to forget her and instead gird himself for whatever it might be they were riding into. He tried, but he couldn't do it.

A S THEY TRAVELED northwestward, trailing the herd, Mitch learned tips from Joe about tracking, not that there was much challenge involved. Hoofprints and cow pies and a swath of ragged-chewed grass made the task simple enough.

On the second day, their first full day out, they woke to a steel blue sky that, as the day aged, gave way to a gray haze of clouds far off. The mass perched atop the high-rock peaks looked like a giant cat, waiting, twitching and watching them.

As the hours passed, sunlight dimmed to a gray glow. Already they'd seen sign, as they rode into higher country, that winter was on its way. This hammered the post in for them.

"Won't be long now," said Joe. "We'll wish we had our winter gear. Not much call for heavy mackinaws down in Texas, at least not like they wear in Montana."

"Maybe we'll do what we need to by the time the cold hits."

"Don't bet on it," said Joe, nodding toward an even darker gray mass pillowing up along the skyline ahead.

A little while later, they approached with caution several low shapes they'd been seeing for some time, recognition dawning on them the closer they rode. They drew alongside and stopped.

As Joe looked down at the parched, puckered remnants of four Apaches, a breeze tousled a long gray-and-white feather. It danced a moment, almost free, yet still tethered by a frayed red thread of sinew before settling once more along the man's sleeve.

"A shame," said Joe. "Never thought too ill of them until they played us false." He looked ahead once more. "Best move on."

"Should we bury them?"

Joe looked at Mitch with squinted eyes. "I admire your kindness, Mitch, but they're far from men anymore. They're where they need to be. Now let's go."

That night they donned what few extra clothes they had—an extra shirt, thicker socks, and one thin gray wool blanket each. It was a cold one, despite the meager little campfire, and they wrapped up and sat with their backs to boulders, spelling each other on watch.

The morning broke cool and bleak, and with it came a breeze that sliced and carried the portent of stiffness, the promise of heavy weather that rattled their teeth and hunched their shoulders.

"If there's any luck left in the world, we'll find Cook and Sycamore alive." It was, Mitch realized, something to say to fill the silence between him and Joe.

The older cowboy said nothing as he drained the last of the tea from his tin cup and resumed strapping what little gear he had onto the saddle. The topic of what lay ahead was raw, but they had to talk about it.

What few times they'd nibbled the edges of it hadn't been enough to decide much of anything. They both knew they needed to fight, to bring the battle to the killers and thieves. They also knew they would likely die in the trying.

The day offered close, cold views of the foothills in which they had encamped and, beyond those, the crags of the mountains themselves. As they rode through the coolness of the air and the increasing whistling wind, two things happened at once; neither was expected, though one was welcome.

Ahead was the reason they'd lost easy sight of the cattle trail—a talus slope had poured from the mountainside above. Mitch wondered how that could be.

Joe had ridden ahead, scouting the freshest cattle sign. He disappeared from Mitch's sight for three, four minutes. What was Joe doing, inspecting that riddle of scree for sign? It didn't look possible for the herd to have slogged over that.

As the younger man was about to nudge his mount forward at a quicker clip, Joe emerged again, out from behind a massive slab of jag-edged rock that looked as if it had been cleaved off the mountainside above by a mighty hammerblow from the heavens, then slid down, settling in place for eternity. But it didn't look to Mitch as if it could host a rider behind it, so tight did it seem to hug the mountainside. Soon he saw he was wrong.

Joe rode up, glancing over his shoulder now and again along the several-hundred-yard ride as he made his way back to Mitch. He said nothing, but held a long gloved finger to his moustaches and nodded toward the stone.

Up until then the trail had been obvious and easy to follow. They were trailing nearly eight hundred beeves and a couple of dozen riders, after all. But the farther north they rode, aligned with the slope to their left, the more Mitch began to doubt his judgment. "How is this possible?"

Again Joe held a finger to his mouth. Instead of following the silent directive, Mitch said, though in a lower voice, to the man riding beside him, "Why quiet?"

Joe sighed and nodded ahead once more. They kept riding. Then Mitch saw the reason—a dead man. He lay slumped on his right side, his left arm hung forward, not quite hiding the glint of a metal star on his vest. They rode within twenty feet of him, with Joe leaning low in the saddle, looking in every direction at once.

"We going to bury him?" Mitch said, unable to turn away. He looked to be dead about the same length of time as the Apaches.

Joe shook his head and kept looking up, around, and beyond the dead man. Then Mitch understood and did the same, sensing they were in a place of danger, as if the dead man was not warning enough.

Joe glanced quickly at Mitch, then nodded beyond the corpse. The trail they'd been following, wide enough for a half dozen work wagons to roll through, side by side, widened, and appeared to darken and bend to the right.

Had the thieves run the herd through here? It was the most unlikely thing Mitch could imagine, but there was sign everywhere, the sort only many head of cattle will leave behind: hoofprints and dung. As if reading his mind, Joe pointed a low finger toward a jag of stone. Some cow had shoved too close and left a clump of hair behind.

Joe still wasn't talking. He'd pulled a revolver and rested it atop the saddle horn. Mitch did the same.

If they could remain undetected by whoever had come through here, if they were even still ahead of them, they might survive. To do what, he had no idea.

They still hadn't decided on a plan. All bets, it seemed to Mitch, had been called.

They rode forward. Of course they had to, but it seemed so strange to be riding into the base of a rocky mountain. They left behind the grassy plain, the brooks, the trees, the scree-riddled slope, and the dead lawman. As they walked, with his senses pricking to every detail, questions sprouted in Mitch's mind like grasses poking out of parched soil after a big rain.

Who would take a herd of cattle into a mountain? And why? Why hadn't they kept driving them along the base of the eastern slope all the way north to a market? Were they going to sell them somewhere else? Hell, maybe they weren't going to sell them at all.

None of it made sense, and for the moment, it seemed wiser to keep his mouth shut and his eyes open, not losing sight of Joe. The only thought that gave him some sliver of relief was that since they'd been left for dead, the men they were following may not be expecting them, and so might not have left any lookouts behind.

They'd find out.

The raw-rock trail was, Mitch hoped, a pass through the mountains. It was more of a chasm that, as they rode forward, grew taller and narrower. Gray light lit it well enough, though for how long, who knew? The day was one of uncertainty. The sharp bite in the air promised more cold and they did not know where this pass led.

Mitch hoped they would get to the other side of the mountains before light failed them. The idea of spending the dark hours surrounded by a mountain of stone was gruesome.

The pass angled left, westward—as near as Mitch could figure—and the walls grew taller. Soon they were looking up the jagged, sheer rock walls that lined their way, jutting one hundred feet into the gray light. And pinned against that gray light, he saw clouds the color of a scuffed knife blade.

A gust of wind from somewhere ahead brought with it a whiff of . . . What was that? And then he knew—cattle. It wasn't that fresh-dung-hair-and-sweat smell of worked-up beeves, but it was further proof they were on the right trail.

A whistling wind sliced from behind them and tugged at their hats, dallied with their horses' tails, and made the animals skittish. Neither man spoke, but Joe coughed once and the sound of it, along with their horses' shoes clinking and nicking rock, echoed up, spiraling and slamming into the walls before bouncing off again. Each slight echo made them both wince.

Within moments of Joe's cough, as if the very sound had beckoned it down from on high, a pelting drizzle fell on them. The sky darkened and the cold raindrops turned into stingers of ice that funneled down hard.

They plodded on, collars upturned, bandannas pulled high, hats tugged low. Mitch felt bad for his horse, whose ears drooped and twitched with each fresh pelting. He swapped the revolver from hand to hand, flexing his frozen fingers. Soon he saw his breath.

This was not weather they'd seen much of back in Cawlins. He wasn't so certain he liked it. Still, he tried to remind himself of the blazing pain of the sun barely a week before, back in the low country, when he'd been certain he was about to expire and end up little more than puckered buzzard bait.

He and Joe both had been played right out to the end of their strings, their faces cracked and bleeding, puckered and ruptured by the sun, and then Bakar had shown up. He wished the old man was along with them now, but Mitch was glad they weren't dragging him into the pit of danger they were riding into. No way would he ever do that to Bakar or anyone else.

Mitch looked up and realized it was a whole lot darker than it had been minutes before. He also could not see Joe. He almost called out to get his bearings. He reined up and peered ahead. Shifting his head side to side as if that might help him see into the pelting gloom. Darker there, for certain, and the sleet had become snowy, hard nuggets now a couple of inches deep.

Mitch heeled the horse into a walk once more, his right hand clutching the reins and his shirt collar tight about his throat. Wouldn't matter if he shouted, his teeth rattled like castanets and the wind whipped up sounds on its own, providing a mocking accompaniment and playing tricks on his ears. He could swear he heard his name, as if someone were calling him. He perked and held the horse still. There it was again.

And then he saw a dark shape, tall, moving toward him in the sleeting gloom. Despite the freezing air, he felt cold sweat stipple his top lip and prickle his neck. He raised the revolver, ready to thumb back the hammer.

"Mitch!"

It was Joe.

"Here!"

A moment later, the big man was beside him. "Found it, a way out. Follow me!"

They rode deeper into the pass, and the darkness thickened. They plodded on like that, with Mitch close behind Joe, though he could barely see him. Joe must have known, because he shouted, "Almost there!"

They angled right, then left. The sheer rock walls, what Mitch could see of their imposing presence, were now no more than twenty feet apart. How anybody could shove a herd of cattle through that passage was a mystery to Mitch.

When he was about to shout to Joe to make certain they weren't lost, the light in the gap brightened enough that Mitch could once more see the outline of Joe and his horse. The wind whistled louder and the icy pellets drove harder, and Mitch felt colder than he'd ever felt in all his days. He was certain his teeth were about to rattle loose and drop out of his mouth.

Joe slowed and held out an arm. Mitch stopped alongside his friend and Joe leaned over. "It opens up there." He nodded ahead of them. "Slopes down and opens. I expect we're through the pass."

He nudged his horse forward and they walked another fifty feet. The pass seemed to end. The brightness before them broadened and the wind sliced in at them from the north.

Before them the landscape brightened, enough that even in the low light of dusk in a harsh blizzard, Mitch saw what appeared to be a long stretch of open land angling northward to their right. It was wide, some hundreds of yards across before another big bulky mass of mountain lined the far edge.

Mitch leaned close to Joe. "What is this place?"

"Valley, I think." He motioned with his head. "I thought I saw light before, northward. Lanterns maybe or a fire. We're safe. The wind's coming from that direction. Might be able to smell smoke. If there's someone up there, they can't hear us."

He reined hard to his left and angled back inside the passage until they were somewhat shielded by the last cornice of rock they'd passed. It provided a bit of shelter and wind block. Not enough for comfort, but better than the open end of the pass.

They dismounted and Joe said, "You still have the matches the old man gave you?"

Mitch nodded and patted his thin coat. His hands were too shaky to reach inside to the inner pocket yet, though.

Joe hopped over to a dark corner hidden by shadow and shouted to Mitch. "Hey! Come here!"

Mitch led his hunched, head-bowed horse, clunked his head on rock, and cursed. Then lowered it and reached before him with a hand. "Joe?"

"In here. A cave, sort of."

Mitch's spirits roused. Maybe they'd make it through the night, after all.

"And wood! Been used before, I reckon."

Joe's voice hadn't sounded this alive, this excited since weeks before on the trail. Mitch could already taste a hot cup of tea. Though right then he'd have drunk plain ol' water if it was warmer than the snow they'd been trudging through.

He reckoned once they'd had a hot drink, they could give thought to where they were, what they might be facing, and, most important, whose fire that was northward in the canyon. If it was a fire. If it was a canyon.

Questions skittered through Mitch's mind as he worked alongside Joe in silence with shaking hands to help arrange what little tinder they had, their teeth chattering in counterpoint to the gusting wind.

"You mind tending the horses while I get this blaze going?" Joe sounded testy, something unexpected.

"No, no, that's fine," said Mitch, standing.

He should have thought of that himself, should have set right to it, given Joe's bum leg. He usually tried to be more thoughtful in such matters but he'd been slipping lately. Too easy to blame it on the blow to the head. Even now it bothered him, a dull ache that had not gone away, even though he was surely on the mend.

Mitch made his way back out of the small grotto and found the two snow-plastered horses standing where they'd left them, hipshot, heads bowed, and bodies drawn, as if doing their best to shrink in on themselves.

Not for the first time did it occur to Mitch that horses got a raw deal in life. They were expected to lug some other critter around on their backs all day, eat poor feed, go for too long without enough water, then stand around, sweaty and tired and worn down to the nub.

Pretty much how he felt, too.

CHAPTER THIRTY-TWO

"YOU HEAR THAT?"

The half-breed who called himself Gray—
nobody knew why—glanced at the fat Mexican the others called Fatty. Then Gray looked back to his plate of
beans and grunted, in part because the Mexican was
always hearing sounds he made himself, and in part
because of the beans.

Beans. He had grown to hate them. He'd never been
fond of them, and now he could not stand to look on
them. It was a food fit for dogs and he was no dog. He
was Gray, like the color, and he was, by God, a man
among men. At least that's what he had grown accustomed to thinking first thing each morning.

It was a way of reminding himself of his mother's
fondest desire, the one thing that drove her to work
twice as hard as any man he had ever met—so that one
day, he could "be something."

But all her work had weighed her down until he saw

her collapse and die in a field behind a stringy old mule. Somebody else's field and somebody else's mule. That was the most important lesson he'd learned from his overworked mother—never work for anyone but himself. That and to regard himself as better than anyone else he would ever meet.

And while he did that each morning, liked the way it made him feel, in fact, it didn't go far in helping him pay his way in the world. But he'd be damned if he was going to walk behind somebody else's mule plowing their field. No. Still, that didn't mean he wouldn't take money for doing work someone else didn't want to do.

In recent hard times, though, such notions had conflicted with his actions, and so he'd only wanted to make a lot of money this one time, then get away from what he had become. Away from this man his mother would have hated. He often thought of her and wondered what she was thinking of him now, looking down at him from somewhere up there, floating high above the living, watching, watching, watching him.

She would not be impressed with him—that much he knew for certain. Neither was he. Maybe he wasn't much better than anyone else, after all. The thought sagged him a little. Then he looked at the fat Mexican, a sweaty man even in a blizzard who thought no further ahead than the next meal due him for stealing other people's cows for that rich bastard Simms.

Looking at the Mexican reminded Gray that he was at least better than that man. It almost made him smile. Almost.

"I said, did you hear that, man?" The fat Mexican farted again, chuckling, and cuffed Gray on the upper arm.

The four other men seated with them around the little campfire at the south end of the herd stopped clinking their wood spoons against the tin plates, paused in their wolfing down of beans, and looked, lips dripping bean juice, from Fatty to the half-breed.

They hoped it would play out as it had months before—what the half-breed did last time somebody poked him in the chest. It was Monty Pringle, that dandy who wanted to be a cowboy. He'd felt the sting of the half-breed's gleaming blade. Its needle tip had left a quick circle of red around the tip of the offending finger, a red that bloomed bright and drizzled the dandy's blood in a growing puddle between them on the dusty earth even before Pringle could scream. Then he'd screamed. Oh, boy, did he yelp it up.

Of course he was gone the next day. He'd run to Simms to complain, bleeding pointer finger held high as if to test the wind's direction. He had said he was going to draw the money owed him and ride on. Said he wasn't going to share a camp anymore with a half-breed who was treated like he was a man same as the rest of them. *Good riddance,* they'd all thought.

But later, nobody had seen him ride off. And nobody dared to question Mandrake Simms. He was downright spooky. For a boss he was tolerable, usually fed better than the run of beans they'd had lately from Craven, the lousiest cook ever to draw a breath. But Simms also kept them in liquor and had enough men around that they all didn't have to bust their backs tending to every little thing, not like some ranchers they'd all worked for now and again.

Something about Simms made everyone shut up and work. Even when they whooped it up and drank hard, nobody dared yammer about the boss man. He had a habit of popping up where you did not expect to see him. Spooky.

And then there was Gray himself—that odd half-breed; half-black, they all supposed, though nobody knew for certain. And the other half, well, that was not clear, either. But it didn't matter—he was all mean. And he was about to dole some of that mean out on ol' Fatty.

For his part, Gray knew what the men were expecting. He was to blame, of course, for he had set that ball rolling when he'd lopped off that fool's fingertip a long time ago now. But he didn't feel like repeating himself. That would be bringing himself down to the filthy level of the fat one, the same gut pile the rest of them crawled about in.

What he was interested in was finishing his beans, no matter how foul they were, and then figuring out how he was going to leave this place. For he had noticed a worrisome pattern these past few months.

Lots of men hired on. Judging from the faces he'd seen come and go, new folks were regularly replacing those who weren't there anymore. Yes, lots of men went away. But where did they go? Not many trails into or out of Cattle Canyon, as the men called this place. There were a whole lot of buzzards up at the north end, though, in that tiny spur canyon to the northwest he'd seen only once, fetching a couple of strays.

"What you gonna do, 'breed?"

It was the fat man. Gray set the spoon on the last of his greasy beans, set the plate down on a rock, and stood. He sniffed once and cleaned the corners of his mouth with his thumb and finger. He didn't look at the Mexican or anyone else; then he walked off into the dark.

He heard the fat one giggle. "Maybe he don't like the smells I make. I know he didn't hear that last one, huh?" He giggled again, but was hushed by the others, whose whispers by then Gray could only guess at. Probably words warning the fat one to be careful and look out all night, sleep with his eyes open, that sort of thing.

It would do him no good. When he grew sober, the

fat one would recall what he'd done and come around him tomorrow, mewling for forgiveness. Gray had heard such before from others.

A man could only excuse that sort of behavior now and again. If he lashed out more than once or twice in a row, he would not be mysterious or frightening to them. And yet, if he did nothing, he would be yellow in their eyes. And Gray knew he was not that. Not yellow. He was Gray, a man among men.

He allowed himself a thin smile in the dark as he lit a cigarette and sought quiet shelter from the incoming storm. Already the sleet pricked at his skin. He would need what sleep he could get before his turn to watch over the herd in the early hours. And if he didn't get a little sleep at least, he might decide tomorrow to gut the Mexican.

He might do it anyway. He could do whatever he wanted to the fat, smelly bastard, and nobody would tell Simms about it. They would not dare.

Gray sucked one last pull of smoke from his cigarette and sighed as he dropped it to the already whitening earth.

Tomorrow. He would see what tomorrow would bring his way.

CHAPTER THIRTY-THREE

"WHAT DO YOU think we ought to do?"

The question surprised Mitch. In his brief but close time with Drover Joe Phipps on the drive, he could not recall the man asking his opinion.

"Well," he said, trying to not look as simple in the head as he felt at that moment, "I've not given it a whole lot of thought. I was thinking about the food and the cold, and then I figured we'd talk about it once we ate."

Joe nodded, prodded the little flames. "Sure, yeah, I was only trying to do what you usually do."

"What's that?"

Joe smiled. "Fill the air with words."

"Do I do that?"

The older man rubbed the knee of his wounded leg. "Sometimes. But then again I can't blame you. I had to ride with somebody as shut mouth as I can be, I'd be apt to be chatty, too. Oh, heck, don't pay me any mind. I'm sore and tired and cranky."

"Well," said Mitch once more, hoping to change the subject, "there was that light you saw to the north a ways. Seems like whoever took our herd and . . . everything else, seems like they didn't get too far."

Joe bobbed his head in agreement. "This icy business can work for us. We're too tired, and we don't have a plan as yet. But as they're not likely to be moving about, we might use some of tomorrow to rest up, then sneak down there, see what we can learn of them, how many there are, if the far end of this place is open to the north."

Mitch nodded. "But . . . you can't go."

That sparked Joe's eyes. He looked at Mitch over the rim of his steaming mug. "What?"

"With that leg of yours, Joe, you'd slow me."

"So you expect to do it all on your own?"

Mitch shrugged. "Unless you have a smarter idea, I'd say that's the way it has to be. I'll be careful, but we have to know what sort of snake we're dealing with."

It took a long minute before Joe slowly shook his head in agreement. Nothing much more was said before they dozed.

THEY WERE COLD before they woke, and it was the frigid air that nudged them awake. Mitch cracked his eyelids. Cold and bright. He groaned and recalled where they were and what they were doing. Despite the freeze, he'd been having a nice dream about Evie. Even while he was in the midst of it, he knew he should be thinking about anything but her. That was the past, and to Mitch, his past was a dead thing, dead as the men they'd buried.

"Oh, I'm stiff," said Joe. "G'morning."

"Morning, Joe."

They'd slept side by side, shoulder to shoulder, huddled sitting against the wall. Mitch had left the saddle blankets on their mounts, tied them in place, to help the horses to stay warm. They offered them water, then meager rations of dried grasses and a handful of oats from the old man, but there was little more they could do for the poor beasts.

They'd propped the saddles before themselves in the little grotto, and used them to huddle beneath as much as they were able.

The first order of business for Mitch was to relieve himself, then tend the horses. Not necessarily in that order.

He stood as much as he was able in the little rocky space, and stretched, then shuffled to the entrance, bent low, and groaned. "Hey, Joe."

The cowboy joined him at the entrance and uttered a rare blue word. One of the horses was down, unmoving, and covered with a thin scrim of ice. It was obvious the beast was dead. And it was Joe's mare, Cloudy. He didn't speak and Mitch kept his mouth closed, too.

The other horse, the brown Mitch had ridden, was still upright, but it breathed hard, laboring to pull air in and push it out again. Its head hung low and thin tendrils of ice hung from its nostrils.

Mitch felt as low as he'd ever felt. Despite his fussing over the horses the night before, they'd lost one, likely both.

Joe hobbled over, his wounded leg outstretched, stiff from sleep, and nudged the downed horse. "Oh, Cloudy. You've gone stiff," he said, rasping the back of his glove over his tight mouth and chin. "I half-wondered how long we'd get out of these two." He looked up toward the sliver of gray sky above. "It was a boon to us that the old man found them, but they were looking poorly even then. And our riding them with so little decent feed at hand clinched the deal, I'd say."

"You think the brown here will fare the same?" Mitch rubbed the ill horse's neck.

"Yeah, nothing for it. Too bad," said Joe, patting the horse. "Wasn't the nicest night, but a healthy horse might have lived through it."

They were silent a moment more. Then Mitch said, "I guess we should talk about what I need to do."

"Oh, you mean to make something of that meager plan we talked about last night? The one where you leave me here and scout the canyon, see what we're facing?"

Mitch couldn't tell if Joe was angry with him for saying what he had. He'd not meant it that way.

Joe offered a tired smile. "Okay, yeah. But first things first. Let's go up to the mouth again and see what we can see."

The crusted snow was at best three inches deep, hard enough on top they had to poke through with each step. The sky beyond the steep rock walls lining their path was a mottled gray, nothing indicating the blue of the day before.

"Is this what winter's like up here in the north?" said Mitch.

"Naw," said Joe. "Winter's cold and snowy. This is Mother Nature's way of offering a taste of what she's about to lay on the table."

It was agreed that Mitch would indeed be the one to scout the canyon. Joe didn't give him much in the way of specific instruction, but kept on him with that fatherly stare that made Mitch more aware than ever that though Drover was only ten years his senior, he had done a whole lot more living outside of one little town and off one rough-patch ranch than Mitch ever had. It was a vexation to Mitch even after he'd nodded yes and yes and yes to all of Joe's departing thoughts that were not so much questions as statements.

Finally, he paused once more by the one dead horse and the other nearly so, wheezing and rasping out its last hours, still upright on locked bone legs. "You know, I have been around the tree a time or two myself."

It was a phrase he'd heard somewhere and believed it meant he was experienced in the ways of the world, though he couldn't be certain. "And I intend to make it back alive so you can harangue me some more." He knew his face was red and he didn't care.

Drover Joe offered a nod. "Glad to hear it. Keep that in mind." Then he turned and limped back toward the little grotto and didn't look back.

Mitch felt badly about snapping at Joe like that. For Joe not to put up much of a fight about going along, too, must mean the cold was bothering that leg more than he let on. He'd caught him a few times with a wide-drawn mouth and half-closed eyes, rubbing the leg above the wound.

It was slow to heal and they had nothing to ease the pain. Even the old man had been unable to offer anything more than the scanty last herbs from which he made a poultice. He'd boiled and wrapped it about the wound; then, when it grew cold and dead feeling, he'd boil it again. He claimed its magic hadn't yet been drawn from it, though they all knew that it was little more than an old steaming, sodden cloth nesting a few dissolved leaves.

"Okay, then," said Mitch, poking his head into the gray day beyond the gaping, toothy mouth of the pass. His task was simple. Stay unseen and learn what he could.

"Stick close by the east edge, and keep to the scree as much as you're able so you don't leave too many tracks in the snow." Joe had followed that with: "It's cold enough that this crust will be with us all day. Could be a hindrance, could help us. I'm not certain which yet."

But what Mitch saw when he got out there and looked to his right, northward, meant his job would be anything but simple. First off, the canyon was a whole lot bigger than they'd seen late the day before, when the heavy weather had sullied their view. Though this day was itself thick with the promise of further storming, the air was clear enough for a good view of the expanse before him, reminding the young man from Cawlins, Texas, once more that there was more to the world than wide-open spaces and blue skies.

There were also oddnesses that a person would later think about, notions that would make him wonder why people did the things they did.

The canyon was a valley—a long, narrow valley. Mitch wasn't certain what the difference might be, but Joe had called it both a valley and a canyon, so he guessed it didn't much matter. It was also half-filled at the far end with a big herd of cattle. Most of them could be their herd, though a few head were black, some white with black patches. Those appeared to be hornless, though distance prevented him from seeing clearly.

He bet the cattle were fed up with the cold and with not moving. They'd churned the snow in vast swatches to reveal mud and, more surprising to Mitch, green grass. Much green, in fact, glowed through the punched snow. "Huh" was all Mitch could think to say.

He kept tight to the wall and breathed easy and out the left side of his mouth toward the gap in the rock behind him, lest his steaming breath on the morning air draw the eye of one of several men moving about on horseback.

He thought back on the attack. There had been what seemed like dozens of men—though some of them had been the Apaches, Joe had said. It didn't matter now. There were many of them, and he and Joe were but two. And on foot, and without much in the way of provisions.

Once more, Mitch mumbled, "Nothing to lose," and wished he had Joe's spyglass. It had been good of Joe to give it to the old man, who had obviously coveted the item. But it mattered little now, for Mitch didn't have it and had to rely on his eyes and nose and ears and legs to gain what further information he might.

He eyed the scene, watching the cows move, and noted a slight breeze riding north to south, carrying with it the mildest trace of cattle smell, dung and hide and wet hair. He heard the far-off sounds of cattle bellowing, the random chesty declarations of cows that wanted to move, to be fed, to be more comfortable than they were. He could not blame them.

The canyon was perhaps an eighth of a mile wide, with the same sky-tall spires and columns and sheets and ledges of granite they'd been surrounded with while riding through the passage. A snaky black trail cut roughly down the middle length of the canyon—a creek, he decided. That would explain the green grass.

Mitch could not see the far end because the canyon itself curved northeastward. Beyond the herd, though, Mitch thought he saw something sizable and square in shape covered with the stained white-gray canvas of a tarpaulin, with snow clinging to it. Clouds of smoke rose nearby it before teasing apart on the breeze.

The herd's noise grew louder as Mitch watched. The canyon was wide enough that the beeves weren't packed tight, so they milled loosely. Mitch saw white and brown between the beasts, shot through with more spots of green.

Here and there a rider's whistle rose up. There were no men at this end of the herd, presumably because there was nowhere for the cattle to go. The south end was closed off, rounded as if scooped with a giant spoon and, he guessed, also bedded with green grass beneath.

He thought briefly of the sickly horse behind him in the passage, and though he knew it was too late, he still wished he could offer the beast this warmth and sunshine and green grass one last time.

He didn't know what more he might learn from where he stood. But neither did he think he would remain unseen for long, even if he hugged the gray rock of the eastern wall. He began easing himself back a step at a time, trusting that if he were to make a sudden move and someone happened to be watching, he'd be seen.

Then a sudden gust carried voices to him. They were men's voices, and he saw three riders along the east edge, side by side, talking. He thought for certain he saw the hat of one of the men bob in a nodding motion. Then Mitch heard the words "Montana" and "storm" and he thought he heard the word "tonight" float to him.

Could the man mean the storm from the night before? Or perhaps they were fearful of a fresh walloping? Though Mitch was not of this cold northern place, he was a critter, same as any other on the earth, and he recognized portents. He'd bet money they were talking of a coming storm. Stringing the words into meaning, he figured they were going to drive the herd away from the valley before tonight.

That must mean they were fearful of being trapped in the valley by snow. How much would they get this early in the season? By Mitch's calendar, it was still September.

More important, that meant the men who dealt

them such a raw hand and left them for dead would be leaving. Then what? He had not thought much beyond finding these brutes. Back on the flat, healing under Bakar's care, Mitch had had plenty of time to consider all this, and it still bothered him that he wasn't certain what he'd do to the killers and thieves should he find them.

He was certain they deserved death and worse for what they did. But could he be the person to dole it out to them? He bet Joe could. When it came down to the nub, could he kill if he wasn't being attacked?

"Yes," he said, nurturing the painful image of a dead Rollo, Chet, the Kid, and all the others, and he knew he could do it. He had to do it. Now he just had to make certain they got the chance. Or all this hate, all the deaths, would be for nothing.

Random sounds from the three talking men rose into the air, but nothing more that made sense as a word. Mitch squinted past them, noticing that the herd had changed shape. The pawing, bawling beeves slowly roved here and there as they do, to reveal more of the middle and far bits of the canyon. The next thing Mitch made out in the distance held his breath in his mouth. It was unmistakable.

Cook's wagon. Had to be. He recognized the canvas covering, patched all over with whatever cloth the man could lay his hands on over the years. The familiar contraption sat parked away from the west wall, facing northward. The area about the wagon looked to be set up as a long-term camp.

Conviction set his teeth, remembering afresh that Cook and Sycamore, as near as he and Joe and Bakar had been able to tell, had been taken with the raiders, for they were nowhere to be found among the dead they'd lugged and buried.

He'd seen enough. Mitch shoved back into the colder, darker passage and walked back to talk with Joe.

As he neared their spot, he saw the lump of the first horse, still crusted with snow and, beside it, another. The second horse was down. Mitch had only been gone perhaps an hour, but it had been time enough for the beast to succumb to its affliction. He walked nearer and didn't see blood, so he knew Joe hadn't done for it, something he thought the horse-loving man might have done to ease the horse's struggle.

Mitch looked at the brown steed. The horse's ribs were no longer heaving, its muzzle no longer offering even the slightest puffs of hard-won breath.

"Hey, Joe," said Mitch, trying to sound happier than he felt. He peered into the little rocky cave.

Joe was there, leaning against the wall as he had been all night. But he was awake and staring at the little fire he'd managed.

Mitch bent low and made his way the few feet into the space, keeping low. "Turns out, I didn't get far at all," he said.

Joe leaned forward. "Was it safe? You weren't seen, were you?"

"No, no. Nobody saw me." Then he told Joe all he had seen and heard.

The older man leaned back once more and played his fingertips thoughtfully in his chin hairs. They'd each grown beards, no choice otherwise. It pleased Mitch that his came in stronger than he'd supposed it might.

On the topic of growing beards, Evie had once said, "Just because you can do a thing doesn't mean you should." She was wise, no doubt, but she wasn't here with him to tell him he shouldn't be hairy.

"We won't have an icicle's chance in hell to take them once they're on the trail, not all those men, all spread out." Joe sighed. "Our best chance would have been to trail them well behind and get the law on our side once we reached a town of some sort. Likely foolish of us to dally with death anyway. We know what they're like."

"But that's not a possibility anymore." Mitch looked toward the dead horses but a few yards away. He needn't have, as Joe understood what he meant.

"You're right. Now we're afoot. And winter's closing in and baring its fangs. And from what I recall, we are many days' ride to anywhere."

"Let alone walking."

"Right. And I don't fancy sitting here all winter, carving off hunks of frozen horseflesh for roasting. Besides, those horses won't freeze up for another month or two anyway, come real winter."

"We're sunk. Unless . . ." Mitch looked at Joe with a raised eyebrow.

"Oh, boy, you quiet ones are the most frightening of all when you get a notion." He settled back and sighed. "Let's have it."

"What do you think my odds of sneaking in and getting a couple of horses might be?"

"Without being seen? Without them seeing tracks and following? And most important, without me?"

"I could get them, bring them back here. We could ride back the way we came. We'd have a head start on them."

"You're forgetting something."

"What's that?"

"They're not blind or deaf and it's daylight."

"That's three things."

"And here's a fourth: You said it sounded like they were fixing to leave before tonight's storm."

Mitch sagged. "Yeah."

"Take heart, Mitch. That means we have to gamble

a bit. I've never been much for cards. Money comes too hard to waste it in such a frivolous way, but that doesn't mean I haven't studied on it some."

"What do you mean?"

"I mean"—Joe groaned to his feet—"gather your goods. Nothing you'd regret leaving behind. We'll go together to find a couple of mounts."

"Then what?"

Joe shrugged. "Then we really gamble."

A few minutes later, outfitted with the leanest kit they figured they'd need should they live through this foolish exploit, Drover Joe Phipps and Mitchell Newland peered once more around the edge of the stone cornice and up the length of the valley.

"They don't look to me like they're about to make a move," said Mitch. "At least not tonight."

Joe nodded agreement. "That's good for us. We can sneak in a whole lot better under cover of the dark. Trick is to find where the horses are before darkness falls. We'll have the snow to help us see."

"What do we do then?"

"Then we ride up and get on out before anybody sees us. Simple."

They stood for a few moments, breathing shallow and watching the herd, the men, the campfire smoke, the wagons, each thinking a hundred thoughts and not daring to give voice to a single one.

Finally, Mitch spoke. "Joe."

"Yep?"

"This is crazy, right?"

"Yep."

CHAPTER THIRTY-FOUR

Dusk in high country descended, heavy with the weight of the coming storm. Mitch and Joe were as ready as they were ever going to be.

They'd dropped back inside the mouth of the gap to wait and double-check their weapons. Gunfire too soon would bring down certain death, so their revolvers and rifles would be used only when they found themselves backed up and snarling, turned away from hope's final door. If they needed to dole out the bitter taste of pain and revenge before then, bare hands and the silent menace of their broad-blade hip knives would serve.

In that thinning span of time before departing the stone gap, the weather began fulfilling its foul promise. What had commenced as a light, soft snow soon gave over to errant gusts from the north that lashed downward with increasing furor. Riding the winds' coattails, the once pretty snowfall thickened with each moment.

Mitch made the mistake of looking into the swirling,

dizzying snowfall and had to close his eyes for a moment. It was a pretty sight, but stunning, too. He'd never seen so much snow all at once, and with no end in sight.

Joe wasn't bothered. "Could be worse, Mitch."

"How so?"

"Give it an hour."

The darkening air had taken on a chill that slowed their hands, and kept them stiff, despite the extra socks each man wore as mittens. They'd cut holes in the toes so that they might poke their fingers through when needed. Otherwise they kept them balled into fists that clutched rifles and balanced their awkward low walking as they hugged the east wall.

They'd draped the saddle blankets over their shoulders, and they wore them as thick, smelly ponchos crudely tied across their chests with leather strips cut from the saddles they'd left behind.

With each slow, cautious step forward, scree slid away from their boots. Mitch grew convinced that nothing but a crackling blaze and a pot of bubbling coffee could ever warm him again. He felt like a child whenever his teeth rattled from the cold. Joe was in obvious pain but never said a thing about it, other than offering up a grunt now and again. He kept swinging that leg, working to bend it at the knee and keep it limber.

And so they made their way along the base of the east cliff face lining the valley. Snorts and low bellows from cattle rose up in the cold air. The storm would be both a boon and a curse, Joe had whispered once when they halted to breathe and assess the land before them.

They'd crept to the southern end of the herd, where the cattle had ranged far apart from one another. As far as Mitch and Joe could tell, they were unwatched by any men, on horseback or otherwise. If they could move down among them, slowly, the beeves would provide the two men with the best chance they'd ever have of getting over to the horses.

It was comforting for them both to be back amongst the herd. Even in the low light from the snow's glow, Mitch was able to read a few brands, mostly Bilks' critters. And then he made the unexpected discovery of one of his own, a steer from the Twin N. It gave Mitch a brief stab of happiness such as he'd not felt in weeks, maybe months.

It was a cow, sure, but it was what the beast represented that gave him more than happiness. It gave him hope. After all, despite all the viciousness they'd seen, all they'd been through, he and Joe were still alive.

Joe must have felt much the same because Mitch noted the man moved stealthier, more catlike than he had before. They edged through the herd without causing a ruckus, creeping closer with each snowy, shuffling step, toward the far northwest corner of the canyon, where they hoped they'd find the remuda.

They'd seen a few horses along the far-east edge, close by what looked to be a makeshift shelter, a spot where men were likely to hunker.

The cattle were disinclined to be riled, as the nasty weather chastened everything it touched, turning even the rowdiest critters into hunched beeves, heads facing southward, tails tucked, while the slicing north wind whistled up their backsides and stinging pellets of icy snow peppered their rumps.

Still, the two men took no chances and moved easy among them, offering low, soothing sounds and hoping the ornery beeves were too cold to lash out with hard, quick kicks. It happened anyway and twice Mitch stifled a groan, knowing he'd have purple welts along his shins and calves.

They were still some feet, perhaps twenty, from the west edge of the canyon and the herd's edge when Joe, who'd been in the lead, held his hand out and Mitch felt it pressing into his chest. Joe pointed to his ear, then northward. They halted and held there, crouched among the cattle.

Within moments, Mitch heard voices, not steady, but jags of words carried to them from ahead. Then he smelled something familiar and sharp, not a cow's earthy tang, but something he hadn't smelled in weeks. For a moment it confused him; then he placed it—tobacco smoke.

They held and listened and the voices carried to them, along with the pungency of the smoke. In the troughs between gusts, phrases carried down to them: "Last of . . . Apaches . . . paid in cows." "Supposed to . . . Montana by now . . . Placer City . . . mine camp. Boss . . . top dollar."

They traded a quick nod of mutual understanding. They didn't need to hear any more to confirm their suspicions that the thieves intended to sell the beasts much as Mitch, Joe, and the crew had intended. Then Mitch smelled horses.

Joe waited a half minute; then with a quick jerk of his head, he bade Mitch to follow. Within seconds, a fidgety flank shuddered under Joe's outstretched sock-covered right hand. The beast sidestepped and offered a low, throaty chuckle.

"What's the matter?" said a close voice. "You gonna cause the whole place to bolt you don't simmer yourself, boy."

One moment Mitch was crouched behind Joe; the next Joe had rotated his rifle so that he held the barrel and forestock like a club. Then Drover Joe Phipps stood full height, a black shape emerging against the pelting snow, swinging the gun wide as he rose.

Even in the whipping wind, Mitch heard the harsh

smack as the walnut stock met a man's skull. The out-
law dropped like a sack of wet meal. By then Mitch had
snagged the lead line and kept the jumpy horse from
thrashing into them.

The horse was bareback, and from what Mitch had
heard, there had to be at least one other man nearby.
Why was this horse unsaddled with a rider standing by?

"Here!"

It was Joe's harsh whisper. Mitch held the line
tugged by the spooked horse and found Joe a dozen
feet beyond where he'd dropped the man. He saw the
answer to his question. There was a campaign tent,
narrow and peaked, tall enough for a man to crouch in,
maybe deep enough for him to stretch out in, which
from the looks of the unlit interior was what the man
had been doing or had been about to do.

That's what the irregular snapping sounds were, the
wind hitting the tent like a drum beaten by a child.
Sounds they'd heard as they approached this far wall,
but hadn't paid attention to. What an odd outpost.

Mitch eased, let the rope slide through the stock on
his hand, and the becalmed horse stood, still wild-eyed
but calmer.

He saw no other horses. There was no campfire, no
lantern, which worked in their favor, but it meant Mitch
couldn't see the other man. Maybe he'd ridden off
northward. Joe ducked into the odd tent and Mitch
looked left, then right, for all the good it did him. There
was no way anyone could see more than two, three yards
in any direction, especially north.

Inside the tent, the wind's whipping lessened enough
that he could hear Joe, who in a low whisper said,
"Canteen. Here." He handed Mitch a canteen and they
shared it. While Mitch sipped, Joe found a cloth-
wrapped bundle and grunted in pleasure as he handed

half the contents, two tall biscuits, to Mitch. The third
he jammed in his mouth and stuffed the fourth in a
coat pocket. He rummaged a moment more, then said,
"Can't find the man's saddle. That horse'll have to do.
But we need a second mount. I'll go," he said, jerking
his thumb farther along the valley.

"No, I can do it. You stay here and find the saddle,"
said Mitch, knowing Joe would balk at the suggestion.
Mitch didn't care. They needed a second horse, and
despite his efforts of earlier, Joe was still slower than
Mitch.

Then a horse snorted from north of them and a man
said, "Earl? Where you at? And where's your fire? If
you ain't the laziest . . ."

There was no response from the head-knocked
Earl. Joe looked at Mitch and jerked his chin, indicating he should reply.

"Huh," said Mitch in a loud voice, hoping Earl was
as he looked to be, not a man filled with the need to
chatter, especially on a stormy night.

The horse snorted again, closer, and Mitch backed
out of the tent, hoping he would not be easily seen in
the spitting gloom.

"Hey, Earl, what you playing at?"

He'd been seen.

Mitch kept his head low. His hat was still jammed
hard on his head and tethered beneath his chin by the
stampede strap.

The horse rode closer. Didn't sound like the other
man they'd heard, but no matter, it would be the second mount they needed. Then they could backtrack,
maybe skirt the herd, and make for the passage, thread
through it to the eastern edge of this odd place. From
there, they could ride northward, putting distance between them and this nest of vipers before they turned

on them whenever the storm lulled and the results of their presence were discovered.

Something told Mitch it wasn't going to happen that way.

"That you, Earl?"

Mitch nodded his head. He cut his eyes to his left and saw that Joe was trying to shove his way out under the back of the tent, but it was tied together, slowing him.

"Help me with this horse," the man yelled. "I'll spell you. Boss says to go on up, get you some supper."

Mitch nodded and, without raising his head too high, tried to grab the reins and steady the horse. The man slid from the saddle and stomped in place. "Can't get the feeling back in my feet. I hate the cold. I surely do."

Any second now, thought Mitch, *he'll see I am not his friend. Then what?* He didn't dare look to his left once more to see if Joe had escaped from the tent. But he got his answer when he saw the limping cowboy out of the gloom rounding behind the newly arrived horse.

"What's the matter with you, Earl?" The man stepped closer, peering. Something tipped him off, because he reached for his revolver, but it was beneath his buttoned coat, so he fumbled with the buttons.

"Hold there now," he said, his uncertain voice rising in pitch. He sensed something behind him as the horse jerked sideways. The man half-turned to see what was going on.

That's when Joe swung that rifle once more, from left to right, but the newcomer was quick, set already to a role of skittishness, and dodged the blow. The rifle stock slammed into the saddle and the man jammed hard into Joe's midsection with a lunge and a punch, all at once.

Joe folded in half, the wind pulled from him. His rifle dropped. The horse reared and the reins slipped through Mitch's grasping hand. He growled a curse and tried to poke his fingers back into a usable position, but they fouled in the sock end. He raised this rifle, but the man didn't seem to care. He spun low to his left and, with a savage, guttural shout, barreled toward Mitch.

Mitch was about to sidestep when something grabbed his boot and upended him. He crashed backward into the tent, pulled down by a revived Earl. The new horse stomped in a tight circle as the cattle, a dozen feet to their right, churned farther away. The confused horse snorted and shoved its way northward.

Joe gained his knees and launched himself in a cat-like spring at the back of the newcomer, who still fumbled with his coat, trying to get at his revolver. Joe had already unsheathed his big knife.

Mitch flailed, jamming his rifle butt at the revived Earl as the other man's shouts of anger and surprise dissolved into a burbling, gagging sound.

The newcomer's voice tailed off, high and squealing, and he jerked and spasmed, trying to lurch away from Joe, who stood behind him, one arm wrapped about the front of the man's grimy sheepskin coat.

The man's arms flailed wide apart, but at about the same time, his sounds dwindled, his arms stiffened as if he were reaching for something only he could see. Then he sagged and dropped forward, leaving Joe standing spraddle-legged behind him with his big knife in his right hand.

Even in the snow-whipped gloom, Mitch saw the length of the blade was coated with something slick and thick.

A burst of humid stink clouded Mitch's face, then dissolved, as if a cow had belched. But he knew the smell of warm blood. He jerked and kicked at the grasping efforts of Earl, who had half-risen but seemed to have trouble gaining his feet. *Good,* thought the young man as he jerked his rifle back once more and swung the stock around hard.

It slammed into the side of Earl's head, flecking gore as his ear peeled partway off and a gash in his scalp burst wide, spraying blood in a wide arc. Earl swayed on his knees but a moment, then his right hip buckled and he flopped once more to the ground, his leaking head smacking the snow. The gash Mitch had dealt continued to bleed, pumping in spurts and starts, and the man's tattered ear hung at an angle not useful to the human head. Not that Earl would ever again need to hear.

Joe, chest heaving, limp-walked over to Earl and thrust a hand between the man's thick coat collar and his neck. He paused there a moment, then shook his head and looked at Mitch. "He's done, Mitch."

Mitch didn't think this was the first man he'd killed. He was fairly certain that honor went to one of the nameless brutes of this same gang of range pirates back during their initial attack.

"They both . . ." Mitch tried to gain control of his breathing. It came harder than it should have.

Joe nodded. "Looks like it. We have to get out of here."

"You think they'll be missed?"

"Yeah, soon. That horse might turn up wherever it came from and it won't have a rider. They'll come looking. We don't want to be here when they do. Only thing we have going for us is this storm. Let's use our heads, make it work for us."

Mitch was already forming ideas. "Only thing we can do is follow this edge on up. We've gone too far now. We'll leave this valley alive or dead."

Joe smiled.

Mitch rolled his eyes at his own comment. At least Joe had the good grace not to say, *How else would we leave?*

But then he did, and chuckled, a thin sound in the wind and snow, with two men, dead by their own hands, at their feet. Joe bent to the second, the one he'd knifed, and grasped him by the shoulders. "Help me drag them into the tent."

Despite the weather, no snow stuck to the spreading stain on his dark, wet back. They got him inside, and then they dragged Earl.

"Anything in there of use to us?"

"Nothing save a few shells I already grabbed," said Joe. "And the canteen and those biscuits."

"We going to ride?"

"The one horse?" said Joe. "No saddle?"

"You, then. I don't have a shot-up leg."

"Neither do I, Mitch. I have a limpy leg, that's all. No, let's leave it here. Less of a target that way. We should have grabbed those coats, though." Mitch shuddered at the thought of pulling on the dead man's bloodied clothes, despite the promise of warmth.

With no more palaver, they nodded to each other and melted into the darkness to their left, close to the foreboding black rock of the canyon wall.

They walked on, keeping the hunched, lowing herd to their right, and their ears perked for sign of horses and men. Then a gust brought with it the pungent tang of woodsmoke before whipping it away. It meant they were drawing close to something.

Long minutes passed. They weren't traveling fast, given the weather and their caution. Each man did his best to keep his chattering teeth quiet. When one or the other came up to something of concern—a mass that could well be another tent, something large and covered with snow—they communicated with head nods and shrugs before poking it and moving on. So far, anything of concern had been snow-crusted masses of rock tumbledowns from the cliffs above.

The thought that all that rock face could give way, shear off, and crash down did little to comfort Mitch's rabbity mind. And wouldn't winter's harsh weather, its ice and snow and gales and who knew what else, add more weight to rocky crags high above, straight over their heads?

"Mitch!"

Young Newland jumped, spun toward the voice, backing up at the same time and grabbing for his gun. It was only Joe. The man had leaned close and whispered in his ear. Now he made calming motions with his hands.

Mitch eased. He needed to rein in the wandering ways of his mind.

Joe shook his head, telling him much the same thing, then nodded ahead. Before them, a snow-covered shape squatted in the dark. It was larger than the rocks they'd passed, and dark until about five, six feet up, where a low white line glowed.

"Shack, I'll wager," whispered Joe. The wind was against them, whistling at them from the shack's direction, northward. There was no way their close-whispered voices could carry upwind.

A gust flipped up the front of the older cowboy's hat brim and sandlike snow pelted his face. He closed his eyes and readjusted his hat.

"I'll scout it," said Mitch.

Joe grabbed his arm and leaned close. "What's the plan?"

Mitch grinned, recalling one of his father's favorite phrases. "It'll be like a drunkard's story."

"How's that?"

"We'll make it up as we go along."

Joe nodded.

"There," whispered Mitch. "That crack. I'll try to see how many are in there. From the tramped-down snow, I'd say that's the way to the crapper."

"Uh-huh," said Joe, understanding raising his eyebrows. "Then what?"

"Depends on how many there are."

He could tell by the droop of Joe's big moustaches that he didn't much like the skeletal plan. But they had little else going for them. Mitch continued on, Joe beside him. They crept to within six feet of the shack. It was a gappy affair obviously not intended for winter-long habitation. Likely the thieves hadn't planned on being caught here during foul weather.

A lamp's low glow sliced vertical rays that angled outward onto the snow. A burst of laughter was joined by another before settling back into an erratic murmur. No words were clear, but it sounded as if the speakers, at least two voices, might be drinking. Or they were at least excited about not being out in the hard weather.

Joe hugged the near corner, a couple of feet from the plank door, and kept his rifle ready to level down on whoever came out, should they catch sight of him and Mitch.

Mitch bent his hat brim back and eased himself up to the nearest gap, a crack central in the twelve-foot-long sidewall of the shack. The rough-sawn planking must have been brought in by wagon. His frozen cheek could barely feel the splintery grain of the wood, but his nose pulled in a piney scent released by the scant heat coming from inside.

From the looks of the semipermanent structure and the men they'd crossed so far, they could tell that this was one large planned operation. Which meant there was a lot of money being made. And a goodly portion of it was Mitch's, and by relation it also belonged to the men he'd befriended—the ones who had died because someone was greedy enough to set up such a den of deceit and murder.

Mitch held his left eye close enough to the wood that his lashes touched the coarse surface. Still, he kept the eye open and held his breath. It would not do to be seen by anyone in there. Then a nasty thought caught him. What if they set fire to the building? He dismissed the vicious notion as soon as it came flitting into his cold-benumbed mind. Too cruel even for these bastards. Or was it?

He caught sight of a boot, and another, with different trousers above it. That made two men accounted for. How many more?

The voices mumbled low, a bench Mitch could partially see shifted, squawking wood on wood. A man stood, yawned, and moved away toward the door, revealing a squat sheet-steel stove, the sides of it glowing and warped from overuse. Through the crack Mitch felt a sliver of its meager heat. He glanced to his right.

Joe heard the sound, too, heard the boots on planks making for his end of the shack, the door's end.

The man paused—Mitch guessed the fellow was tugging on his coat—muttered a crude joke that made him laugh, and then shoved the door.

Joe had flattened himself against the side of the shack. The man would not be able to see him until he returned from whatever brought him out. Likely to urinate. Which, given the weather, meant there was no way he was going to make for a privy, wherever it sat at the end of the filled-in path in the snow. No, he'd make for the corner of the shack. Right where Mitch and Joe stood.

By the time the man descended the single step into
the snow, Joe had raised the rifle high to deliver a blow
to the man's head. But he hadn't reckoned on the man
being as large as he was.

Never had Mitch seen such a big man. He was nearly
a foot taller than Mitch or Joe, who each ran north of
six foot by a couple of inches.

The brute passed Joe before he caught sight of
Mitch, who remained in a crouch, but had levered a
round and held his rifle aimed at the man's bulk.

"What the . . . ?"

The big man spun to his right as Joe stepped forward,
swinging. The brute raised his right arm and the rifle
collided with it. Mitch heard something crack, but the big
man didn't go down. He growled like a bear and rammed
his shoulder into Joe, pinning him between the shack
and his bulk. Boards cracked and Joe groaned. Somebody inside the shack shouted and made for the door.

Mitch cut wide behind the man and slammed his
own rifle into the big man's head. At least that's what
he aimed for. The stock caromed off the side of the
man's pate, then slammed his shoulder. The blow did
not drop the brute. It angered him.

At least it got him away from Joe, thought Mitch,
dodging the growling bear-man's mighty swinging reach.
Joe, when the beast let go of him, had dropped to the
snowy earth like an armload of firewood.

By then, a man from inside the cabin had shoved his
way outdoors and cranked back on the hammer of his
revolver. He shouted something in Spanish and cut
loose with a shot. Mitch heard an "Oof!" and wondered if he'd been hit. Other than cold, he still felt
okay—he wasn't out of the game yet.

He saw Joe flailing in the snow, scrabbling at the
splintered boards above him, gapped enough that part
of the inside could now be seen, casting an irregular

low gold light on waists, legs, and boots as each man shuffled and struggled.

The newcomer's gun went off again. Joe remained upright and swinging, grabbing for his own revolver. It looked to Mitch as if he'd dropped his rifle.

The shots would attract others, many others. They had to get free of here or they were dead men. The big beast, whom he was now stuck with, kept growling and cursing and trying to snatch Mitch's rifle. Mitch couldn't let him have it, but he struggled to keep away from those big mitts that landed blow on blow, sloppy and poorly swung, but numbing when they connected.

Mitch managed finally to squeeze a shot that he guessed drove like a tiny, angry bee into the big man's broad gut. If it did end up there, it didn't slow the man. He worked the lever to try another round, but never got the chance.

While his hands were occupied, the giant swung a wide, fast blow that slammed into Mitch's still tender head. It drove him down to his left knee.

He saw that Joe was still in hot combat with the other man, and Mitch looked back up in time to see the big man sagging. Mitch dove out of the way as the giant, holding a hand to his gut, managed to get a knee beneath himself.

Drops from between the man's fingers dripped to the snow, blew with the wind, and spattered into the air. The tiny stain leached larger, nearly as large as the man's great eyes that looked on Mitch with wonder and then anger. By then, it was too late. He dropped the rest of the way, slamming to the snow on the spot where Mitch had been.

The young rancher, dizzied by the brute's blow to his head, gasped as he shoved once more to his feet, resisting the urge to shake his head. Snow gusted in his face and he dragged a gloved hand down, wishing his double vision would settle and help him choose which of the two Drover Joes needed his help most. He decided it didn't matter. Both were to the left in his field of sight and the man Joe fought to his right, lunging for his friend.

Mitch raised the revolver he'd shucked from its holster and, without giving it any more thought, cranked back on the hammer. He let loose a bullet that drove into the man's left side. He dropped to the snow and spasmed and groaned, blood geysering from the wound, then slowing to a pumping trickle as Joe stepped over him. He retrieved his fallen rifle.

"Mitch, you okay? We have to get out of here!" He limped over, one leg stiff, but quick, and snatched the swaying younger man by the shoulder. "Pick up that rifle and let's go!"

Mitch gritted his teeth hard and nodded, bent for what he thought might be his rifle, a long, dark shape half covered with kicked snow. It was. He didn't recall dropping it. Joe snatched at his sleeve and dragged them behind the cabin.

Their tracks could be followed, but if they trailed off into the dark once more, it would be a few minutes before someone followed with a lantern. Already they heard horses and the shouts of men north of them, from where they assumed other members of the gang were nested in, waiting out the weather.

"Now what's the plan?" said Joe, perturbed that Mitch's plan had led to naught yet again. "We boxed ourselves in. Unless we can figure out something to do and fast, we're holding the ends of our ropes."

"We have to keep going, see if we can get horses. It's our only chance to get out of here."

They hustled onward and heard shouts and saw lanterns cutting the gloom. The mass of the herd was off to their east, a couple of hundred feet away. For several minutes, the only sounds were far-off shouts of men, growing fainter, and their own hard breathing.

They appeared to be following a trail of sorts that wound through boulder piles and led to a broad cabin that looked to be built out of the rock wall itself. They knew it was a cabin because the front of it glowed, with two windows flanking a door; the effect was that of a broad face leering at the gloom of the storm.

The roof was low but broad, perhaps twenty feet deep. The lower edge, which overhung the windows and door by a couple of feet, was barely sufficient for a six-foot man. Out front a hitch rail hosted two snow-covered mounts that stood hipshot and sullen, their faces angled as much as they were able away from the wind.

Mitch and Joe ducked behind a boulder pile and regarded the scene. They would steal the horses, then make for whatever opening there might be at the north end of the canyon. For all its bluster and bravado, the storm had been busier with shoving out wind than shaking out snow. It covered everything, but it hadn't built up to anything they couldn't run their way out of on solid horses.

The duo hunkered behind the boulders, rifles at the ready, and watched the cabin. As with the other cabin, an inferior to this in every way, there was little sign of activity. That changed as soon as they ducked their heads down.

A figure crossed behind one of the windows; then they heard the door rattle, followed by a thin, squeaky sound. A lean man with a face in shadow stood outside the open door a moment. He put his hands to his mouth, and they thought he might be going to light a cigarette. Then he shouted.

His sudden voice shocked them and the horses tied a couple of yards before him. They shied, jerked their ropes, then settled, ears twitchy.

He bellowed again. "Rubens! Where have you gone to? Rubens?"

As if in response, a lone steer lowed.

"Head of the snake, I bet," said Joe in a low voice.

Mitch nodded. "Kill that and the rest dies."

"Or so we hope. One way to find out." Joe began to stand, but Mitch laid a hand across his arm. The man under the shallow ramada turned and, after snapping out a cursed oath, retreated back into the warm-looking house.

"Last place we need to be is stuck in that cabin, pinned down by the rest of these killers."

Joe sighed. "Yeah, but we have to be somewhere, and if he is the head of this outfit, we might be able to use him as bait."

They waited too long. Four men on horses thundered from the north out of the pelting gloom and jerked their horses to a stop before the house. The other horses skittered in place, jerking at the intrusion. One man slid down and shouted something to the others, then walked to the door, stomped in place, and knocked.

That seemed formal to Mitch, and it told him that this had to be the headquarters. How were they going to get out of there alive? Suddenly the only thing that mattered, more than vengeance, more than cattle, was their lives—his and Joe's. But now it seemed that Joe was in this to kill as many of the killers as he could, and if he died in that canyon, so be it.

"They'll be tracking us soon. Won't take anyone with skill to see our trail, even filling in with snow as it is."

"Let's wait these men out, then see if we can't get a couple of those horses out of here."

Within another half minute, the last man to enter the cabin left it, followed by another man. They all mounted up, and the same man who'd ridden up before barked orders once more. The only word Mitch could make out was "kill." They rode off, not twenty feet to the right of Mitch's and Joe's rock pile.

"That leaves one horse," said Mitch.

"Wonder if the boss man is still in there." Joe stood. "Can't wait any longer. I'll take care of him. You get the horse and ride on out of here, Mitch. I'll catch up."

But the young cowboy didn't buy that any more than Joe expected he would. "Ha," said Mitch, standing. "And leave you to fend for yourself? Nope. We're in this together. Besides, I'm not so dizzy now. I imagine you could use somebody to deal with the men you can't handle."

Even through the whipping murk, Mitch saw Joe offer a weak smile. They walked steady toward the house and ducked under the first window they came to. They stood beside the door, rifles ready, coats unbuttoned for easy access to revolvers and knives.

When Joe nodded, Mitch thumbed the latch and shoved the door hard inward. He kept low, with his rifle bristling outward from his gut, ready to pull the trigger.

He was mostly seeing one of everything, though when he stomped forward, as he did when he entered the cabin, his world split into a fractured version of itself, as if he were seeing through a mirror that had received an accidental elbow, webbing it into shards that somehow held in place.

Joe shoved in beside him and they crouched side by side, facing what looked to be a single room. A nickel-detailed woodstove ticked with the cold blast ushered in through the open door. A stuffed armchair sat beside the woodstove and a blue oval braided rug sat an-

chored in the center of the floor. Two chairs and a small
table spilled off the rug, filling the left side of the room.
Beyond that, in the left-rear corner, a half wall partially hid a single bed.

The rest of the cabin bore plenty of signs of
occupancy—a man's clothes strewn over chair backs;
boots leaned against one another; a tin-front single-
door cupboard stood open with a half loaf of bread
peeking out of it. And that was it, no sign of the man
they had expected to see.

"Must have been one of the riders who left," whispered Joe as he walked forward with caution, eyes
peering side to side, taking in the entire room, lest they
miss something. He spun to his left, jerking the rifle at
the crude low wall half-blocking the bed. Nothing.

Mitch had stepped to the side, closing the door,
keeping an eye on the outside, and staying away from
the windows. "You see any reason why we shouldn't set
fire to this damn place?"

He took in the relative comfort in which the man
who was obviously the boss of the outfit, the head of
the killers and thieves, lived. And it bothered Mitch
more than much of what they'd been through since
they'd been left for dead amid a field of their friends'
buzzard-riddled bodies.

"Haven't heard a better idea all day. But we best get
to it. They'll figure us out, and someone will be back
here, I'll wager, and soon."

Joe crossed to the stove and hefted the gray agate coffeepot on top. He grunted and looked quickly about him.
There on the table stood an enameled tin cup beside a
china teacup upside down on a saucer. He flipped it over,
filled them with steaming black coffee, and handed the
tin cup to Mitch.

They both gulped down the hot liquid, sucking in
cool air to ease its heat.

"Been a shame to let that coffee go to waste." He held up the pot. "More?"

"Nah, I'm good," said Mitch, looking out the window.

Joe nodded and set the coffeepot carefully back on the stove, which Mitch found amusing, considering what they were about to do. The older man pulled open the squeaking front door of the stove while Mitch kept watch.

He smelled smoke and glanced at Joe, who caught his gaze. "You having second thoughts?"

"Nope," said Mitch. "It's the least we can do."

"You bet." Joe stuffed in three twigs of dried kindling, caught the ends, then without hesitation walked to the bedding and set it alight. With another he managed to get the strewn clothing smoking, then flaming, and the last he set on the seat of the stuffed armchair, where it quickly inched up the blanket draped there.

He noticed a book, wine red covers, spread-eagle on the chair's arm. He didn't stop to read the title, but snatched it up and tucked it under his arm, then made for the door. "Let's go. We'll ride double if that horse hasn't left us yet."

"What are you going to do with that book?"

Drover shrugged. "Not sure, but a book's a special thing, Mitch. You can't go around burning them, not without consequence."

Joe thrust the book, not an overly large volume, into his coat pocket, and untied the fidgeting horse's reins. "Let me mount first. If we have trouble, you can slide off faster than me. Curse this leg."

He climbed up while Mitch watched the dark to either side, expecting at any moment to see riders burst through the snowy, blustery night. Joe extended his arm and helped haul Mitch up behind the cantle.

As they rode away, northward into the spitting snow and dark, each man glanced back and smiled. Flames lit the two windows, filling those eyes with a flicking orange light that radiated into the night a dancing glow even the wind-driven snow couldn't tame.

"Keep an eye on our back trail!" shouted Joe.

"Yep!" Mitch didn't need telling. So far they were safe, no sign behind. Joe kept a watch ahead, the slow-moving, snow-covered mass of cattle to their right. Darkness ruled to their left, interrupted with juts of rock. Snow pellets lashed the night about them.

Joe bent his head to the side and said, "This night is starting to look like a carnival event I attended once in Gallardo. All manner of people and tents. It's getting foolish. We need to make tracks and this keeps happening."

Mitch didn't understand at first, then looked toward where Joe inclined his head, pointing ahead of them. There was another tent, different from the first, larger and sagging with the building weight of snow.

Outside stood a saddled horse. They slowed and a man poked out from between the loose flaps of the tent, holding a lantern. He seemed as surprised to see them as they did him. He raised the lantern, but the snow prevented him from eyeing them well.

He was wide at the hips and bore a large belly that sat atop thin legs wrapped in tight trousers with silver conchos studding the outside lengths. He wore a poncho and a sombrero tugged down tight over his face so that the brim nearly touched a long hawk nose above icicle-laden moustaches.

The man hooked the lantern's bail on a leaning post with a branch nub at the top that seemed carved for this purpose. He shivered and hugged himself. "Hey! They get 'em yet?"

Joe groaned in frustration, made a move toward his revolver. Behind him on the horse, Mitch gripped Joe's arm and in a low, growly voice said, "Yeah, said they want you down there."

"He'll take the horse!" hissed Joe.

Too late, Mitch realized his mistake. They had to let it play out now.

"Huh? Me? Why?"

Mitch sighed. "Dunno. Said to make it fast."

"Me?"

"Yeah."

"But what about the prisoners?"

"Prisoners?" said Joe, too loud.

Mitch prodded him with his right hand. "Yeah, we'll deal with them."

The wide man shrugged. "Okay. But it's odd, huh? Where they at?"

Mitch hesitated.

Joe piped up. "Past the fire, down at the end."

"The end?" whispered Mitch.

"Want to get him as far away as we can," whispered Joe.

"What fire?" said the man, turning and looking into the night. Sure enough, when Mitch and Joe followed his sight line toward where they had ridden from, there was an orange glow in the sky.

"Oh, ho, ho! What's burning?" said the fat man.

"Cabin," said Mitch.

"Oh, that ain't good. Simms, he's going to be on the warpath. And I don't wanna be around when that happens." The fat man tightened the cinch and mounted up. "You two look new. What's the matter, couldn't find another horse? Ha! Say, you stay clear when he's angry, huh? Fatty ain't never wrong. And I should know because I'm Fatty!" He smacked his belly and laughed, a ragged sound that ended in a cough. "You sure they are down at the end?"

Both Mitch and Joe nodded and watched as the man, bobbing in the saddle, tucked low and made for the far end of the canyon.

"Hope he gets lost," said Mitch.

"I hope he starves to death," said Joe. "But not before he's half-eaten by snakes and wolves. Now, let's see what he was on about when he said 'prisoners.'"

With Joe keeping an eye on the blowing trail leading to and from the tent, Mitch bent low and nosed his way inside the tent. It was dark and still, and smelled of unwashed man and spilled booze. He flung the swaying front flaps up onto the side of the tent and assessed what he saw in the gloom of the old campaign tent.

And what he saw pulled his eyes wide.

CHAPTER THIRTY-FIVE

Fatty rode up, trying to catch his breath. He'd never enjoyed riding, less so lately since he'd gotten fat. Too many frijoles. He heaved himself out of the saddle and wobbled as he hit the ground, only because he landed on an icy patch.

The boss, Mandrake Simms, turned to look at him. "You're supposed to be watching the prisoners."

Fatty held the reins and looked about for help from his fellows. "But you sent for me." There were four of them clustered about two bodies at their feet and they looked away.

"Hey, what happened to Earl and Rink?"

"Somebody killed them. And no, I did not send for you." Simms' nostrils twitched. "You've been drinking again instead of working, haven't you?"

"No, no, boss. I . . . a fire. . . . There's a fire, boss."

"Fire? What fire?" Simms' eyes sparked hard anger even in the low light.

That look was what Fatty had warned the new men

about. And it came to him that he did not want to be
the one to tell Mandrake Simms that his cabin was
burning. Let someone else do that.

"You're a drunken idiot and I am busy." Simms
looked back at the dead men at his feet, then looked to
Fatty. "You're not even worth the effort of killing right
now. Get the hell away from me. Get back to the prisoners! And don't you dare leave the canyon. I'll deal
with you later." He turned back to the men.

"But I—"

Mandrake Simms spun back around to face the big-
bellied Mexican, a slender-bladed pigsticker in his hand.
As he spun he swung the blade left to right, then stepped
back. Even in the darkness, the other men saw that the
long blade's color was different, darker, and it stretched
as if lengthening toward the snowy earth. It dripped.

"You should have taken the opportunity I so gener-
ously extended." He wiped the blade on the mewling
man's shoulder, leaving a dark smear. Then he stepped
back and sighed. "Stupidity is not knowing when to
shut up."

The other men crept backward away from their boss
and the oozing gut pile that was quickly becoming a
dead Fatty. He was still standing, but then he collapsed
at the knees and pitched to his side in the snow, his guts
spilling and slopping beside him.

As Simms gazed down at the stilled form of Fatty, a
long, loud fart leaked out of the newly dead man.
Simms stepped backward and said, "Oh, my word." He
tugged the bandanna up over his face and tried to sup-
press the gag that bubbled up out of his throat.

"Hey, boss."

"What?"

The man pointed northward along the west canyon
wall. "Looks like Fatty was right. About the fire, I mean."

Simms squinted into the snow for a moment, let out

a "Gaaah!" and ran to his horse. "Mount up! Mount up! My house is burning!"

Knowing what would happen to anybody who got to the cabin at the same time as Simms, and having yet more proof of his abiding madness in the form of their now dead pard Fatty, none of the men wanted to ride too close on the boss' back trail. Trouble was, they couldn't see so well in the dark, with the snow spitting hard into their faces.

They hung back and rode slower than they might have, following along the trail that cut closer to the miserable-looking herd rather than the one that hugged the rock wall. A couple of times they thought they heard the boss shouting back at them, but the wind ripped the words all apart, so it sounded like more of his crazy screaming.

None of them would have followed at all if they weren't earning decent money, and with the promise of a whole lot more decent money very soon. It was money they'd already have if Mother Nature hadn't reared her head and delivered this foolish early-season storm.

And then they saw the cabin. The boss was already off his horse and running back and forth before the blaze. The licking flames hadn't yet enwrapped the entire structure, but would be soon.

"Get off those horses!" Simms stood before the open door waving his arms. Already his face was reddened by the heat and his clothes steamed.

"What are you waiting for?" His shouts trailed off into screams. "Julio and Roddy, get in there and get my strongbox, in the back corner, under the bed. Pry up the floorboard, the one with the knothole!"

Still the men didn't move. A growl rose up out of Simms' throat and ended in him spitting a wad of smoke-induced phlegm at them. "Okay, then," he said, and wagged his revolver at Roddy. "Get in there and get my goods! Now!"

Nobody could see it happen, but shots flew like flower-driven bees straight for Roddy and Julio. Roddy offered up a strangled scream that cut off when he landed on his head in the dark.

Julio writhed in his saddle and had enough wit about him to yank on his reins and drum his boots into his hopping horse's barrel. As the frightened beast lurched forward, Simms squeezed another shot and it hit Julio in the center of his neck and drove him forward, slumped over the saddle horn and looking as if he were expressing affection in a most unusual way toward his horse.

He bounced a moment, then dropped, his body whapping the snow and sending clouds of white spraying, and his right boot still in the stirrup. The horse dragged him off into the storming night.

As soon as the shots began, the other men spurred their mounts and jerked the reins, hunching low in the saddle and making for anywhere but where they were. Each, on riding away, winced and held his breath as more shots, intended for them, chased them into the night. They did not stop, and made for the southern end of the canyon and the passage through which they'd driven this last herd.

Mandrake Simms saw he was alone and growled and howled, kicking at the snow and raging at the sky with a fist-clutched revolver. He sent another shot skyward, then jammed the gun back in its holster. He still had one more at his hip.

All this took place in less than a minute, but it was enough time for the fire's fingers to creep their way out from under the roof, feeling around the edges until they looked as if they had a full purchase on the roof itself, as if they were about to lift it off and fling it into the snow-peppered blackness.

He growled once more, and regretting his affinity

for not wearing a hat, he pulled his coat's collar up high about his face and charged into the burning cabin.

The interior was barely recognizable to him, but he knew where everything lay, as he was the one who had put it all there. The men sometime before had built the cabin under his direction, but it was at best a flimsy affair not intended for long-term, let alone cold-weather, use.

On a supply run, he'd been able to have men fetch back furnishings and accoutrements that made life more bearable in this hellish canyon. Among them was a woodstove not fully up to the task these past few days of storming weather.

He cursed himself again for not getting the herd out of there before the storms hit. He'd been lazy and dithered, hoping by waiting a few more days he might pressure the miners in Placer City for even more money. Every day without food, he told himself, was another day their desperation, with the coming winter in mind, would drive them to pay more and more and more.

He still believed in the logic of this plan, but in this instance, he'd waited too long. And now he was being attacked. Him attacked! Was it his own men turning against him? Those foul Apaches seeking more beef? Some unknown band of thieves? And why in the midst of a blizzard?

Why not? Wouldn't that be the way he'd go about it? So the attackers were clever. Well, he'd show them clever.

He fumbled about in the bright, smoky space, coughing as he slammed too hard against the table. Then he nearly upended himself shoving a chair out of the way, and more by instinct and memory than sight, he made his way to the back corner. He felt the bed and dropped to his knees.

The air was better there, but the bedding was ablaze right by his face, licking upward at the ceiling, and the stink—a raw, more-than-burned-wood stink—gagged him, dragged coughs up out of his throat as if a tiny, scaly fist were raking up and down his windpipe. He couldn't draw in a full breath, but was too close to the prize, his cashbox, to give up now.

He bent lower, his right cheek touching the floorboards, and groped with his fingertips for the knothole. There it was. He tried to jam a finger into it but his glove was too thick. He growled, coughed, and tugged at the fingertips of the glove with his teeth.

"Why?" he howled, and his ragged voice ripped apart in a coughing jag while his fingers groped once more for the knothole. He'd lost it and could no longer breathe.

Blackness, this time from within his own head, crowded his blurry, stinging eyes and he knew he was about to pass out. *Surely,* he thought as he forced himself to turn away from the far back corner, *surely the cashbox will survive the fire. But if you don't get yourself out of here, Mandrake Simms, you won't survive to enjoy the money.* He staggered, gasping, dropping to his knees, lurching forward once more.

He wouldn't live to enjoy the pretty, long views of the California coastline, the wonderful meals served by a dapper waiter, everything carried on a silver tray with a domed silver cover lifted to reveal a delectable feast laid out for approval or dismissal. And the champagne. Yes, all that and more would never be his if he didn't get out of there.

And so it was that Mandrake Simms lost consciousness, thinking of what his hoped-for riches would bring him. But in the dark corners of his mind lurked the notion that he was going to die, to die without having done much of what he had promised himself he'd do in life.

Even when he pitched forward, from the longest crawl of his life, and smacked face-first into the snow, even then he did not revive.

CHAPTER THIRTY-SIX

"JOE! HEY, JOE! He was right! Joe, there's folks in here."
Mitch heard the man climb painfully off the horse, tie it on a flimsy hitch post behind Mitch, and join him peering into the campaign tent.

"Hey in there!" growled Joe, impatient to get the hell out of there while they were able. They'd not get many more opportunities to escape. This valley was acrawl with killers and thieves. "Get on out here! Show yourselves!"

A dragging sound greeted them; then a voice said, "Joe?" It was a quiet voice made timid by the storming night, by the coldness of the unheated space, by the situation itself. "Drover Joe Phipps?"

Mitch and Joe stared at each other a moment; then Joe shoved into the blackness a half step behind Mitch. "Yeah, it's me."

"And Mitchell Newland! Who's in there?"

A croaking laugh greeted them from somewhere in

the dark, but all that was visible to them was a dim, dark shape.

"Can't be," said the voice. "Can't be."

"But it is," said Joe, halfway down the tent's length but cautious now, wary that it might somehow be a trick. A trap. Killers behind them, mystery men before them, blizzard about them. This was a hell of a spot to be in.

Mitch, slightly ahead of him, dared to poke his head farther into the darkness. Both men had their rifles poised, ready to fire.

Then that voice said, "It's me . . . Cook."

They hurried to the dark end of the tent and felt at the dim shapes with their hands. There were two men, each lashed tight to a boulder. The rear of the tent had been set up over tumbledowns from the cliff above.

Mitch fumbled for his sheath knife, pulled it out, and sawed through the ropes, trusting that what he was feeling was rope and not the fingers or arms of the tied men. The second man was awake, too, and made muffled shouting sounds that were not words.

Mitch grabbed that man and Joe grabbed the first man and they dragged them backward toward the opening, where thin light from the snowy night helped them see who they might be.

One of them was, indeed, their old friend Cook. The other was Sycamore Jim, and his mouth was stuffed with a balled-up kerchief and wrapped with a bandanna. Mitch tried to untie this but the knot was too tight. Sycamore looked at him with one dark-circled eye, wet and red, and one eye purpled and so swollen the eye was not visible, only a thin, hairy crack across.

"I'm trying, Sycamore. Hang on." Mitch abandoned the idea of untying it and put the knife to work once more. It took longer than he would have liked because the blade was dull, but it worked in the end and Sycamore's face twitched and his mouth remained in that puckered rictus of pain, even though nothing bound it any longer.

With his hands finally free, Sycamore reached up to massage his swollen, painful face and tried to speak.

It sounded to Mitch as if the man were drunk and half-asleep at the same time. "Don't talk, Sycamore. Let's get out of here. We can talk later."

Joe had been freeing Cook from his bindings and helping to ease the man to a standing position.

"They kept us alive." Cook sounded weak, tired, and old. "Beat us whenever the urge grabbed them. Tried to get me to cook for him. I said no. Beat on us some more."

"All the time," said Sycamore in his garbled speech. He was still working his cheeks and lips with his fingers.

"Yeah," said Cook.

"Anybody else?" said Mitch.

Cook shook his head. "No, no way. They drove us off with the herd. Took my wagon, my mules. I think they're here somewhere. How you two make it? I saw you all get shot."

"Later," said Joe. "We're all that's left. Counting you two, there's four of us against all of them."

"I ain't a gambling man," said the haggard cook, "but those odds ain't good."

"Nope," said Joe. "We have to go. You two ride the horse. We'll walk until we get to another. Bound to be one close by."

"Oh, there's lots of horses," said Cook. "But they're all across the canyon, east of here, up at the mouth."

Joe considered this as he hustled them out of the tent, following Mitch, who scouted the night to make certain it was clear.

"You know your way around here, boys?"

"Some," said Sycamore, wincing as Joe helped shove

him up behind Cook in the saddle. "Most of the gang hole up by the horses and a little south of that, along the far side."

"Yeah, east side," said Cook, nodding. "Hand me up some snow, Mitch. I am dry."

"Me, too," said Sycamore.

Mitch did, and as they hustled along at as quick a pace as Joe could muster out of the laden horse, they each ate several handfuls of snow, sighing as if they'd tasted the nectar of the gods.

"How much farther to the end of the canyon?" said Mitch.

"Hard to tell," said Cook, "with all this snow."

They moved eastward, with Joe alongside the right stirrup doing his best to hobble faster and Mitch on the left side, holding his aching head with one hand. They each swiveled their heads fore and aft every few seconds, wondering when they'd see killers emerge out of the gloom.

The herd, to their right, had thinned enough that Joe suggested they cut across. "Tell us when you think we're even with the horse herd. They won't be able to see us too well. Might be able to find horses and get away before anybody knows."

"How much ruckus you cause so far?" said Cook, wobbling from lack of strength. "I could use a biscuit, I tell you. They ain't fed us in a couple of days."

"I expect they were set on killing us. Kept us for sport, is all," said Sycamore, trying to help Mitch by looking behind them.

"We've caused plenty of upset so far," said Mitch, not without a hint of pride. "Set fire to the boss man's cabin."

"You did what? Oh, man," said Cook. "That means ol' Simms—man's name is Mandrake Simms—he will be in a killin' rage."

"You know that fella you run off who was watching over us?" said Sycamore. "Fat Mexican fella?"

"Yeah?" said Joe.

"That's Fatty. He's a talker and a drinker," said Sycamore.

"The two mix too well, I've learned in life," said Cook. "You liquor a man up, he's more often than not going to talk all manner of things to death, making less sense with every swallow. He'll tell the boss you run him off and Simms will be on your trail. He's a devil, he is. Kills folks for lipping off to him. I never seen the like."

"The horses, Cook. We getting somewhere close so if we cut across the herd, we can come out near the remuda?" said Joe.

"Yeah, sure, I expect so. But I can't tell, what with this snow and all."

"We'll take our chances. Mitch, you good with that?"

But Mitch was already tugging the reins to the right, eastward, parting the miserable-looking, snow-covered cattle before them.

There was no way of knowing how far they had to go, nor if they were going to emerge from out of the herd smack-dab in the middle of a gathering of the hired killers. With no choice, they kept on.

Worried as he was about Cook and Sycamore—the two men looked as haggard as he'd felt when he was first revived by the old man out on the plain—Mitch knew they had bigger worries at that moment.

The cattle through which they were riding weren't much of a threat. They had, long hours before, given up thrashing amongst themselves, their brute anger and unreasoning frustration with the relentless cold and snow having played itself out. Now they stood muted and dulled and covered in snow. They parted with a grunt and the odd halfhearted swipe of their heads.

No, the real danger lay in the storm or, more important, in what it hid from them.

Of course, it also hid them from danger, too, from being seen by the killers and thieves. There were dozens of them around somewhere. And if their suspicions were correct, they had set a course through the storm, through the herd, straight for the heart of a nest of men who would do them the most harm.

And so, thought Mitch, *we must be the ones to harm them first, hard, deep, and quick.* With this sudden thought, another came to Mitch: "You two need guns."

"Here," whispered Joe. "Have one each from us." They handed up revolvers.

"Fine, but we best keep our yappers shut. I ain't worth much, but I am sure not interested in getting my Cajun self shot to pieces." Cook's hoarse voice was more a hissed shout than a whisper, but its intent worked on them.

They walked on for a few minutes more, Joe and Mitch flanking the horse and working their way with caution through the beeves. Sycamore touched Mitch on the shoulder, then did the same to Joe. As he did so, he and Cook both bent lower in the saddle.

They slowed the horse until they stood still. Not fifty feet ahead in the sleeting gloom a glow shone close to the ground. Fire or lamplight. This told them they were close to the edge of the herd, and there were men ahead, the very ones they had expected to run across. To find them, though, was still surprising.

Mitch felt ill prepared. They hadn't planned for this. There were too many men alerted to their presence in the valley, hunting them with blood in mind, angry because they were paid to be angry.

Mitch and Joe had at one point heard shouts and shots, but that had been much of an hour before, and back along the west edge and south of them, from where they'd walked. Now there were four of them. And one horse.

Better than a punch to the face, as Mitch's father used to say, then giggle and stare off over the dry land and drink more whiskey. Looking toward the sea, guessed Mitch. The only place, he'd once told Mitch, where he'd been truly happy.

Mitch blinked hard to dispel the past and heard Joe's low, whispered voice. "You see any horses?"

None of the other three answered. They saw that glow, likely a lantern, maybe from a tent. A gust rippled through and hunched the horse, despite its burden, and flipped up Mitch's hat brim. He turtled his neck down deeper into his meager collar and squinted, trying to see horses that weren't there. But neither were there enemy men. Yet.

"Well, look at what we got ourselves here," said a coarse, close voice on Joe's side loud enough to be heard.

Their heads pivoted to see a tall man in a big, shaggy buffalo robe coat and a matching furred hat, pointed at the peak and with no brim. A voluminous snowy beard, covered in the same white fluff as his shoulders and hat top, testified to the fact he had been out of doors for some time. He looked as crusted over as the cattle.

"I wondered if I might find such as yourselves if I kept myself to myself, and away from the idiots hugging the stove yonder. Now I'll wager you all are the very coyotes we're scouting. What's more, I'll wager Boss Simms will look kindly on a fellow such as me was I to bring you to him. And it's an extra consolation that I beat that mean-eyed half-breed Gray to it. Yes, sir, me and me alone. Ha!"

Joe worked slowly to raise up his rifle, to make it easier to swing around and shoot this windbag, but the man was having none of it.

"No, no, no." The man hefted a dark shape to his shoulder. They all saw it for what it was—a double-barreled gut shredder. "That's not how we're going to play this, cowboy." The man jerked it from right to left. "Now, what you gonna do is chuck that rifle to the ground over this way. Then keep walking that horse forward toward the light, like you was good little moths."

They did as he said, resisting the urge to fight him or hammer the horse with heels and flee.

"Yeah, and once we get there, you two on the horse, you're going to get yourselves down nice and easy. Don't think I don't recognize you. I know you're them prisoners. I know you two well. Heck, I should. I'm the one who doled out the first round of beatings. You recall that, you two? Been a long time since I was in a bar fight, so I thought I ought to keep a hand in, if you know what I mean."

Cook couldn't help himself. "Takes a big man to beat on another man all tied up."

"What was that?"

Cook shook his head. "You heard me all right, I expect."

"Yeah, yeah, I did. And I will let that one slip by. But not again. Once is all I will allow."

The men on the horse kept their mouths shut. They didn't want to, but they knew the capabilities of their captors, and this fellow had been one of the worst. Tobacco spittle from his filled, pursed mouth had sprayed with each kick and backhand and punch he'd landed.

They remembered, too, the blind anger that grew worse among all of them, far worse the deeper the rustlers dove into the bottle of rye whiskey they'd passed around.

They walked and the fur-covered man yammered.

One by one, Cook, Joe, and Sycamore realized that Mitch was not among them. Somehow he'd slipped away, hidden by the darkness and snow. Maybe the storm was good for something, after all.

They knew better than to assume that he'd been hurt and lay dying in the midst of the herd. No, Mitch was plenty clever enough to be planning something. Whatever it was, and whenever he might come out with it, they hoped it was quick.

CHAPTER THIRTY-SEVEN

Mitch had been in the habit of leaning forward, ducking behind the horse's barrel, taking the moment free of pelting snow as a gift so that he might better be able to see into the dark about them, beyond and above the backs of the cattle. He'd leaned once more when he heard the thick, hollow clicking of a hammer being yanked back into the deadly position.

At the same time a stranger's voice sounded, close by, on the opposite side of the horse. Joe's side. Mitch did not raise his head, but kept apace with the horse as they walked slowly forward. From what he could glean of the man's yammering, the fool hadn't seen him. He knew he had to keep it that way if they stood any chance of staying, if not free, at least not yet caught and shot.

As the man began threatening Cook and Sycamore, telling them who he was, as a bullying reminder, Mitch saw his opportunity—a gap to his left between two steers. They were angled such that he was able to dart into the dark cleft and stay low. The entire time, he kept tight—puckered, his Pa would have said—expecting to feel a brutal blast of that fool's shotgun ripping through the night and tearing him apart.

But it didn't happen and Mitch did his best to stay low and disappear into the herd. But he didn't rove far, and kept pace with them as they walked closer to the light.

He took stock of what he had on his person that could serve as a weapon. He'd given one revolver to Cook, but he still had another revolver, as well as his loaded rifle and another ten or so rounds. He also had his hip knife and his trusty Barlow folder that Pap had given him when he was nine.

Unbidden, an image of the old Basque came to him, and he heard the man telling him how it was good to be a free man, not beholden to anyone other than yourself, except perhaps also to your dog and your mule. That, to the old man anyway, meant no debt owed to other men, certainly no bank money and no debt to society. *Don't break laws,* the old man told him, not in so many words, but the notion was there.

Easy for him to say, thought Mitch. He wasn't the one who had had his life nearly stripped free of him.

Mitch had paused, waiting for his friends to walk on with their captor, far enough ahead that his further movement wouldn't attract the shaggy man's attention. When it felt as if time enough had passed, Mitch angled northward, keeping low and cutting his way through the cattle.

He ignored the harsh pangs of hunger writhing in his gut, despite the dire situation in which they found themselves. But thirst, now that was something he could deal with. He gnawed on snow he scooped in his glove—he'd shucked the sock mittens some time ago in favor of the needed extra dexterity his old leather gloves afforded, even if the fingertips were full of holes.

The snow numbed his lips and revived his fatigued senses to a level of keen alertness.

CHAPTER THIRTY-EIGHT

SNOW, SOOTHING AS it can be to a stiff joint or a burned finger, can also feel so cold it is itself a source of burning pain. And so it was that a surge of hot agony jolted Mandrake Simms from toe to top-knot, and he spasmed awake with a groan. He came to, facedown, gnawing graveled snow.

Shoving up onto an elbow, he looked about himself into the bleak, snow-specked air, wind gusts riffling his hatless hair, shoving between and beneath the parted halves of his gray wool coat.

"Gaah," he moaned, tasted grit, and spat, then indulged in a longer moan as his plight came back to him. He smelled smoke and glanced past his prone legs toward a black, sizzling, smoking mass, random tongues of flame licking, dancing about it.

"My cabin," he tried to say. It came out as a mumble through crusted, blistered lips. "My money . . ."

The whispered words carried away, teasing apart into the bleak dark night of the long valley where cattle and men milled, all seeking a way out, away from this hellish place in which they found themselves trapped by a madman.

Simms felt a surge of bile rise up his gorge, flood his mouth and nose, shove up and out with blood. He let it pump out of him, soak into his bedraggled waxed moustache, then trickle down his face. He felt better. His body ached wherever skin had been exposed. He touched the top of his head with his fingertips; his leather gloves were pocked with small burn holes showing blisters beneath.

His head felt awful on top, the hair, once a fine thatch of gold, now felt puckered, shriveled, knobby, as if he'd been carved from wood by a poor craftsman. He imagined his face was the same, and a small laugh barked from his blistered lips. He didn't care what he looked like. He was alive. And unless the cashbox could be found whole, he was a pauper. But a living pauper, one with a reason to keep on living—to kill those who had done this to him.

No, mere killing was too good, too simple and easy for the vermin who had ruined his life. He would offer them death, but not for a long time. First he would pick them apart, removing tiny slices from each of their hides until he had removed a hunk for each dollar he figured he'd lost because of them. It was enough to live for.

After a time, he rose up on his knees; then he stood. Pain pulsed through him, but it did not matter, for he had nothing any longer to lose. Nothing.

He smiled, his puckered skin splitting about his mouth with the effort. It was time to hunt.

"Simms."

Mandrake jolted stiff, stood still a moment in the whipping gray light of early morning. He was hearing voices now.

"Simms."

There it was again. *I hear it not because I'm crazy,* he thought, *but because it is there.*

He let his hands drift down toward his gun belt, thinking that he should have pulled the revolver. He wasn't thinking straight.

"No."

Simms held his hands at gut height. "Who are you?"

"Turn around."

Simms did, and a dozen feet behind, there stood one of the men in his employ. He sighed. "Good it's you. I was worried you were one of the invaders. You know what they did?"

When he finally shut his mouth, Simms recalled the man, though not his name. Not that he knew any of them by name. More by type—the dumb ones, the quiet ones, those willing to kill for a bottle of booze. But this one, he had always been different.

Even in the swirling-snow dimness, Simms remembered this one. A tough root. Hard to figure. Men like him, Simms was secretly glad they were on his side, working for him. But wait. If that was the case, why was he calling him by name and holding a gun on him?

Simms eased his hands lower. He'd be damned if he was going to be held up like a simpering victim by one of his own men.

"No, no." The man wagged the gun up and down like a nodding head.

Simms raised his hands a couple of inches and held them there. "What are you doing, you dolt? You work for me, you remember? You want to get paid, you'd damn well better put that gun away and follow me. I need you to do something." Simms turned and his right leg collapsed at the knee. He fell to his left knee, then dropped to his side in the snow.

For a flicker of a moment, he thought he'd stepped

wrong. Then a pinhead of pain in the middle of the soft cavity behind the knee joint blossomed into a full leg of hot pain. He grabbed for the spot and felt a knife lodged there. That brought up a sharp scream as he scrabbled with his blistered gloved hands in the snow, turning to face the bastard who had thrown it.

"What . . . ?"

"Toss away those guns."

Simms hissed and clawed at the snow.

"Now. Or I'll shoot off parts of you."

Simms gasped as he shifted on the reddening snow and unbuckled his gun belt. He shoved it toward the man.

Gray stepped closer, dragged the gun belt toward him with his boot toe, then bent and lifted it. He buckled it and draped it over his shoulder. "Now pull out the knife."

"What?" Simms could barely understand what the man was demanding, so hot was the pain in his leg.

"Give me my knife."

"What?"

"Do it. Toss it to me."

Simms groaned and with his right hand reached behind his bent leg and closed it over the knife's ebony handle. He gasped as the half-buried blade shifted against tendons and meat and bone.

"Now."

Simms gritted his teeth and pulled hard. The knife came free and fell from his hand. The man nudged forward and slid it back out of Simms' reach. He sagged and blackness began to cover over even the pelting white snow. The man's voice brought him around again.

"Now those gloves."

"What?"

The man sighed. "Stop saying that. The gloves. Take them off."

"But they're my gloves."

"Not anymore. I want them."

"You want my shirt, too?" As soon as he said it, Simms regretted it. The man was crazy and he might have given him the idea to strip him down and leave him to die in the snow.

"No. Just the gloves."

Sucking in a cold whisper of air, Simms used his teeth to tug off his leather gloves.

Gray looked at them quickly. They were charred at the fingertips, but still useful. Better than the ones he now wore. He looked at Simms' hands, the fingers spread in the snow, propping the burned man up. There was something wrong with one of his hands. The tiny finger on the right hand was no bigger than that of a two-year-old child. And it was gnarled, withered like a stunty branch on a tree that grew poorly.

Gray looked at the gloves he held in his hand. They would not be any good. They would be tainted. He tossed them to the ground.

"I want your money."

Mandrake Simms felt the first prickling of hope in many long hours. "Money?"

"The cash. From all summer. Where is it?"

Simms thought about this. The man was correct to assume he had money, but he did not know how much there was or where it was hidden. "Then you will let me go?"

The man did not respond right away. Then he said, "Sure. Okay. Where is it?"

"I . . ."

The man sighed. "Hold out that hand."

"What?"

"I said to stop saying that." He toed Simms' right hand. "That one, lay it out flat. Farther away from you. Okay."

"Why?"

Gray ignored his question, but kept the revolver aimed at Simms' quivering blanched face. He pulled the same black-handled knife, and quicker than Simms expected, he sliced the gnarled little finger right off the man's hand, close to the root.

Mandrake Simms had screamed earlier when he'd been stabbed in the leg, but now he merely grunted and stared at his hand. The severed pinkie barely bled and hardly hurt at all. *The snow,* he thought. *It's gone numb.* But he stared at it anyway. The embarrassing bane of his life, the little dirty shameful thing that had always been with him, was now gone. The thing he had not had the strength to do away with . . . gone.

"Thank you," he said to the man.

"Huh?"

Simms did not repeat himself. He kept staring at the severed withered little finger in the snow.

"It was your power. You don't have it anymore."

"My power."

Gray nodded. "It's gone." He nudged the finger with his boot, then flicked it off into the night.

Simms whimpered, then nodded. "Okay."

"Where is the money?"

Mandrake Simms licked his crusted lips, then told the man where to find his strongbox. Somehow it felt like the only thing he could do.

The man walked away, toward the smoldering cabin.

Simms sat in the snow for a long time. His leg had stopped bleeding. *Now what?* he thought. Then he began crawling, crawling across the valley.

CHAPTER THIRTY-NINE

SEVEN MEN HUDDLED in the tent, hugging the sheet-metal stove. It was not a small tent, but it was only made to hold two or three men at a time. Seven made it tight, but nobody minded much. The night had turned savage and Simms was on the prowl and so were the raiders. On this of all nights. Each of the seven brooded, staring at the glowing stove and suckling off the bottle when it circled around to them once more.

They each knew only what they'd been told. Somebody had said there was a whole passel of men bent on stealing the herd. That they chose the storm to do it in spoke much of their nerve.

Others said it wasn't but a pair of men, three at most. Still someone else suggested that they were the ghosts of the men they'd killed this last time. They discussed the possibilities in between swigs. Soon all seven men were sweating from the liquor, the stove, and the small space with so many bodies. Then a gust of wind would shove at the tent and set the lantern to swinging, and their faces would leer with the lurching shadows and they would fall silent once more.

"Yes," said Antoine, finishing the bottle. "They will be the ghosts of the men from the last time. That last herd."

Most of the listeners chuckled, but a few shivered and crossed themselves and muttered words of fear and whispers, silently begging for forgiveness and salvation.

Then they heard a shouting voice that made them all jump as if jerked by ropes.

"Hey, you silly women in the tent!"

None of the seven men moved.

"I can see you, fools! Get out here! I caught me a bunch of rustlers!"

The voice sounded familiar to them. And then the voice laughed at what it had said, and by the laughter they knew it was Big Bonn, a large fur-clad man. And hadn't he said he caught them?

"It's a trap set by the spirits," said Antoine.

No one moved. Finally one of the men, Shub, sighed. He untied the flaps and poked his revolver's barrel out, then widened the gap, parting the tent flaps. He squinted into the dizzying snow. The sky was not so dark, but for a moment he could not see who was there, save for several dark shapes. Then his eyes became used to the gray light.

Shub turned back to the others. "It is Big Bonn. He's not alone. Maybe he's telling the truth."

MITCH EMERGED FROM the herd, shoving his way between the humped-up longhorns. They were sullen and lumpish, reticent to shift themselves as he trudged low among them, paralleling the slow progress his friends made as captives of the big shaggy brute.

The brute stopped them about a dozen feet before another tent; this one was on the large side and equipped with a woodstove. From the glow within, Mitch saw the silhouettes of many men, five, six, maybe more. He didn't know what to do and wished Joe were with him. *No, damn it,* he thought. *I'm here and he's not, and he and Cook and Sycamore need my help.*

Mitch still carried a rifle and one revolver, and as far as he could remember, he had enough bullets for a few choice shots. At least enough to get into trouble. The only thing he did not want to do was shoot his friends. Beyond that, he was too tired and too angry to care if he hurt or killed the others. It had been a long night, and though the sky was beginning to lighten, it was far from over.

Then the big man shouted at the tent. He was calling them out. Then the men in the tent would come out and kill his three friends and that would be that. *So,* Mitch reasoned, *I have to do something.* And the only thing he could think of to do was shoot the big shaggy man. He was close enough to do it; at least he hoped so. Trouble was, Joe was standing to the man's left.

Mitch whispered, "In for a penny," and gently cocked the rifle, wincing at the sharp metal-on-metal sound it made. Nobody noticed. The tent flaps opened. Any second now they would all come out.

Mitch raised the rifle, sighted down the barrel, hoping the new day's lessening snow and early light would be enough to guide his bullet past Joe and toward the shaggy one. The light from the tent moved outward, its glow reaching the shaggy man, the horse, Cook and Sycamore atop it, and beyond, Joe's shoulders and head.

Mitch saw the shaggy man's hairy coat and, above that, the silly hairy hat. He aimed for it and squeezed the trigger.

* * *

A GUNSHOT RIPPED through the unfolding situation right as Joe had decided to try something desperate. The buffalo-coated man had made them toss away their guns, but had not made Cook or Sycamore hop down off the horse. He also had not checked Joe for other weapons. Joe still wore his sheath knife on his left side.

The shaggy bastard hadn't gotten close enough on the short walk for Joe to pull the knife and lunge at him. But it was act now or forever regret it. So Joe slithered his fingertips up, slipping the leather thong looping the handle in place. He slid out the knife and hefted it.

One second more and he would bend low, lunge to the side, and drive the blade hard and fast into the middle of that shaggy mess. First, he smacked Sycamore's boot and shouted, "Hee-yaa!" Then he bent his legs to lunge. That's when the gunshot from somewhere to their left, the north, cracked the early-morning air.

Joe checked his lunge and watched as the big shaggy brute whipped away from him, pitching as if clubbed in the head with a length of stovewood. Even in the dim light Joe saw blood spray and spatter the snowy ground. The shot had cored the fool's big hairy head. He would never move again.

Joe's rap on Sycamore's boot and the accompanying shout had confused Sycamore and Cook but a moment. The two men had crouched low, holding on to the horse as the beast lunged forward, straight at the tent and the men shoving out of it.

That shot had to be Mitch, thought Joe, not bothering to look as he bent low and snatched up the dead man's rifle. There might also be a revolver there, but he didn't have time enough to rummage. There were men in that tent ahead—how many he'd find out soon.

He didn't have long to wait, for Cook guided the

spooked horse true, knocking down the first man to emerge from the shelter. It stomped him in an effort to get away from the jerking shape of the wind-buffeted tent and the shouting, writhing mass of men within.

Sycamore rolled off the horse's rump and hit the snow, pitching toward the dazed and stomped man. He grabbed up the revolver still clutched in the weak man's hand, and with no more thought than that he'd had enough of these vicious, killing, torturing brutes, he thumbed back the hammer and sent the mewling bastard to his death with a close-up shot to the throat.

The man bucked and gagged, and blood spumed, then settled, along with the man's spasming. The stench of hot gore rose in the air, twitching the young man's nostrils. He vomited bile but did not slow a whit as he joined Cook, who had wrestled a rifle free of another emerging man's grasp, slamming him in the face with the butt.

Cook delivered several rounds into the swaying tent alive with thrashing shapes of shouting, cursing men. Screams replaced the cursing, and blood spattered the canvas. A crash accompanied the howling voices and thick smoke boiled out the flapping doorway.

Joe edged wide southward and kept an eye behind, lest their ruckus should draw unwanted attention. The bottom edge of the tent rose up from the snow and a man's flank inched out. Joe waited until the man emerged and rose up from one knee to half-standing height. Joe shot him in the chest, sending him sprawling backward against the tent.

The movement jostled the writhing mess further and the swinging light from within dipped as the lantern fell free of the rope running the length of the tent and crashed atop the woodstove, which had already been knocked aside. It took seconds for the tent to bloom into a boiling, smoke-spewing orange pyre.

Four men remaining, shot to pieces and confused, scrabbled to escape the inferno enveloping them. As the canvas dissolved in licking flame, they burst out screaming, arms flailing and bodies alight, into the dawning morning.

By then Mitch had bolted over to help his fellows, and each of them shot at the careening, screaming men as they howled and thrashed in circles. The killings, though a grim act of mercy, were also as bold and cruel a thing as any of them had ever done. But as they shot, each man thought of their friends slain in the attack so long before on the hot plain, and they were steeled.

They grabbed what other weapons they could find and stalked as a group, backs to one another, bristling with guns, in silent agreement, resolved to end the madness in which they found themselves.

Thus they marched for much of an hour, nerves jangled and alertness coursing through them as if they had each downed a pot of Cook's thickest morning brew. They moved as a single beast, exchanging little more than head nods indicating a direction, a boulder to search behind, a last tent to investigate. They found no other souls alive or dead at the north end of the canyon.

Their last stop was Cook's chuck wagon. It was in good repair and had been drawn up beside the camp's existing chuck site. The remnants of a fire fizzled and smoked. Nearby, they found two other living creatures, Romulus and Remus, Cook's mules, standing hipshot and tethered in a small corral with a slight overhang along one side.

"My boys!" The big man handed Sycamore his guns, broke ranks, and walked between their heads to encircle their necks with his big arms. The men gave him a couple of minutes. Then, in silent agreement, he backed away from the mules, took up the proffered guns, and they resumed their patrol.

Beyond the mules' small corral, a rocky arm formed one side of a much-larger corral, within which milled a couple of dozen horses, among them Champ, Trooper, and Rascal, Sycamore's mount, on which he'd been forced to ride to the canyon when he and Cook had been captured.

The men climbed into the corral and after a few minutes of coaxing managed to reacquaint themselves with their prized mounts. Champ nosed Mitch's pockets for dried apple slices, raising a smile on the young man's face. "Soon, pal. I promise. Just hold tight for a while longer."

There were three dead horses in the corral, but the rest were in decent flesh, though hungry and unimpressed with the storm.

The morning was coming around bright, with a clear sky. The snow shrank, dripping off high-up rocks that felt the sunlight long before it reached the canyon floor. Despite the all-night blow and near constant lash of pellets, the snow hadn't accumulated to more than six inches.

Sunlight warmed the beeves and soon their wet backs steamed. Beneath the slush, green grass poked up, and the ravenous animals nosed aside the snow and cropped as they roved.

The men began to relax and consider that they might live through this, after all, though vigilance was foremost in their minds. Weary but determined, they made their way down the west flank of the canyon, pushing the herd slowly before them.

A third of the way down, the cattle, wary and stepping with caution and ears perked, parted around something in their midst. The closer the men drew to it, the slower they, too, walked. Soon they saw it was a man.

The blackened, bent creature before them looked as though it had crawled out of the gates of hell and barely lived to tell of it.

They looked past him at the ragged furrow he'd left behind in the snow. He'd dragged himself a fair piece.

"That's Simms," said Cook, his voice cold and low. "Boss man."

"I reckon he's felt better," said Sycamore.

"You don't look so good, mister." Mitch looked at the man as if he and the boys had stumbled on a steaming gut pile in the woods.

"He wasn't in that cabin when I set it alight, Mitch."

"I know he wasn't, Joe."

Instead of whimpering and asking for help, the quietly seething man pushed up higher on his elbow and showed them a thin smile. Then he laughed, a ragged chuckling sound that ended in a cough. He spoke in a soft, croaking voice. "Do . . . you have . . . any notion of what . . . you have done? You fools. You—"

"About to ask you the same thing, mister," said Mitch. He stepped forward, and stood over the sprawling man. "Why? Why did you do all this?" He waved an arm wide to take in the entire valley and its dead and ragged denizens.

"Couldn't find it in all the smoke . . . my money . . . in the cabin . . . oh, you fools . . ."

"Money." Mitch snarled the word. He bent low and snatched the other man's blistered, knobbed head and bent it up to look at him. His voice grated out low and hard. "You killed our friends. You made us kill men. All for money."

Mitch stared at him a moment longer, then shoved the charred head away from him as if it were a diseased dog.

Simms shook his head. "No, no, no . . ." He chanted the small word as if talking to himself. So fixated were they by his hideous face, by what he was saying, that they didn't see his right hand fumble at his waist.

"The ocean . . . eggs . . . champagne . . . no, no, not

right. Send it back if it's not right. Start over again. More champagne . . ."

Too late, Joe saw the dim flash of light on polished metal. "No!" he shouted, his hands up, but he lunged forward too late.

The man on the snow at their feet had shoved up onto an elbow, then plunged a long, thin blade into himself, angling up, a heart stab. He sucked in a quick breath, his eyes jerked wide open, and his mouth did the same, as if he'd been told a great secret confirming something he'd long suspected. Then his stiff torso eased as the last of his life drained away and he sagged, eyes still wide in surprise.

No one moved for long moments.

"Well, that was something," said Sycamore.

Maybe because they were all beyond tired, maybe because they all had been through so much viciousness, and all of it because of the man who had killed himself at their feet, Sycamore's comment snapped a final taut wire they all felt pulling at them.

Cook shook his head. "Boy, you got a knack for words. . . ." Then he smiled and ran a big hand up and down his face as if scrubbing it.

Joe's shoulders began to twitch; then Mitch smiled. Soon they all were chuckling as they turned away and walked back toward the cook tent, though still glancing back, in case they'd been followed.

"I expect you all would like some hot coffee," said Cook.

They spoke over one another, affirming the big man's suspicion.

"How hard would it be for you to make a batch of your famous biscuits?"

For a moment, Mitch's request hung in the air while they all watched Cook's stonelike, craggy face. Then the big man smiled.

"Now you done it," he said, turning to his chuck wagon. "My mama always said if you want something done, you ask a busy man. Elsewise it won't get done...."

In another few minutes they made it to the chuck site. Cook busied himself with gusto, rummaging, crashing pans, and mumbling about how somebody changed everything all around, and how was he ever going to find anything in his chuck box ever again ... ?

Mitch, Sycamore, and Joe smirked and prodded the fire back into life.

"Aha!" Cook turned to face them, a familiar green glass bottle held high in his grimy right hand. "At least one of those idiots had the good sense to keep Mother's tincture safe. I think we all should have a dose or two, ward off whatever we might have come down with in this nest of fools."

Mitch, Sycamore, and Joe high-stepped it for the re-muda, the herd, anywhere but back to the chuck wagon.

"That's fine," said the big Cajun. "You'll be back. If you want yourself coffee and biscuits, you'll be back."

CHAPTER FORTY

THEY WAITED A full two days to assess their odd
situation. In that time they determined that unless
they were going to be set upon by some of the outlaws
who'd hightailed it out of there, they were the only
people left alive in the canyon. They gathered weapons
and ammunition, righted the chuck wagon around, and
tallied the herd. They found they still had most of their
beeves, plus a dozen stragglers from other herds.

They dragged all the dead men by rope over to
Simms' burned cabin, where they laid them out side by
side. They felt over the dead for valuables and gathered
their meager take in a sack—pocket watches, folding
knives, weapons, tooled gun belts, and the like—vowing
to use the proceeds to further enhance the money they
would send to the families of their dead fellows.

If no family members could be traced, they would
use the money to help build up a new herd and pay
whoever might come forward for a fair share, should
that day ever come.

Their efforts, they knew, were wishful, for there were only four of them, and they still had to drive the herd the rest of the way to Montana Territory.

"We've been through a whole lot more of a challenge than that, boys," said Drover Joe over coffee that second night, after a hearty meal by Cook. "We're solid."

"You bet we are," said Mitch, raising his cup. The others did the same. The next day would prove them right or prove them wrong. They had spelled each other for night watch and sleep, though each wished for a whole lot more of the latter.

The morning was another warm, bright one, and any remaining snow was nested in small piles in clefts beneath rock rarely out of shadow.

They decided that Cook was going to ride east of point and keep the herd moving and straying along the farther half of that edge. Sycamore would wrangle the remuda to the best of his ability at the rear, not giving distant chase to any horses that might break for freedom.

He also would share drag with Mitch, who would help with the remuda and keep a constant roving effort along the rear of the herd and the latter half of the west edge. Joe would ride the rest of the west flank and point, scouting as he was able.

The arrangement, while not without its challenges and need for constant vigilance, worked pretty well—largely, said Joe, because the storm and the lack of decent feed kept the beeves and horses weak and tired. This slowed the critters, and the four men were able to move the herd at a slow, steady pace.

Their luck held, and then changed late in the morning of their third day out. A gang of riders from the north rode at them hard and fast. Joe spotted them while they were still a quarter mile away and rode over to tell Cook, who armed up. Joe made the circuit, warning Sycamore and then Mitch, who rode forward with him, along the west flank of the slow-moving herd.

Neither man spoke, but each thought the same thing: They were about to go through hell once more, and this time there were only four of them.

As the riders drew closer, sunlight glinted off something shiny high on the chest of the lead rider. Joe grunted, but still held a rifle across his saddle, ready to swing. His double-gun rig, too, was loaded and ready. The other men were similarly equipped and waiting.

The riders, a dozen in all, spread apart as they approached. Joe and Mitch held in place and the herd slowed to a stop behind them.

The man with the star on his chest rode up while the rest halted. "Morning."

Joe replied in kind. Mitch nodded.

The man looked them over, then looked at the herd and, to the east, took in the chuck wagon.

As he did, Mitch assessed the lawman. He was a slight man, beyond middle age, with a dapper black wool suit coat, striped breeches, and stovepipe boots that looked as if they received regular polishing. On his head he wore a low-crown black beaver hat and his face wore a trim, clipped gray moustache that did not extend beyond the corners of his mouth. His gun rig was simple, no adornment or carvings on the leather enfolding a single walnut-handled revolver.

"Mighty small crew for a herd this size."

"Yep." Joe kept his gaze level.

The lawman—sheriff, so his badge read—made no attempt to haul on his iron. He canted his head and squinted an eye.

It looked to Joe as if the man were about to smile.

"You wouldn't happen to be . . . Let's see." He snapped a finger a couple of times, trying to recall some-

thing. Then looked at Joe. "Joseph Phipps? And you"—
the lawman looked at Mitch—"Mitchell Newland?"

Their surprise must have been obvious, for the lawman smiled widely and touched his hat brim. "Pleased
to meet you then. I'm Sheriff Longley from up Montana
Territory. And these are my, ah, volunteers, you might
say." He gestured to the eleven men behind him. They
were largely a smiling bunch who nodded to Mitch and
Joe. A few even offered a hello.

"I'm confused," said Mitch. "How do you know us?"

"Thought you might be. An old man rolled into
Placer City a few days back, told us all about you. He
goes by the name of Bakar or some such. Travels with
a dog and a mule and seems to set quite a store by
them. Anyhow, we'd have been here sooner, but the
blizzard slowed us. Early-season storms can be brutal."

Mitch and Joe exchanged raised-eyebrow glances
and then sighed. "Ol' Bakar," said Mitch. "Imagine
that. Saved our fat from the fire again."

"Hell of a fellow," said Joe. Then to the sheriff,
he said, "We'd sure appreciate any help you men can
give us in getting this herd to your town. We're about
done in and weren't sure until this very minute we were
going to make it."

"Mister," said one of the men behind the sheriff, "if
this herd is bound for Placer City, then there isn't a
thing we won't do to help you get it there. Right, boys?"

Whoops erupted along the line of newcomers.

"I'm going to go tell Sycamore and Cook," Mitch
said, then kicked Champ into a sprint.

Pretty soon Joe and the other men heard, even
above the lowing and bawling of the cattle, a distinct
loud "Yee-haa!"

"Gents," said Joe. "If it's all the same to you, now
that you're here, we'd like to call it a day, maybe set up
camp. We're played out."

Longley nodded. "I'd like to hear your story," he said. "I'm missing one of my deputies and I fear he's met a hard end."

Joe nodded. "We did come upon a dead lawman, I'm sorry to tell. Back there in a hellish canyon." He sighed. "If we can convince Cook to brew us up a pot of coffee, I'll tell you all I know."

The lawman nodded. "Sounds good."

"Any of you men know about herding cattle?" said Joe.

Most of them nodded.

Longley leaned forward. "They weren't always hungry miners."

L ATER—AFTER COFFEE and the full story from Joe, Mitch, Cook, and Sycamore—Sheriff Longley, true to his word, left behind eight of his men to help drive the herd. He took the remaining three men with him and made for the hidden valley to inspect the situation and bury his dead deputy.

EPILOGUE

OKAY, THEN." THE man in the spectacles and the black bowler looked up from his desk. "Here's the tally for your herd." He spun the paper and slid the paper over to Mitch. "Would you like this in cash or on a draft at the bank in Silverton?"

Mitch eyed the figures.

"Hey, Mitch." It was Joe, standing outside the depot office. "Come here a minute, will you?"

Mitch slid the tally sheet off the desk and looked at the cattle buyer. "I'll be right back."

The man sighed. "Very well."

Mitch joined Joe and the boys on the boardwalk out front. He noticed Joe held a slim wine red book, the very volume from the cabin they'd set afire, his long finger marking a page. In small gold type, the cover bore the words A CHRISTMAS CAROL BY CHARLES DICKENS.

Joe nodded toward the east end of the bustling little mining town.

A wide work wagon, pulled by two brace of horses

and freighted with lashed-down goods, rolled into view at the far end of the rutted street. The wagon was followed by another smaller work wagon. Both were flanked by several riders. On the driver's bench sat a straight-backed young woman who looked awfully familiar.

Mitch squinted and craned his neck forward. "Evie?"

The wagon rolled straight toward Mitch and stopped.

He stood on the raised boardwalk looking over at her. She stared right back at him, not quite a smile on her face.

"Well," she said, "aren't you going to say hello?"

He shook his head and stepped down from the boardwalk. In two strides he made it to the wagon as she hopped down. He stood before her, his eyes wide. "Evie!"

She nodded. "Yes, it's me. And you remember Carmelita?" Evie gestured behind her toward the second wagon.

A plump, dark-haired woman with a wide smile waved from the driver's bench of the following wagon. "Hello, Meetchell!" Then she wagged a finger. "I told you! Just like the swans!"

Mitch smiled and looked at Evie. "But . . . we fought. I thought it was too late. . . ."

"It's never too late, Mitchell Newland." Evelyn Bilks reached up, wrapped her arms around his neck, and pulled his face down to hers. They kissed, and when she pulled away, she said, "I like the moustache, Mr. Newland. Tickles."

It was then Mitch detected the presence of Golly, the Bilks family's farting bluetick hound, asleep in the boot well of the wagon. "Hi, Golly! Glad to see you . . . I think."

The next five minutes were filled with hugs and renewed hellos as Cook, Sycamore, and Drover Joe caught up with Evie, Carmelita, and her family—husband,

Juan, and their son and two daughters, all of whom worked for Corliss Bilks.

"But, Evie, what are you doing here? You and them . . . that was it? All the way from Texas? Don't you know there are range pirates and . . . and worse?"

She shrugged. "We were fine. Except for a little snow a week or so ago. We cut wide and stuck to the plains. We would have been here sooner but . . ."

"Evie, I told you I'd come back to you . . . if you'd have me."

She shook her head. "Mitchell, you're not listening to me. That day you left? I packed, too. I was going to follow you . . . at a distance."

"What?" He shook his head. "Evie, that's crazy!"

"That's what my father said."

Mitch lost his smile. "Your father."

She returned the somber look, and she looked down at their entwined hands. "Well, he won't bother us any longer."

"What do you mean?"

"That day when he found out I was going to follow you, he grew so angry, such rage." She shook her head. "It laid him low, Mitch. Doc Shelby said it was a brain stroke. He lingered for weeks, and then he died. Oh, Mitch." She laid her head against his chest and he hugged her.

"I'm so sorry, Evie."

She wiped her eyes with a hankie and sighed. "So I sold the ranch and . . ." She looked at Mitch once more. "And I lied to the banker, Mitch. I sold the Twin N, too."

"What?"

"I told him we were married. It took a little doing, but he believed me. Then we followed you, Mitch."

For the first time he could ever remember, Mitch saw doubt and fear in Evelyn Bilks' eyes. He'd only ever seen strong conviction there. More than anything else, that look convinced him she loved him beyond all measure.

"Oh, Evie," he said, holding her at arm's length once more. "I don't care. You're all that matters, not some played-out patch of dirt. But you could have been killed traveling all that way!"

"So could you, but you lived," she said.

"Barely," he said.

"What's that mean?"

He shook his head. "I'll tell you later."

"Ahem."

They all turned to see the man in the spectacles and black bowler standing on the boardwalk before the depot office door.

"Mr. Newland, I'm pleased to see you've met up with old friends—truly I am—but I have a business to run, and I prefer to conclude our transaction sooner than later."

"Of course, I'm sorry about that. Where were we?"

"Payment for your herd, Mr. Newland . . . will that be in cash or bank draft?"

Mitch glanced at Evie. "I need to check with my partner." Then he handed the sheet to Drover Joe.

"Your eyesight going, Mitch?" said Joe. "Evie's your partner."

"Evie's going to be my wife." He hugged her close.

"And don't you forget it, Mitchéll Newland," she said.

"I'm talking about my other partner. Drover Joe Phipps, are you interested in owning half the Newland-Phipps spread?"

Drover Joe looked from Mitch's smiling face to Evie's smiling face and felt a sense of belonging, a bond he had not known his life was missing. He smiled, too, then tapped his chin with a long finger and looked up at the clear blue sky. "Hmm, I think Phipps-Newland sounds stronger. Don't you think so, Evie?"

"I can't say I disagree."

"Details, details," Mitch said, and stuck out his hand. The men shook on it.

Mitch turned to Cook. He wished Bakar, Pep, and King Louis had still been in town when they'd arrived. He had a feeling Bakar and Cook would get along well, but the old man had been gone many days by then.

"Cook? I hope you and Romulus and Remus will stay, too. If we're going to build up the biggest ranch Montana Territory has ever seen, we'll have mighty need of you as head of . . . well, whatever you'd like. We can build you a fine cabin. Anything you want."

"Oh, I do appreciate the offer, boys. And I might show up again one of these days. In the meantime, I'd be obliged if you could keep on ol' Rom and Remus, let them ease out their days on good feed. I'll take my share for now and light a shuck."

He rubbed his arms. "It's too cold up here for the likes of me. I'm liable to come down with chilblains, and then I'd need a steady dosin' of Mama's tincture." He looked over at them. "And I'm not so sure I could take that."

"Where will you go, Cook?"

"I expect it's time to visit that ol' sainted mama of mine."

"She buried down in New Orleans?" said Mitch.

"Buried? What? No, no, just because I call her 'sainted' don't mean she's dead. That woman will out-live all of us!" He smiled. "Yep, first thing she'll do is box my ears. Then she'll lock me in one of those gator hugs of hers. She outweighs me by a fair piece." He nodded solemnly.

Joe raised his eyebrows. "My word."

"You ain't kiddin'," said Cook.

"I reckon I'll miss you, Cook." Sycamore folded his arms and dragged a boot toe back and forth.

"Aw, don't go blubbery, boy. You ain't shed of me yet." He popped the young man on top of his hat, squashing it down about his ears.

"How about you, Sycamore?" Mitch looked at his grinning friend as he tugged his hat up and reshaped it. The young man had been quiet while they all talked of future plans.

"Oh, I . . ."

"You have anywhere you need to be, son?" said Joe.

Sycamore looked at his boots and shook his head. "No, I reckon not."

"Well, that's good," said Mitch, exchanging nods with Joe. "Because we're in sore need of a ranch foreman."

The young man looked up. "Who? Me?"

"Well somebody's got to do the hard work around here," said Joe, clapping a big hand on Sycamore Jim's shoulder. "Those two will be too busy being married. And after that drive, I'll be too busy hibernating for a spell."

Sycamore Jim puffed his chest and smiled wide. His Adam's apple worked up and down a few times. Finally, he said, "Well . . . well, that's something, that is. That is something else!"

THE MAN WHO called himself Gray rode southwest, picking his way through the tailings of snowfields, reaching back now and again to check the buckles on a saddlebag that held a charred cashbox, heavy with coin and full of promise.

Ready to find
your next great read?

Let us help.

Visit prh.com/nextread